In the year of ou~~r~~ ~~excavated an unmarked burial site on abbey grounds, hoping to prove the~~ *tales sung by bards were true…that six hundred years earlier, a famous warrior had walked their lands. What they found surpassed their wildest hopes: the mortal remains of two humans, along with an engraved leaden cross identifying the pair as England's renowned King Arthur and his wife, Guinevere.*

When news of the findings broke out, kings, bishops, and other political figures all laid claim to them, lobbying fiercely even as they questioned the authenticity of the remains. Battle threatened to break out. The Bishop of Glastonbury, distressed by such greed and aware of his own mortality, sought a way to protect the findings for all time.

Success, however, was fleeting, for though the remains and associated artifacts were kept as holy relics in the abbey treasury, then later placed on display in a carved tomb, the passage of time brought to England a break from Roman Catholicism, followed by the Dissolution of the Monasteries. In the sixteenth century, King Arthur and Guinevere were once more lost.

The relics—or reports of their whereabouts—have resurfaced from time to time, yet they remain unrecovered. The magic of Camelot has captivated the imagination of generations, for the ancient prophesy lives on: one day Arthur will return, a living king, to rule an England greater than ever before. But that day will never come unless the second, oft-forgotten part of the prophecy also lives on. Those sworn to protect the prophecy toil in secret, knowing that the great leader who was struck down by the sword of a son will someday be raised by the loyalty of a daughter—as long as their mission does not fail.

For those seeking to part the mists of time, the quest continues…

Entrusted

ALLEGRA GRAY

PROLOGUE

England, Glastonbury Abbey, 1536

"It has begun. More than two hundred religious houses disbanded." Abbot Whiting paces near the small window of his study. He is not a man given to pacing. The movement, even more than the grimness of his tone, makes me nervous. The meager light of fading day filters through the window, emphasizing the lines etched on his face. "Buildings destroyed. Faithful observers of the religious life turned from their homes, forced to act as beggars until another house can take them in."

"There are reasons..." his companion offers. A prior. An important one, by the look of him. The stream of religious men coming to seek advice at Glastonbury has increased to a near flood of late.

I shrink backward, trying to blend in with the wall. I should not be here—but it is too late now, for the men have forgotten my presence. To leave now would only draw attention. But this is not a conversation meant for a serving girl's ears. Not even a serving girl favored by the abbot himself.

"Reasons? Insufficient annual income? Improprieties in the order? *Pfft*. Excuses. You know this as well as I."

The prior inclines his head in silent acknowledgment.

"Do not be fooled. You think they will stop with destroying the lesser monasteries? No. This is merely the beginning. The small houses serve only to whet the insatiable appetite of the crown."

"'Tis treasonous to speak so."

I feel dizzy. Things are bad in the world outside the abbey's walls. I'd known that already. But *treason*?

"Indeed. I do not deny the gravity of the matter." The abbot enunciates his words carefully, which only makes the situation sound worse. "Neither do I believe a held tongue will save us. I fear Henry will not stop now until each and every monastic house in England is dissolved."

The prior puts a hand to his heart, and in the movement I see the flash of a cross—a square cross—embroidered at the hem of his undersleeve. Hardly noticeable, but working for such a meticulous man as Abbot Whiting has trained me to be observant. Still, it makes no sense. My eyes must be playing tricks. No one has used the square cross in decades—not since the most notorious group to use it was disbanded, hunted down and persecuted.

"We must be prepared," the prior agrees. "You know of what I speak. Do you have a plan?"

"I do," the abbot answers.

There is a pause. I shift positions, and the rustle of my skirt against the wall catches Abbot Whiting's attention. Is it my imagination, or do his eyes rest on me just the tiniest bit longer than necessary? I wonder what he is thinking—though in truth, it is best I do not know.

I wish I was anywhere but here. Normally my duties are limited to the outer rooms. But Sam was ill today, so Mother stayed home with him, sending me in her stead.

The prior nods, slowly. "And until then? What will you do?"

Abbot Whiting bows his head. "What I have always done. Pray."

CHAPTER ONE

Audrey

England, Autumn 1538

"I have good news," Abbot Whiting announces.

I jump, startled from the solitude of my work. I hadn't even heard his footsteps as he approached.

"Good news?" I clutch my dusting rag. This morning's visitors looked like they bore anything but good news, and the abbot hadn't looked too happy when he left with them earlier. "*One by one, they fall. These men will stop at nothing.*" The words of the dark-bearded caller echo in my mind. Shortly after he spoke them, the abbot dismissed me from the room. That's not so unusual, these days. Everyone has grown cautious.

"A rare thing, these days," the abbot admits. "But, yes. At least some of today's news is good. The French convent I wrote to some months ago has agreed to become a sister convent to Buckland. They are also an order of hospitaliers, and they will accept as initiates the Englishwomen who originally intended to take their vows at Buckland."

"That is…kind of them, indeed." A thousand thoughts race through my mind. Buckland—the very convent I once hoped to join. I applied last year, and was approved. How could I not be, when the abbot himself recommended me? I still have my notice. It states that, although my application was approved, I would have to wait until alternate arrangements can be made to house and train new novices. I knew what that really meant. With King Henry having broken ties with Rome, the prioress at Buckland wasn't certain of the convent's future. She would not make promises to hopeful young women that could not be kept.

When the notice first arrived, I'd been determined to wait. The church was so big, so powerful. Surely something would give. But a year passed, and things only got worse.

The abbot clears his throat and I jump again, guilty of drifting into memory rather than paying attention to him. His eyes twinkle. He knows, but he doesn't chastise me. "It *is* kind. Though the French prioress did mention that, with the influx of new sisters, she will be forced to ask that only dowered nuns and novices make the journey. Her establishment has an endowment, but cannot cover such a sudden expansion. Still, I believe the sisters will work something out. And as for you, Miss Thorndale? Will you go to France?"

"I have no dowry, Father Abbot."

"You have the pasture rights to your land. Instead of paying your allowance directly, I could send the funds to the French convent. I believe the amount would be sufficient."

I squeeze my eyes shut. I want to go. Oh, how badly I want to go. Everything in England, and my life in particular, is a swirling cesspool. To escape it all, to enter a French nunnery, would be a dream come true. Quiet. Safe. Secure. A year ago, I could have said yes.

The death of my parents changed everything.

"Be good, and take care of Sam." My mother's dying words. So simple, and yet so difficult to honor. Longing shoots through me at the memory. Oh, how I miss her.

My little brother Sam is eleven, an age when most boys can look after themselves fairly well. But Sam...well, too often, people do not see Sam's good heart. They cannot see past his twisted leg and his stammer. He still needs a protector. That means I have to fill the role—which also means I cannot leave Glastonbury any time soon.

France is too far away for me to look after Sam, and I can hardly bring him along. I open my eyes. "I cannot. I must stay here. For Sam."

His gaze, old but sharp, takes in everything. "I was afraid that might be your answer. Your father's relatives cannot take him in?"

"No." The answer is more complicated than that, but I don't elaborate, lest I speak ill of my few remaining relatives.

"I suppose my good news is not so good after all."

"It is good. Just not for me," I whisper. The frustration, the hopelessness of the situation sticks in my throat, keeping further words from forming.

"True. Several dozen faithful sisters, and a few aspirants, will benefit. I do not disagree with your decision, Miss Thorndale, though I understand the sorrow it brings. Indeed, I think you have made the only good choice you can, and are the more noble for doing so. I am only sorry to see the opportunity pass you by, for I am not certain another one will come along."

"I know."

"Know also, then, that your position here is secure for as long as Glastonbury is under my governance."

Neither of us knows how long that will be. A week? A year?

I nod. "Thank you, Father Abbot. I am finished here, unless you have need of something else?"

Normally I love my work in the quiet of the abbot's house, but today I can't wait to escape. I know who is next in line to take the veil. If I do not go to France, Mariel Smythe, daughter of one of the local landowners, will go in my place. Mariel has a respectable dowry and nothing to tie her to home.

She will go, and I will keep doing what I have done for years—working at the abbey, seeing to the needs of the great and busy church, and to the abbot himself. He has ensured both Sam and I have positions that keep our bellies from going empty and our hearth from going cold—at least for now. I am no stranger to the injustices of life, but that doesn't always make them easier to bear.

"No, Miss Thorndale, nothing else. A pleasant afternoon to you, and God Bless."

Picking up a tray of dirty mugs, I close the door behind me, imagining that as I do, I am also shutting the door on the dreams I once held.

If Glastonbury Abbey should fall, I am in trouble.

I take the mugs from the abbot's house to the kitchen to be washed—I can drop them off and collect Sam at the same time. We always walk home together, even if it slows me down. It's safer that way. Glastonbury is usually a safe town, but tensions are high, and by working at the abbey, Sam and I obviously sympathize with the Church—and Sam is an easy target.

Sam works in the kitchens, washing pots, chopping vegetables, and any other chore he is directed to do. He is keenly aware the others that share this work are girls. There are serving lads, of course, running back and forth between the kitchen and the hall where the monks dine, or the room where Abbot Whiting dines when he entertains more elevated guests. But since Sam's hands work better than his legs, he is not suited to the work of the servers, or the stable boys or the shepherds, with whom he would much rather spend his time. This is the sore point of Sam's life.

He knows he should be grateful to have any position, but all too often, I spend the walk home teasing and cajoling him out of a sour mood and back into an impish young lad.

Today is not a good day.

When I arrive, Cook is in a right rage, going on about some apricots that have gone bad. "Shipped in from France, those were." He rounds on Sam. "What good are you if you can't keep the root cellar in good order?"

"I didn't open the box," he mumbles. "I thought they were dried."

The cook's eyes bug out and his already-red face grows a shade darker. His lips twist.

I jump in. "It's my fault, Master Cook. I told Sam we were to hurry that day, and to just set the box on the shelf to keep vermin away." I don't actually remember the day the apricots arrived, but it sounds like the sort of thing I would have told Sam.

Cook looks back and forth between us, and I sense his anger diffuse. It's completely unfair, but everyone knows I am the well-behaved, well-liked one of the family. I'm pretty, if not in a conspicuous way. More importantly, I am whole. Sam does his best not to hate me for what cannot be helped, and I do my best to rescue him from situations like this.

"He should've seen to it first thing next morning, then," Cook grumbles.

"It won't happen again," Sam promises.

Cook doesn't look like he believes that, but he finally shrugs. "Go on with ye."

Sam gathers the parcel of bread and cheese that will serve as our dinner, and the two of us set off toward the town, Sam's limp more pronounced than usual.

"You shouldn't have done that, Audrey," he says, after several minutes of quiet.

"Done what?"

"Stuck up for me. It was my fault. Cook was right. He thinks me an idiot. It doesn't help when I act like one."

Sam is one of the most honest people I know—which, for a boy his age, is saying a lot. But sometimes he is too hard on himself. "It's not you, Sammy. Everyone was on edge today."

"It is me," he insists "It's always me."

I hate the tone of defeat in his voice. I sense that no amount of teasing and joking will lighten his mood today, so I remain quiet.

"Why is everyone on edge?" Curiosity, at least, always gets the better of him.

I stifle a sigh. "Same reason as always, at least lately. The monasteries continue to fall. The big ones now, too. The abbot doesn't say it in so many words, but he is all but certain the assurances from the king—written letters saying Glastonbury would be left untouched—will not hold."

"Oh."

These problems are too big for Sam. He absorbs them, then returns to his previous line of thought.

"It would have been better if I'd never been born," he mutters. His toe kicks at the dirt. With his limp, it's hard to tell if the kick is intentional or just a result of his uneven gait.

I don't know what to say—especially because a secret, ugly part of me agrees. It's not that I don't love him, because I do. He hadn't asked to be born, and he hadn't asked for a twisted leg, so I can't blame him for those things. But his birth was hard on Mother, too. After him, she was unable to have any more children. Worse, we both know that if he *hadn't* been born, I would be on my way to France instead of Mariel. I'd be safe, serving God, and cared for the rest of my life.

Since I can't think of anything to say, I sling an arm around his shoulders. Of course, that just makes it harder for him to walk. I drop my arm, and we trudge home in silence.

We've just passed the baker and the alehouse when a cheery voice penetrates the gloom of our progression.

"Ho there, Mistress Thorndale. 'Tis a delight to find you still here." Tobias Seybourne, sometime adventurer and younger brother to John Seybourne, greets us with a smile. A shadow at his jawline gives him the roguish appearance of a traveler, but does nothing to diminish his charm.

I smile back. Tobias flits in and out of town like a bird, never failing to bring cheer when he arrives, but always leaving just as quickly.

"And where else should I be?" I ask.

"'Tis high time thee get thyself to a nunnery, is it not? If that is still your intent."

"Nunneries are becoming increasingly hard to come by in these parts," I reply lightly, unable to resist the teasing lilt of his banter. I won't be leaving for a convent anytime soon, but that isn't Tobias's burden to bear.

"So they are." He walks companionably beside us for a minute, then reaches into a satchel at his side. "Perhaps the scarcity of nunneries will work in my favor."

He is flirting, but I know better than to take it seriously. "Master Seybourne?"

He grasps the item in his satchel, pulls out a wrapped parcel and waives it triumphantly. "There. You see, if you had gone off to a convent, I might not have run into you this afternoon, nor your brother Sam here, and these lovely blackberry tarts might have gone to waste."

"Tarts?" Sam's face lights up.

"Packed for me by a kind innkeeper. I thought to bring them to my brother, but now that I recall, he does not have nearly the sweet tooth of someone else I know."

"Me?" Sam bounces on his good leg.

"Master Sam, has your fondness for sweets outgrown that even of your sister?"

My cheeks grow hot. When we were younger, Tobias had come upon me at the stream, my face and hands covered with berry stains and crumbs. I'd received a tiny tart made of leftover dough, an act of generosity from the baker, and I'd fallen to temptation before getting halfway home. Tobias hadn't forgotten.

Sam eyes me. "Maybe not."

Tobias laughs. "Worry not. There's plenty to share." He hands the package to me.

"I cannot repay you, Master Seybourne."

"No one said anything about payment. 'Tis a gift, and only a simple one."

"It will not go unappreciated. Thank you for your kindness."

He flushes a bit.

He probably knows the past year has been hard on Sam and I, but it is kind of him not to mention it. I don't want to accept charity, but Tobias doesn't make it feel that way. I truly think the gift of the tarts is, to him, nothing more than a neighborly gesture.

"Where have you returned from, Master Seybourne?" I ask, changing the subject.

"Just back from London. King Henry's court has returned from their summer progress."

"Are you become a courtier, then?"

'Nay, merely a soldier. I serve among the men at arms. Occasionally I am asked for an opinion, if the king is considering new defenses." He drops his voice. "The king likes those who agree with his ideas, and I am always certain to do just that."

I stifle a laugh. "You sound like the veriest of courtiers."

His eyes twinkle. "I do not know whether to be wounded or flattered, Miss Thorndale."

"Flattered, of course. You are coming up in the world, Master Seybourne." He is, too. Everyone knows that Tobias went off to serve among the king's men, to do what his elder brother could not—try his hand at winning fortune and glory. His mother is quick to speak of his progress to anyone with a willing ear.

Tobias just shrugs. "It's hard to say who is coming up and who is going down, on any particular day. But I thank you for the flattery."

"How long will you stay?"

He hesitates. "I have not yet decided. I am not important enough for King Henry to mandate my return, and yet I suppose I shall go back before too long. There are many...opportunities to be had in London."

"And you hate to leave any path untried," I tease lightly.

"True enough."

We reach the fork in the road, where the well-kept lane that leads to Seybourne Manor goes left, and the somewhat overgrown lane leading to Thorndale house goes right.

"A good evening to you, Miss Thorndale, and Master Sam."

"And to you," I reply. Only now that we were about to part ways do I realize how much he lifted my spirits in such a short time. Sam, too, judging from the renewed bounce in his step. Down the lane, my home beckons, welcoming and yet surrounded by a quiet air of desperation, as though the very house is aware that each day the brambles creep a bit closer, and the hope of being restored to its original glory drift ever farther. There is no staff to care for it as it deserves, save for old Meg, who still comes faithfully, twice a week, to tidy up and strew fresh herbs. We could—maybe—afford a laborer to help outdoors, but I don't dare take on anyone else. If the abbey gets dissolved, I won't be able to pay anyone, and might very well wish I'd done what I am doing, which is to save every coin I can.

"Thank you again for the tarts!" Sam calls behind him. When Tobias is out of earshot, he looks hopefully up at me. "Could we save the bread and cheese for tomorrow and eat these straightaway? Just this once?"

I ruffle his hair. In truth, I'd been thinking the same thing. "I don't see why not."

The future is certain to hold many a supper of bread and cheese. But thanks to Tobias Seybourne, today's supper doesn't have to be one of them.

I fall asleep that night with the taste of blackberries lingering on my tongue, and the words of the abbot lingering in my mind. *Your position is secure…for as long as Glastonbury is under my governance.*

Secure. Tears well up in spite of my closed eyelids. I squeeze them more tightly shut. I can hardly remember the last time I truly felt secure.

CHAPTER TWO

The following week, I watch in silent envy as Mariel Smythe departs for the French convent. As children the two of us were sometimes rivals, sometimes friends. In a way, not much has changed. To her credit, though, she doesn't rub it in. If she were condescending, I could hate her. But she isn't, and I don't. I just envy her freedom. I envy her family, which was not struck by the same sweating sickness which took my parents. The Thorndale family has fallen a long way, but it is not the fault of the Smythes.

I watch the sweep of Mariel's skirts over cool stone, the gracefulness that comes with being assured of one's future. That could have been me.

Instead, Mariel will be the one to travel to another country, to study under a Mother Superior and profess her vows. I wonder if she will be homesick. *I* would not. Once, maybe. But those days are dead to me. England is now a frightening place to call home.

I remember the day I stood in Abbot Whiting's study, more than two years ago, listening to his dire predictions. I never believed they would come true.

It shames me to admit that when Lord Cromwell gave the decree—that is to say, parliament approved it, but everyone knew whose initiative it really was—to dissolve the lesser monasteries, I thought perhaps his reasons were valid. A painful but necessary purge of a system grown corrupt. The people of England would all be better off in the end.

I was so naive. Abbot Whiting saw what I could not—that Lord Cromwell was only practicing, perfecting his methods before moving on to larger targets.

Targets like Glastonbury Abbey. My home.

When Mariel's carriage rolls out of sight, I go back inside to finish up my tasks. Though I have worked at the abbey forever, entering into the abbot's space still makes me nervous. I tiptoe when he is present, and sometimes when he isn't. This chamber belongs to the world of men. Men, with their politics and their struggles for power. Men who make decisions that change the fate of thousands. I both fear and admire them.

I wipe the dust from the tables and shelves, setting everything to rights. Abbot Whiting values order and cleanliness. He trusts me to keep the parlor and library tidy, because I share those same values, as my mother did before me.

I harbor secret hopes—accompanied by an equal measure of nervousness—that Tobias Seybourne might accompany us on the way home again. I know he is still in town, for I have seen him at mass with his mother and brother. I am in sore need of a cheerful interruption to my dreary thoughts.

But Tobias is nowhere to be seen, and Sam is also quiet, leaving me to my thoughts.

The image of Mariel climbing into the carriage, her trunks loaded up behind, swims before my eyes. Jealousy, piercing and bitter, stabs through me. An unbecoming emotion. I try to will it away, but that is easier said than done. What is the French abbey like? Is it as nice as those in England? Nicer? Will the Mother Superior treat Mariel, the English transplant, well? Would everyone speak in French, always? Is the life there as peaceful, clean, and simple as I imagine it to be? Will my life ever be like that?

I scrunch my nose and shake my head in frustration, as though I could shake the very thoughts away. Sam glances at me curiously. He doesn't say anything, but he gives me an awkward pat on the shoulder. I guess he knows what's upset me, and knows also that there's nothing to be done about it.

But he surprises me.

"I'm old enough to earn my keep. Someone will take me in, if you really want to leave."

That just makes me feel worse.

"I don't want to leave." Sam's all I've got left. If I'm not here to look out for him, he'll get assigned all the worst jobs. Cleaning the slaughterhouse, or the outhouses. I refuse to let that happen. Maybe, if Sam had received years of tutoring as I did, he could have been a scholar, but Sam was still young when the money for tutors ran out. It's up to me to protect him, and teach him when I can.

I need to focus on the future I *can* have, not the one that is lost to me.

Marriage is the obvious answer. Already I have offended the butcher's son, Robert, by refusing his offer. I am old enough to marry, and everyone expects I will do so, soon. Though my father made arrangements for us, my position as an unmarried girl is tenuous. My uncles do not stop by often enough to be considered guardians. Were it not for the fact that I work for the abbey, and most know me as "practically a nun already," my reputation would not have survived even this long. It would be easier if I were already widowed.

Lovely. I have just wished death upon a stranger I have not yet married. I heave a sigh. I must start thinking more positively about the possibility of marriage. How else am I to maintain the house and the land?

Just…not the butcher's son. Not when I know the only thing he is after is just that—the house and the land. He thinks to use my misfortune to better himself. His family does not own any land. He thinks I will be swayed by the promise of a full belly and someone to take the burden off my hands.

Not so. Robert is full of himself. Nor can I forget all the awful ways he taunted Sam when we were younger. How could I take such a man for a husband?

Take care of Sam.

Yes, Mother. I am trying.

Mother was taken so quickly, she had little time to prepare. The sweating sickness is often that way. My father lingered longer. Before his death, he did his best to provide for Sam and I—he sold usage rights for our little patch of farmland to the abbey, in exchange for an annual allowance. He knew his brothers, my uncles, would want the land—but he also knew of their disdain for my crippled brother. Like as not, they'd have married me off and turned him out, robbing us of our home with nary a twinge of guilt. My uncles grumbled that I was too young to inherit, but my father put it in writing, and Abbot Whiting himself acknowledged it. They didn't argue after that. They don't help us any, but they leave us alone.

The allowance from the abbey is enough for Sam and I to keep the house, and to keep the hearth stocked with wood. I closed off the empty upper rooms of the house. Too expensive to heat, and with only two of us now, we don't need the space. Perhaps someday the rooms will be needed again, should the Thorndale family fortune once more rise. Our full-time maid, Agnes, found work with another family, and only her mother, old Meg, still helps us.

Sam and I take most of our meals at the abbey, as part of our wages. Like that, we get by. Not lavishly, but enough that I do not have to accept the hand of the first brute to offer it. For this, I am grateful.

But if Glastonbury falls, like so many of the religious houses have already done, Sam and I will struggle, no question. This is what keeps me up at night. I do not have to accept the *first* offer of marriage, but I would be a fool to think I need not marry at all.

I should find myself a nice young man, someone with prospects, and—subtly—indicate my interest. I know this. But the whole idea of marriage—of caring for a husband, of squalling babies and children who might catch the fever, of the endless commotion—it is too much. I hadn't planned to marry. Now I must, but I cannot imagine it. So far from the peaceful pursuit of a holy life I once planned.

Not that men aren't...interesting. Some are. Attractive, even. But I was never one of the girls who giggled at every lad over the age of twelve, and who could hardly wait for babies of their own. I saw my mother's pain, when she lost my baby sister, born before Sam. And then her struggles with Sam—love and pain mixed in equal parts, now passed on to me. Caring for Sam is hard enough. How can I take on even more?

"Audrey?" Sam nudges me as we approach our home.

"Hmm?"

"Are we expecting company?"

I frown, following his gaze. Smoke puffs cheerfully from the chimney of our house. That isn't right. Sam always banks the fire before we leave in the morning. I could do it faster, but he takes pride in the job, so I let him. He never forgets—and even if he had, this morning's fire would have long since burned out. "No, I'm not expecting anyone," I say slowly.

"Huh." I can tell Sam is disappointed. He probably hoped one of our cousins was passing through. They are more pleasant than their fathers. But the disappointment on his face quickly gives way to the same feeling I jumped to immediately—suspicion. Sam is smarter than people give him credit for.

"Stay here," I tell him.

"No. I should go. Check things out."

I sigh. "Oh, Sam. Don't go all 'lord of the manor' on me right now. You've a noble heart, brother. But I'm lighter on my feet."

With that, I dart to the side, approaching the house from an angle so that, if anyone is inside, they won't be able to see me. It's *possible* one of our cousins has come by—but it is also possible that thieves or some other questionable characters have noticed how often our home is empty and pinpointed it as a likely place to hide out for a spell. We keep up the little yard as best we can, but there's no denying the air of dereliction that hovers at the fringe of the property, as though nature is just waiting for us to have one more stroke of bad luck before reclaiming the land.

I creep closer, quietly as I can. I don't hear any voices, nor any movement—at least, not over the unnaturally loud beating of my own heart. Finally, I gather my courage and push the door open.

A fire crackles merrily in our hearth, but there isn't a soul in sight. Then my eye catches on the table, where a square of brown sacking is neatly folded, with a blackberry tart and a small pile of almonds sitting atop it.

Tobias.

Relief, and something more that I'm not ready to analyze, flows through me. He must know what time we usually arrive home. Last week's gift of the tarts could very well have been a spur-of-the-moment decision on his part. But today? That is something more, and the kindness of the act warms me as much as the fire. Coming home to a cold hearth after a long day is one of my least favorite things.

I can't help the smile that tugs at my lips as I poke my head back out of the door. "It's all right, Sam. Come on in."

A few moments later, Sam shuffles in. "Who was here?"

"Master Seybourne, it would seem."

Sam's eyes land on the tart. "So it would, indeed." He sizes me up. "Is he courting you?"

I laugh him off, hoping the heat rushing to my cheeks doesn't give me away. *Is* he courting me? No more than he courts any pretty girl in town, I should think.

"Of course not. But we must remember to thank him for such a neighborly gesture." The words make sense as I speak them. After all, Tobias Seybourne could do much better than me.

"We must," Sam agrees, though his expression says he's still convinced our neighbor has more than neighborly intentions.

Later that night, I lie huddled in bed, awake. Sam sleeps soundly on his side, and with the fire still burning on my other side, I am comfortably warm. I can't stop wondering. Tobias is pleasant and charming. Even better, he treats Sam like any other person. Of course, he knows what it's like to have a cripple in the family. His older brother John is one. A humpback. Nothing extreme, barely noticeable but for the self-conscious way he holds himself.

Then again, it doesn't take extremity for the townsfolk to whisper behind your back, wondering what sin resulted in the punishment of deformity. The curvature in John's back didn't show up until he was a lad about Sam's age. Though he was older than me, I knew from gossip that he'd gone from being a sociable child to a near-recluse in the course of mere months, as his friends all cut him off. Tobias had witnessed it all from a younger sibling's perspective. As eldest, John had still inherited Seybourne Manor, and the informal title of Lord of the Manor that went with it. But he hadn't been able to join the lists, to become *Sir* John the way his father and grandfather before him had.

Tobias is the one who went to court instead, who might someday be knighted. A second son and an adventurer. But also a young man with a good heart, who returns to his brother time and again, never forgetting to put family first. Nor does he forget his less-fortunate neighbors.

No wonder the maids all bat their eyes at him. He is easy to like.

I roll my eyes—at myself—without bothering to open them. It would never do to go losing my heart over Tobias Seybourne, no matter how affable he is. I need stability—a plan to fall back on if Glastonbury should fall. Tobias, for all his charm, has never left a stone unturned, nor a path untraveled. Doubtful he knows the meaning of the word stability. But he did ensure I was warm and fed tonight, and for that, I will remember to thank him.

I sleep restlessly that night. The following morning, Sam and I arrive earlier than normal at the abbey. In spite of the hour, a number of people bustle about. I drop Sam off at the kitchens and make my way toward the abbot's house, waving hello to acquaintances along the way.

Abbot Whiting himself stands near the entrance to the gardens, in close conversation with a man who has his back turned to me. Their conversation looks private. I drop my gaze...but just as quickly I glance back, curious. I shouldn't spy. But every day now, I live with the fear that the end is coming. Like sand running from an hourglass—only I can do nothing to stop it. Every whispered word, every cloistered conversation, might be an indication. King Henry has gone too far to turn back now. Besides, the man with his back turned looks familiar.

The abbot nods. His companion sweeps a courtly little bow, and my spine tingles in anticipation. As the abbot lifts a hand in parting and turns toward the cloisters, his companion turns the other way, toward me, and a flare of recognition sweeps through me as Tobias Seybourne strides toward the very gate where I stand.

"Master Seybourne?"

"At your service." He sweeps me a bow, and his over-the-top gallantry makes me giggle.

I recover my composure quickly. Though I enjoy his flirtation—a first for me—I want information more. "Actually, it appeared you might be in the abbot's service."

His easy charm takes on a measure of guardedness. A subtle change, but there nonetheless.

"I serve England," he answers with a smile. "Always and ever."

"May she ever prosper," I answer in turn, as I ought. Interesting, though, how he phrased his answer—almost as though he wants me to know it is England, rather than King Henry himself, that he serves. But they are supposed to be one and the same.

I need to stop prying. Tobias, for all his kindness, isn't going to tell me anything. Not what he and the abbot discussed, not his intentions for the future, and certainly not where his allegiances lay—we both know his answer to my question is an evasion. As well it should be. Even if he does serve more than one master, it is better—safer—if he is the only one who knows it.

"Thank you, Master Seybourne, for the kindness you did us last evening," I tell him, and the honest gratefulness in my voice puts us both back in more comfortable territory.

"My pleasure," he tells me, the guarded look melting away. "It was nothing."

"Nothing to you, but not to us. In times like these it is comforting to have such a thoughtful neighbor."

He flushes a bit, which I find charming. It may all be a part of his courtier's charm, but I fall for it.

I bid him good day. If only it could all be so easy.

◈◈

The encounter with Tobias rattles me. I go about my work, trying to pretend everything is normal. But I can't stop thinking about his guardedness, or about yesterday's visitors. Were they the king's men? Is the fate of the abbey being decided, even now?

In the afternoon, the visitors return and spend several hours in counsel with Abbot Whiting. Since they are closed up in the study, I am forced to occupy my time elsewhere. I fetch supplies, replenishing the candles and ink that the abbot uses so often. He says he reads or writes long after the sun has gone down. I think he must have trouble sleeping, too.

As I go back and forth, venturing into other parts of the abbey, I see that everyone else is just going about their daily routine, nothing out of the ordinary. It calms my fears, somewhat. If Lord Cromwell or his men were here, it would be all anyone could talk about.

Still. Whoever these visitors are, they've given Abbot Whiting cause for concern. He'd been moving slowly this morning, as though carrying a great weight, and the furrows lining his face seemed even deeper. If this afternoon's conversation had been unimportant, he would not have shut me out. He would have allowed me to hover in the background, unseen and unheard, like any good servant.

This time, when the men depart, the abbot does not go with them. Instead, he beckons me inside. He knows I am a creature of habit. I begin to tidy things up, as always. He returns to his desk and sits, heavily. Waves of exhaustion roll off him, almost palpable.

"Who were those men, Father Abbot?" I don't usually ask questions, but I've been fidgeting for hours, wondering what portent of doom has come. He won't hold my curiosity against me—not when I express it so rarely.

"Not who you think."

Not the king's men. I know what he means.

"Do not fear, child," he says, then checks himself. "No, disregard. I cannot in all honesty say you should not fear."

I stop the tidying and twist my hands in my skirts, already regretting my hasty question.

"The men came from Walsingham Priory. Or rather, what *used to be* Walsingham Priory. They confirm what I have heard from other displaced clergymen as well. The dissolutions are becoming more violent. No longer is it enough for monks and men to be turned from their homes, from their very way of life. Now, they are burning buildings, tearing down the very walls they once worshiped under. The priory has been destroyed, with Prior Vowell in full compliance."

I can think of no reply but to stare, wide-eyed, like a fool. This has happened so many times already, and yet I still feel shock, disbelief, that it should happen again.

"Last year," he continues, "Eleven of the prior's men, including the sub-prior, were hanged for treason. This summer, Prior Vowell accepted a pension in return for allowing the king's men to suppress his priory."

"But—" I cut myself off. How could the man accept a pension after those under him had been executed? Abbot Whiting would never do such a thing.

He considers me, his gaze, as usual, discerning. "His decision troubles you?"

I nod.

He looks thoughtful. "You are a bright girl. But think of this. The prior's decision, while seemingly self-serving, may have prevented further executions from taking place. The men who came calling to Glastonbury did so *because they survived*."

I lower my head, chastised. "Aye, Father Abbot." That's why he is an abbot, and I am nobody. He knows how to look at things, to see the things that are not obvious to me.

"I cannot say I would make the same decision, necessarily," he continues, which only confuses me further. "There is a time to acquiesce. There is also a time to make a stand. The difficult part is in knowing which time is which, and whether you are the one called upon to make that stand."

It is a lot to ponder, and I retreat gratefully at the end of the day to the kitchens, where no one talks about making a stand,

and the argument of the day is over whether the brace of rabbits hanging in the smokehouse ought to be roasted or stewed. There is mutton and gravy left from the monks' dinner, and most of the kitchen staff has gathered around to make short work of it, sitting on a jumbled assortment of benches and stools. Sam and I join them. Once, I would have thought myself above eating with the servants. Even when Mother came to work for Abbot Whiting, she was his personal assistant…more like a courtier to a king than a servant to master. A position of favor and importance. A position that might, in the right circumstances, help raise the Thorndales back up.

But, no. Circumstances have never been right, and I am not too proud to eat in the kitchens anymore. Usually, Sam is so anxious to leave his duties by the end of the day that we pack a cold supper. But today, the mood is less formal, and Sam is relaxed. Platters change hands freely, and the allure of the hot meal is too much to resist. No one takes notice of Sam and I— or, if a few of them are gleeful to see us sunk to the level of eating in the kitchen, at least they refrain from rubbing it in our faces. To be honest, I rather like the joking and easy camaraderie of those gathered around.

Cook is abed with a toothache today, I gather from Sam, and his assistant is unused to taking matters into his own hands. That explains the merriment and disorder.

"What a day," Sam says brightly."No one to bark orders, and everyone running amuck. 'Twas fair entertainment. Still, the meals were served and no one went hungry, so all is well."

"What was decided for the rabbits?" I ask between mouthfuls.

"Oh, they're to be stewed tomorrow. Though, like as not, Cook will be back and give different orders in the morning."

Sam doesn't seem to care one way or another, and why would he?

Two of the serving lads nearby debate over whether the fetching scullery maid did, or did not, make eyes at one of them. The women who do most of the baking are trying to outdo one another with stories of difficult childbirths.

I let myself relax against the wall. For this brief moment, nothing is being asked of me, and everything seems so *normal*. I wish it could last. I wish that somehow, some way, Glastonbury could drift away from the notice of King Henry and Lord Cromwell—that we could simply go on as we are, with no one paying any attention, or even aware we exist. Like the Avalon of King Arthur's tales, we might disappear one misty morning, with no one the wiser.

CHAPTER THREE

Tobias

I am composing ridiculous poetry off the top of my head and reciting it to the Widow Barrett, who is neither as attractive nor as intelligent as my flattery makes her out to be. What makes this worthwhile is that we are standing in King Henry's outer chamber, and I am doing it do keep her from approaching the king—and the king knows it.

Widow Barrett is Henry's own age, and therefore entirely too old for his tastes. He would much rather continue playing at chess with Catherine Howard, who is young enough to be his daughter and conniving enough to make him think she finds him attractive. Some days, I think Henry *must* know. Others, I believe he has deluded even himself.

I know Catherine's goal. There are moments, though, as I mince about—trying that much harder each time the widow glances toward her king—that I wonder about my own. Unbidden, the image of Audrey Thorndale enters my mind.

Not one person in my current company would express such simple, uncalculated joy at the gift of a blackberry tart. It would be nicer if they did.

I am the lowest of the low, second son of a mere knight, and yet I have made it to the inner sanctum. Well, perhaps not the *inner* sanctum. The King's privy chamber is open only to those who harbor his darkest confidences or share his bed. Since I am neither a cleric nor a whore, I am as close as I can get.

I hoped earning my way into Henry's circle would mean being a part of something bigger than myself. A grand adventure, exciting moments around every corner. Military campaigns or political ones, seeing the world, knowing I had a hand, however small, in the events that will shape history. Not power—though everyone around me lusts for it—but something harder to define. Some days, the excitement is there.

The Widow Barrett, sensing my distraction, turns once more toward the king. In desperation, I leap to her side, reciting from memory:

"And wilt thou leave me thus?
   Say nay, say nay, for shame,
   To save thee from the blame
   Of all my grief and grame;"

I clasp my hands to my heart, making a show of it, and she cannot help but laugh.

"You scoundrel. You've stolen those lines from Sir Wyatt. I know I've heard them before."

I cringe dramatically. "So I have. But they are no less worthy for having been borrowed." Sir Thomas Wyatt is a dubious choice within earshot of the king, given that the man spent time in the tower for consorting with the king's deceased wife—Anne Boleyn, that is. But Wyatt is back in favor, having been knighted and sent on embassy to Charles V of Spain, so I think I am safe.

Fortunately, the king has finished his game—a win, of course—and is looking to stir up some noise. He signals to a pair of musicians. "Come, play us a lively tune."

They spring into action, and the king winks at Widow Barrett, indicating she may sit near him during the music. That way, I know, he won't actually have to talk to her.

She knows it too, but is willing to snatch at crumbs. Smiling widely, she leaves me thus.

Audrey

I don't see Tobias the next day, or the next. Just like that, he is gone again. Most likely he's gone back to London. It is said the king likes to keep his courtiers close, especially those he finds entertaining. I wish I could be sure, but since Tobias's brother has taken a chill and hasn't been at mass, there isn't anyone I can ask without sounding nosy—unless I run into one of the staff from Seybourne Manor. I do know the gardener there, and one of the maids.

It shouldn't matter so much that he has gone. That's just his way. Here one day, gone the next. I hadn't expected anything else. But somehow this time feels different. He went from leaving surprise tarts at my home to leaving without so much as a goodbye. Did my prying annoy him? I didn't think so, but *something* feels…unfinished, between us. This time, I am *waiting* for him to come back. I can't even say why.

Four whole weeks go by before I see him again. I am ashamed to admit I counted the days.

It's a cheerfully sunny afternoon—a rarity this late in the fall season—and I have finished my work just a bit early, hoping to snatch a few moments to enjoy myself. I step outside the abbey gates, Sam in tow as usual, and find Tobias waiting for me, as though it is something he does all the time.

"Mistress Thorndale."

He doesn't sound angry. My heart does a skippy little dance.

"Might I escort you and Sam home?"

Definitely not angry. He's looking as cheery as the sun itself.

"Why, thank you. To what do I owe the pleasure?" Even I can hear the flirtation in my tone. *Stop being silly*, I admonish myself. Every maid over the age of twelve knows the younger of the Seybourne brothers is a charming adventurer. He may seek success, but I doubt he seeks home and hearth. It will not do to think otherwise.

My self-admonition is to no avail. I cannot help the way I am drawn to his charm.

John Seybourne, Tobias's older brother by two years, is the complete opposite. I wouldn't quite call him bitter—I'm not that cruel—but he is definitely reserved, and understandably so. Though he is Lord of the Manor and a wealthy man, John cannot live up to the standards set by his father and grandfather. No one in town dislikes him, that I know of, but no one particularly goes out of their way to bring him out of his reclusive state, either—at least not unless the gregarious Tobias is also in town.

"Nay, the pleasure is mine," Tobias responds as we set off down the road. "But in truth, I have a favor to ask of you."

"Of me?" I can't imagine anything I have to offer him. Tobias Seybourne has more friends, more influence, more wealth, more *everything* than I do.

"Of you and Sam, really. I thought to do some pheasant hunting, and I need a companion. I was wondering if I might borrow Sam on his next day off."

Sam's eyes light up. But just as quickly, they dim. "I'd only slow you down." His shoulders slump.

Tobias leans his head in towards Sam, making himself seem shorter somehow. More on Sam's level. "See, that's where you're wrong, Sam. You don't have to be fast to hunt pheasant. You do need good eyes, though. Have you good eyesight?"

Sam considers that, then nods.

"Good. We use dogs to flush out the birds, then try to take them down with bow and arrow. If we succeed, the dogs are trained to fetch the bird and bring it back."

"They won't tear it up?" Sam asks.

"No, they know better."

I watch the two of them, knowing the matter is already decided. I am well aware that Tobias does not "need" Sam as a companion. There are plenty of men in the region who are skilled hunters and would happily join him. He's doing this out of kindness—and maybe pity.

I hate to think it the latter—that beyond the simple pleasure of doing nice things for another, he actually feels sorry for us. I try not to be proud, but it's hard.

Still, there's no way I can say no to Tobias's offer. Not when Sam is so excited. With Father gone, there's no one to teach him things like this. And truthfully, even when Father was alive, he wasn't much of a hunter. His eyesight was not sharp, and he'd learned it was much easier get meat by bartering with the local butcher than to hunt his own.

"I have a spare bow," Tobias offers. "We can practice a bit before going out. If your sister agrees, that is."

I shoot him a look that says I know exactly what he's doing—putting the decision in my hands, but making it impossible for me to say no.

It will mean doing Sam's chores as well as my own, but what am I to do? These are things Sam *should* be learning. I certainly can't teach him, and most other people keep their distance from Sam, as though his troubles might be contagious.

For years I've tried to ignore the whispers, the speculation about Sam, and what his leg signifies about the rest of our family. Physical deformity is a sign of corruption, of moral decay. Town folk are suspicious about the sort of man Sam will become. But they were also suspicious of Mother. She must have done something awful to deserve a cripple for a son, they would say. And sometimes, that line of speculation would lead back to me.

There is no question that, deformity or not, Sam is our father's son. His curly brown hair and mischievous upturned nose is—*was*—identical to Father's. With me, though, there is room for question. My hair is pale brown and straight. Not so unusual. My eyes, though, are green—startlingly so. No one in my family has eyes like that. I've heard it whispered that they look uncannily similar to those of a former priest at the abbey.

Since the priest in question moved away some years ago, I am not able to ascertain the matter for myself. I'm not sure I even want to. The man I know as my father never suggested I was anything but his daughter. It seems a disservice for me to question my parentage.

But my father's loyalty doesn't keep people from whispering—and, no matter the color of my eyes, those whispers always come back to Sam. It makes me so angry. If *I* am the illegitimate one, then why aren't they mean to me? But they aren't. My body is unscathed, and I have the favor of being the abbot's assistant. Sam gets it all. He's probably even been blamed for the decline of our family, though Lord knows that began before his time.

Tobias is one of the few people who never treats Sam like there's something incurably wrong with him. And Tobias is definitely one of the few, perhaps the only, who would think to offer to take Sam hunting—to *not* just assume Sam is incapable.

"It's fine. Sam can go. And thank you." I don't have to elaborate. When our eyes meet, I know he understands.

❧

Autumn passes quickly—too quickly, for with each passing day, I know time is running out. Christmas approaches, yet the mood remains somber. In all likelihood, this will be the abbey's last Christmas. All of us turn out to help hang the decorations—fresh-scented pine boughs and wreaths, scarlet ribbons, and my favorite…a hollow gold star with an intricate, lacy pattern cut out of the metal. You place a candle inside, and it casts the pattern of the metal onto the walls nearby, a lovely mix of light and shadow.

In spite of the decorations, a quiet gloom permeates the halls of the abbey. The ranks of refugee monks—those who sought sanctuary at Glastonbury after being forced to leave their places of duty—have grown, but many of our own monks and clerics have left of their own accord. Some, fearing the worst, have taken positions in France or Spain—countries still in accord with the Church. Others have chosen a secular life, or even converted to the new Church of England. There are fewer residents at the abbey to celebrate than in years past.

Even the air feels weighted, like the air before a thunderstorm. Too late in the year for storms, but the feeling persists.

Tobias has remained in town, and he, too, seems to be waiting—though in his case, it isn't clear what he waits *for*. He hasn't said anything about his intent, and I learned my lesson about prying. He's taken Sam hunting a few times now. I have had to learn to roast quail. I wasn't very good at it the first time—but honestly, I could have burned the birds to a crisp and Sam would still have eaten them. Nothing was going to dampen his pride at having partaken in a successful hunt.

Sam is still convinced that Tobias is courting me, but mostly because he has seized upon a way to get a rise out of me. His teasing is well-intentioned, but likely unfounded. If it were true, then surely Tobias would have a problem with the fact that Henry Bledsoe is definitely courting me. After all, we see both Seybourne brothers at mass at least twice a week, and more often than not, Henry is there as well.

Henry is several years older than me. The son of a stonemason, he has a small patch of land just east of Glastonbury. He farms it diligently and has a reputation for kindness among his neighbors. This is a good sign. He does not come off as grasping, upwardly climbing, like so many other new landowners. Still, he may make something of himself through hard work and kindness. I would like to believe this is possible, especially as it is what God instructs of us.

So, yes, I have given Henry Bledsoe indication that his interest will not go unreturned. He stays after mass, and asks me to walk with him. He is an awkward conversationalist. He says he has grown too used to living alone.

But if he is slow to speak, he is also slow to judge, and I deem his interest more genuine than that of Robert, the butcher's son. More genuine, too, than the interest of Tobias Seybourne—in spite of my matchmaking brother's ideas.

Henry will have to speak with my uncles if we are to take this further. He is not a man to be rushed, so I do not pressure him.

If I am honest with myself, I am also in no rush. My feelings for Henry are…I don't know. Mild. Pleasant, but mild. I could live with him, if we were to marry, and he would not be a tyrant or demand too much. This is not a bad possibility. And yet, I find myself waiting—not necessarily for a better offer. It's just the sense that something else, something big, is going to happen soon. Most likely it will be the fall of Glastonbury. When it comes, perhaps my path will be made clear—whether I am to marry Henry Bledsoe, or whether fate has chosen another path for me.

The trouble I am waiting for comes, fittingly, on a blustery December day, after the Christmas celebrations are over. The abbot has been away for several days, lessening my workload to near nothing. When he returns, though, it is as though he has aged another ten years. His skin is chalky, and he moves like a ghost, drifting through his surroundings.

I run to fetch him some hot, spiced wine, thinking the travel has taken its toll on him and he has caught a chill. He accepts it gratefully, wrapping his hands around the mug and breathing it in before drinking. He drinks it slowly, and he seems to come back to the physical world. He takes his seat behind his desk, setting the mug down. He looks about him for a moment, as though trying to remember what it is he meant to do.

Finally, he picks up a quill and pulls a fresh page of writing paper toward him. But his hand trembles when he goes to dip the quill into the ink, and he pauses. His head droops forward, and the quill, forgotten in his hand, drips ink onto the paper. The ink is absorbed, spreading across the fibers—an unsightly blemish from a man who is usually meticulous.

"Is aught troubling you, Father Abbot?"

He closes his eyes for a moment. The lines in his face seem etched deeper than ever. "I would not wish to burden you with my troubles."

"No, of course not," I murmur. "But I've a willing ear if talking will help you think things through."

"You are much like your mother." Before me, my mother served in the same capacity I do now. It's one of the ways I can still feel connected with her. One of the reasons I accepted her place—not that I could have turned it down.

"Thank you, Father Abbot."

"Indeed, I meant it as a compliment." He is quiet for a time, then begins to tell me of the thoughts that burden him. "You have heard, I suppose, that Pope Paul has reissued the Bull of Excommunication against our king?"

"Yes, Father Abbot." Pope Paul's predecessor, Pope Clement, had done this already, which was horrible enough, but then it was held up and not made official…until now.

"All of Christendom now knows the excommunication has gone through. Our country is at greater risk than ever from those who would seize this excuse to band together to depose our king. He will prepare for battle, of course. To do so he will need funds."

"Funds raised by bringing down the final—the greatest—of the abbeys." I complete the thought for him.

"Indeed. I have witnessed too many funerals of late…funerals of friends, and men taken before their time. In October, my colleague John Young passed away just three days before Repton Priory surrendered—for the second time. And I have just now come from the funeral of a fellow abbot who died after seeing his monks turned out and reduced to beggars. I have seen the destruction of Roche Abbey, torn down with such zeal that there are few walls left standing. The local residents wrought much of the destruction, it is said, reasoning they had first claim, and if they did not take what they could, the king's men would do it for them and leave them with nothing. All this weighs heavily on my heart."

I understand, but don't know what to tell him. There is no comfort I can offer.

"It falls to me, I believe, to plan for the disposition of Glastonbury Abbey. The land and the valuables will go to the royal treasury, of course. But the king will not take nearly as great an interest in what becomes of the people. I must look to the protection of Glastonbury's monks, and of certain other…items."

"What items?"

"Items that will be destroyed, desecrated, and then forgotten." He speaks slowly, testing each word. "Some things that should not meet such a fate. King Henry's men value gold and silver. A relic made of gold, they recognize and factor into their assessment of the Church's value. But other relics? These, they warn against. They condemn the practice of venerating certain relics, of incorporating them into one's worship of God."

"The writings of Erasmus," I murmur.

He nods approvingly. "You know of them?"

"I haven't read them, of course," I say, hastily. "I only know what I hear others repeat." Being surrounded by so many learned men, I have retained what schooling I had—perhaps even expanding upon it, though mostly just by absorbing the conversations around me.

"That is fine. You have the meaning of it. What troubles me is that many of Glastonbury's greatest treasures cannot be measured in gold, or even rock and stone."

I'm not quite following where his thoughts are leading, but a little spurt of curiosity pushes me to prompt him. "Father Abbot?"

"In March, Lord Cromwell put out a letter, warning the church superiors against stripping their domains of assets, or concealing valuables, calling it an act of treason to do so. Glastonbury's assets were already cataloged when his men came through a few years ago. They know what we have, or most of it, anyway. There is no sense trying to hide our gold. His letter also said there is no plan to dissolve *all* of the monasteries…but what we have seen in practice says otherwise."

Oh. Well. That much is obvious. The king can, and does, change his mind on a whim. "You are worried that Glastonbury is in peril, and the treasures it holds will end up in the king's coffers."

"Yes—and no." He eyes me. "It's more complicated than that. You must not repeat anything you are hearing right now."

"No, Father Abbot. Never." If there is one thing I am, it is loyal.

"When I combine what I know—what I, myself have seen and heard—with what the monks who have already lost their homes tell me, I see a future in which certain relics of Glastonbury never make it to the king's coffers, but are destroyed instead." He shakes his head sadly. "The idea that the holy relics would go into the king's hands was disturbing enough, but to destroy them? Sacrilege.

"Again, I must emphasize the importance of not repeating this conversation—to anyone. Not even Sam. The Treason Act is too loosely interpreted these days to take chances."

I gulp, cursing myself for giving in to curiosity. Now it is my hands that tremble. I should tell him to stop, that I don't want to hear any more, but my tongue is stuck to the roof of my mouth. I should never have asked what was troubling him. And yet, I have the sense we have set on an irrevocable course, and I must see it through.

Finally, I pry my tongue loose. "I appreciate your honesty, Father Abbot."

"Should Glastonbury fall, the treasures that can be measured in gold and silver will most certainly find a new home—whether it be the royal treasury or a pilferer's stash. It is the others that trouble me."

He rubs his temples, as though even thinking hurts. I begin moving about the room again, straightening things, dusting surfaces…the little, normal, everyday movements that I know, somehow, provide the backdrop of comfort that Abbot Whiting needs right now.

"You remember those visitors from Walsingham? They informed me that the shrine there, the shrine to the Virgin, which the king himself has visited, has been destroyed. The statue of the Virgin removed, the shrine itself despoiled, and the buildings looted. The same happened at Roche Abbey this summer."

Finally, it sinks in, and I know exactly which of Glastonbury's relics—one with no value in gold, but still of immeasurable worth—is troubling him so.

I stop dusting. My tongue, now loosened, does not have the sense to stop.

"If Glastonbury falls, what will become of King Arthur?"

"Indeed. What becomes of King Arthur."

The abbot's words, though quietly spoken, seem to reverberate throughout the room, echoing for long moments afterward.

I trace a finger along one of the abbot's bookcases. So many books. These, alone, are a treasure. But they are nothing compared to Arthur's tomb. A king so great, so legendary, that noblemen today name their sons after him, in hopes of somehow linking the lads to a future seat on the throne. Even our King Henry's older brother was named Arthur.

"The legends say he will return," I muse, for the air feels ponderous and heavy, and I must say something. "I heard it in a poem once, too. The words...they stuck in my memory. Arthur 'shall resorte as lord and sovereyne Out of fayrye and regne in Breteyne,' the poem said." I drop my gaze, feeling foolish. "'Tis fanciful, I know."

I sneak a peek at the abbot, who only shrugs. "I would make a very poor servant of God if I did not believe in the possibility of miracles."

This is what I like about Abbot Whiting. In spite of being a great man, he never tries to make me feel small.

"King Henry, or rather his father before him, has gone to great lengths to prove himself a descendant of King Arthur. The Tudors have fought under the banner of Arthur's red dragon, and have unified parts of Britain in his name."

I am struggling to keep up. "You think King Henry is...King Arthur's reincarnation? That the prophecy has already come true?"

He chuckles. "No, I do not—which is to say nothing against King Henry himself, in that particular regard. But the prophecy says King *Arthur* will return...not that some future king will prove direct lineage to him."

"Oh." I am confused.

"The trouble is, King Henry has already used his connection to King Arthur. So what good would it do him to ensure Arthur's remains are protected and honored? He needs to fill his coffers with gold to fund his wars. But other things, relics and items whose value is more symbolic? Those are more likely to be destroyed, or lost."

"That's...sad."

The abbot is looking at me with a strange expression, as though seeing me for the first time.

"Shall I leave, Father Abbot?" Perhaps I am pestering him too much.

"No, child. Stay. The thing is, I should hate to see the destruction of any relic, but especially not those of our Arthur. I am no prophet, but it would seem to me that as long as he is remembered, and his remains honored, there is hope the prophecy will stand. But if we let him pass unto the mists of time..."

Then I get it. He must think me slow. "You wish to ensure that King Arthur's remains are among those that are not destroyed, but among those that are...well, lost?"

The corners of his lips twitch in a smile. "Clever girl. Yes, lost to those who would let them be destroyed or forgotten. But not lost for all time."

I feel a matching smile tugging at my mouth as he stands, squaring his shoulders. "I fear that I can no longer protect Glastonbury Abbey, nor its living occupants—beyond placing them elsewhere. But, by the grace of God, I can protect King Arthur."

He pauses. "Yet I cannot do it alone. He who stands alone, stands not long. What I *can* do, though, is clear the way for another to protect the king of legend."

"Oh, very good." I clasp my hands. "I should like to think of him, safe somewhere."

He beckons me closer, lowering his voice even further. "Miss Thorndale. I would like to entrust the care of King Arthur to…you."

CHAPTER FOUR

"Me?" I stagger back, mouthing the word. No actual sound comes out. The room tilts, and I reach out, using the back of one of the abbot's large chairs to steady myself. "Surely there is someone else…someone better."

Why would he even suggest such a thing? And to me, of all people. A woman's role within the church is a silent one. Prayer, and reflection—these I know. Not deception and daring. I always thought my quiet nature was part of why the abbot trusts me—why, upon my mother's death, he gave me her position of keeping up his receiving rooms.

But what he asks now…even if I simply followed instructions and never spoke a word…this is no act of silence.

He folds his hands into a bridge in front of him. "Miss Thorndale, what are your plans, now that you are not going into a convent?"

The abrupt change of topic flusters me. "I, uh…I'm not certain. To stay on here, I suppose, as long as you will have me."

His expression softens. "I will have you as long as I am able. But—did your mother speak to you of your future, before her death?"

"She asked me to take care of Sam."

He tilts his head, and I sense he knew that, but was hoping for a different answer.

"Which you have done. But have you not chosen any other path for yourself? Perhaps marriage?"

"Not…yet." He must have seen me walking with Henry Bledsoe, or even talking with the Seybourne brothers.

He nods. "Do you still desire to live a life of service, as you once did?"

"Aye. But that door has closed to me."

"I know. You would not abandon Sam. Your loyalty is admirable. The Church could use someone of such loyalty—and not necessarily in a convent. There is more than one way for you to serve."

"But—"

He flexes the fingers that form the bridge. "I know how much you wanted to go to France. And I know what it cost you to turn the offer down. I would like to see you rewarded…but I am afraid the reward I can offer comes hand in hand with burdens of its own. Miss Thorndale, I would not ask this of you if I did not think you capable."

All I can do is shake my head. There is no way I am capable of this.

Sensing my distress, he appeals to me. "Think of it. The protector cannot be anyone obvious. Those in the highest positions here will be under the greatest suspicion. Even without the matter of the relics, their lives are in danger, should Glastonbury fall."

"But...I can barely take care of Sam. How can I do all this?" I sink into a chair, in spite of the fact he hasn't asked me to. He doesn't seem to notice.

"I do not ask you to do this alone. You will have help." The abbot is warming to the idea, but I can barely hear him over the buzzing sound that fills my ears. "Imagine it. A quiet, peaceful little manor, tucked away inconspicuously in the countryside. You can keep taking care of your brother. And, should all else come to ruin, you will know that you have ensured the safekeeping of one of England's greatest legends."

I close my eyes. It does sound nice. I can almost picture the quiet little manor house. And Sam, safe with me, not worried whether the man I marry will accept him. But the rest...no. It is too overwhelming to think about.

The abbot is just upset, I tell myself. He's come up with an idea too preposterous to consider. Where would I get a manor house? And even if I did, how would I maintain it? It's hard enough to maintain what I already have. Once Abbot Whiting has time to think things over, he will realize it, too.

I stand to leave. Remembering my manners, I bob a curtsy. "I'm honored, Father Abbot, that you would think me capable. Truly, I am. But I fear I would fail—and not just you. I would fail all of England."

The next day, the abbot doesn't say anything about my decision. I spent the night tossing and turning—in spite of Sam's disgruntled complaints. I could hardly lie still, wondering how I would face him again, thinking up what I could say to make him understand that as much as I don't want to let him down, I can't do *this*.

But the abbot never asks for an explanation. He never says anything at all. It is as though that whole conversation never happened. Of course, he is away much of the day, welcoming and arranging lodging for the stream of monks who arrived in the dewy hours of the morning, monks spilled onto the streets as yet another of our sister houses fell.

God's will be done. Submit thyself to the will of Christ Our Lord. These are lessons I have committed to memory since I first learned to understand speech. But is it God's will that Henry be king? That he should cast off a faithful wife, and break the entire country's ties to Rome in order to do so? Is it God's will that those who have pledged their lives to Him should be put out with meager possessions and paltry pensions while their homes burn behind them?

Is this God's will? Or King Henry's?

Those loyal to the crown would say there is no difference.

Others might whisper that Lord Cromwell is the driving force now—that although King Henry set all this in motion, his own personal beliefs are closely aligned with the Catholic Church. Since the wife he divorced and the wife he beheaded are both dead, it is pride, more than anything, which forces him to stay the course. But for Cromwell, there is true seal. In executing the Dissolution of the Monasteries, he can grab power and wealth previously inaccessible. He can change the face of England.

Whose will, then, is being done? To whom do I submit, and know that my submission is the honorable choice?

As the silence stretches on, I wonder if perhaps Abbot Whiting has thought of someone else to take this burden, or dismissed the idea entirely. I should be relieved. Instead, it makes me worry even more, until the whole idea fills my mind, pressing at my temples, begging for attention. I give it a firm mental shove, dusting and mopping with extra vigor, wearing out my body until, by evening, my mind is forced to give in and let me go to sleep.

The following morning is much the same. The abbot is away with appointments, so there is no chance for me to look at him and wonder what he is thinking. He has left a list of people who have hosted him on recent travels, so I compose letters of thanks. I tap my nails against the tabletop as I write, a nervous habit for which my mother would surely have admonished me. I wish she were here to do it. I think of Abbot Whiting's question. *Did your mother speak to you of your future?* Did she? Was there something I missed? Some conversation, mundane at the time, that should have meant more to me?

I should have paid more attention, but the truth is, I didn't, and neither did she. My mother loved me—I do not doubt it—but Sam was closer to her. Even though I was the one following in her path, he was the one who *needed* her, especially as an infant. I grew independent, proud when my capabilities actually brought her back to me—when she taught me to shadow her duties at the abbey. I wonder if she was grooming me for something even greater.

When I finish the letters, I am at loose ends. Having cleaned so thoroughly the day before, there is little left to do in the study or receiving rooms.

That's no good. I need something to keep me busy. Or someone to talk to. Someone who will take my mind off ancient legends and treasonous plots. I hear absent-minded humming drifting in the through the open window, and see Lowdie sweeping the walk below. Perfect. I've never been so happy to join in a menial chore, but Lowdie is just the person to fill one's mind with useless chatter. I hop down the stairs and ask to join her.

"You want to sweep?" she asks skeptically.

I shrug. "I just—am tired of sitting. And my hands are cramped from writing letters all morning." It's a lie, but not a harmful one.

"Come on, then. I'll not turn away good help."

She gives me a smile, and we grab an extra broom from storage. Soon I am being regaled with far-too-detailed tales of her sister-in-law's birthing troubles. I've never attended a birthing, but Lowdie isn't shy with her description, and the imagery of a squalling, bloody baby entering the world is plenty to take my mind off the bones of a long-dead king.

❦

In the afternoon, Abbot Whiting returns. I have returned as well, having finished sweeping with Lowdie and taken my noon meal with Sam. There are no other pressing tasks today, and I hope to be dismissed early, but I wait to ask, in case something has come up while the abbot was out.

He gives me a friendly nod, then retreats to the large desk in his parlor, bending his head over a stack of parchment that looks very old.

He still doesn't say anything, and I am getting up the nerve to ask if I may go. Just as I am about to open my mouth, he starts humming.

I go still. The quiet, haunting melody washes over me. I know that tune.

But I've never heard it sung by anyone—anyone at all— besides my mother.

An awful thought occurs to me. I'm aware of the rumors, the whispers, that suggest my mother might have succumbed to the charms of a man besides my father. Could it have been the abbot himself? Is that why he favors me?

Almost as quickly, I dismiss the thought. Abbot Whiting has greenish eyes, it is true, but they are as unlike mine as two pairs of eyes can be and both be called green. But more than that, I *know* him. I just know, deep in my gut—in my very soul—that this sin, if it occurred at all, did not belong to him.

Too late, I realize he is watching me—watching for my reaction. He stops humming. Our eyes meet in the sudden silence of the room.

"You know this tune."

I nod. I can't speak. I don't trust myself to—though I'm not even certain why.

"I thought you might. Do you know the words?"

I frown, trying to remember. "Maybe. If I heard them again. It is a Welsh song—no? My mother said so…she is the one who used to sing it. I cannot speak Welsh, but I know a few of the words."

He hums a few more notes, then breaks into words. He sings quietly, but intensely. His gaze never leaves mine.

Haltingly, I tell him what I remember. "The song tells of a girl, I think. And something lost. It is at once both sad and—I think—a bit hopeful."

He nods, but doesn't say anything. I sense that he is waiting for me to come up with something more, so I search my mind, trying to remember the times I heard my mother sing it. The funny thing is, in my memories, she only ever sang it for *me*. Not her husband, not Sam, and definitely not in the company of anyone outside the family. Did she sing for the abbot?

My memories don't make sense. Sam was her baby. I remember her crooning songs to him as a baby, and later, he would toddle around at her side in the garden and she would sing silly little songs to him, full of a mother's love. But I don't recall her singing that particular song.

"This song. How did you learn it, Father?" I ask.

"It was passed from generation to generation in my family. My mother learned it from her mother, and my grandmother before that. I did not have any sisters who lived past infancy, so my mother taught it to me. It is one of few regrets I have, that my life's chosen work meant I would not have progeny of my own with whom to share it."

"So you taught my mother?" I guess.

His lips quirk. "No. She was working at the abbey and I overheard her hum it one day. Shortly after, she came to work in the same position you now hold. In all my years, she is the only other carrier of the song that I have met."

Maybe I am slow, but it is not until he says this—*carrier of the song*—that I begin to realize the abbot did not bring this up by coincidence. This is not just some little folk song that he and my mother both happened to know. There is something at stake here. But truly, I am in the dark as to what. This is the awkward conversation I feared, only the topic has changed.

"Did she tell you what it means?"

"No. I remember asking her when I was young. She said she would explain someday. I suppose, for a time, we both forgot. And then when the sweating sickness came—it struck her down so quickly…"

His face falls. "I was afraid of that. Your mother told me that *her* mother—your grandmother—often spoke of dreams and prophesies, of ancient legends, mixing them all in with her everyday life, until your mother was not certain she knew what was real and what was not."

"I don't remember my grandmother. She died when I was an infant."

He seems disappointed, and for some reason, that makes me sad, too. "It's possible your own mother was not certain which of your grandmother's stories were meant to be handed down, and which were no more than a fanciful, passing dream. She and I were working on that, trying to sort the wheat from the chaff, if you will, before her death."

I'm floored. My mother was working with Abbot Whiting on…what? A family history? A book of tales? How did I never know this? I thought my mother and I had the closest of relationships, but now, it's as though I've been told she had a secret life. Maybe she did. Aside from this, there has always been the question of my parentage.

"Why did you never speak of this?"

He answers, but his answer isn't a true answer. "When I realized your mother knew the song, I asked her to work for me directly. Same as I offered you the position after her passing."

My hurt must show on my face, because he offers an apologetic smile. "Your quiet, meticulous ways did not go unnoticed, either. But I think, when you've had time to consider it, you'll agree with me, that the song carried an even greater weight. I did not speak of it until now for several reasons. For one, I did not know how much you already knew, and did not wish to influence what might already be lurking at the edges of your memory. Second, I did not sense you were ready, and there was no need to push—until now." He sighs. "Now, there is need."

"Can you tell me, then? What it means? What you were working on with my mother? Am I to pick up where she left off?"

His answer, once again, is not an answer at all. "Do you know who killed King Arthur?"

"Mordred." I answer right away, despite the incongruity of the question. For some reason, even speaking the name causes me to scowl. I never liked this part of the legend. "His own family."

"A tragic fate. The legends do not all agree…some say he was Arthur's illegitimate son. Others, his nephew. But tragic nonetheless." He rolls his shoulders, as though easing an ache. He takes his time with his next words. "Arthur's sons, and their deaths, were written into the legends. How sad for such a great king to die without a loyal son to succeed him."

I nod. We are back to King Arthur, and I feel a prickle of unease.

"Arthur's daughters did not rise to the greatness of legend. Such is often the case. But the important thing is, they *lived*…and they wrote their own quiet legend, and passed it down in song."

I gasp. The words of my mother's song come rushing back. Snatches of phrases, of faerie stories, tales of a great burden and great honor…

I venture to tell him what I know of the song, guessing at the rest. "A fair maiden, who has lost someone dear. She keeps watch, hoping for his return. Waiting for a sign. King Arthur's daughter?"

His eyes light with a genuine smile, and I feel a sudden…I don't know…a *connection* between us, that was never there before, in spite of the many hours I have spent in his presence. I realize I am speaking more freely with the abbot than I ever have, but I am not intimidated. If anything, energy and excitement rushes through my veins, unsteadying my thoughts. I am frightened of where this may lead, but I have to know.

"I've translated the verses your mother and I knew," he says. "Some of the old Welsh words, I am afraid, do not translate well into English. The nuance of meaning, of emotion…is not always right. Nonetheless, the song holds a certain power."

O'er the misty waters
Ever watching,
Arthur's daughters.

Loyal, true, and strong
They will wait
However long

The king of kings, a man of men,
Brought low by a son grown rotten.
The world has changed
The beauty of his daughters, once heralded
Now forgotten.

A quiet promise did they make
Ere Arthur was borne away
They would watch
And they would wait,
His legacy to guard.

"Arthur was brought low by a son's jealousy and lust for power. But, according to the song, it would be a daughter's love and loyalty that let him rise once more."

It is a very romantic idea. I can't help but be drawn in, a little. "But that was hundreds of years ago. No one even knows the name of his daughters."

His smile grows. "No. But we know their song. Your mother knew it before you, and hers before her…"

Finally, I understand where he is going with this. Why he thinks this dangerous plan is actually my destiny. "You think…" I can't even say it aloud. I try again. "You think…"

"That you are the great-great-great-great granddaughter of King Arthur?" He lifts a hand as though to touch my face, but the distance between us is too great. "I do."

CHAPTER FIVE

I'm reeling, but the abbot isn't done.

"Your mother should have had a coin, or a pendant, as well. Something like this." He reaches into his robes and lifts out a chain. When I see the object dangling from it, the blood rushes from my head and I feel dizzy.

Like my mother's, the ancient metal is worn, both heavy and delicate. A triangle, or, more accurately, three triangles, knotted together in the center. I know instinctively it is of the old world.

It looks odd, contrasted against the abbot's robes. This is not a pendant made by the Roman Catholic Church. And yet, they say Arthur was a Christian king, so perhaps the connection is still there, in this abbot who wears the robes of the Church on his body, and the pendant of Arthur at his heart. I don't know. That is many worlds, many lifetimes, beyond my little world. But I feel as if it is right, too…as if this has always been a part of Abbot Whiting, only I didn't know it.

His knowing gaze pierces me. "You recognize this, do you not?"

"I do. And she did," I whisper. "Hers was silver, though. It belonged to her mother before her, and her mother's mother before that. But the chain broke long ago. She kept it in a little box."

"Do you know where it is?"

I think quickly. I haven't looked for it in years, but I know where it will be—tucked inside the foot of her mattress, where a thief would be unlikely to find it. She'd showed me once, the secret spot she kept her few treasures. My father had kept the household money more secure, in a locked box beneath a floorboard, but my mother had always had her own secret spot for a few personal treasures. I know, instinctively, the pendant was something she kept to herself. It must be there still. "I think so. What does it mean?"

He looks a bit sad. "That's what I was afraid of…that the symbol had been passed on, but its meaning forgotten."

"But you know."

He shrugs. "I know what I have been told, and what I have been able to piece together. There may be details I, too, have missed."

He turns the pendant in his fingers, considering it. "I believe it is a symbol with many meanings. The triangle, of course, a sign of the trinity. But also, if my research is correct, chosen to represent three daughters. Three separate triangles for three individuals, but intertwined, just as their fates are intertwined with that of their father."

"Then…there should be a third pendant."

"There should. Perhaps even more, if the daughters had multiple daughters of their own, or gave them to certain trusted others—people entrusted to keep the watch. We don't know how many were made, nor how many have been lost to time. There may be others who still carry the legacy."

For a moment I hope that he can point me to them—perhaps they are prepared to take this burden. Perhaps there is still, for me, a way out.

"But, save for your mother, I have never met one." He smiles at me as though he has not just dashed my hopes.

We are both silent, thinking about this.

I can't help but wonder why my mother never spoke of this—if all of it is true, and the pendant is more than just a pretty trinket, and the song is more than just a folk tune. Why wouldn't she tell me?

"She was waiting," Abbot Whiting says, guessing at my thoughts. "We were researching the matter—gathering scraps of old poems and songs, and using church records to trace our own histories as far back as we could. She wanted to be able to answer the questions she knew you would have. I expect that desire was influenced by her own frustration at the half-answers and unreliable explanations she'd had from her own mother."

"Instead, I know nothing." I feel heavy with sadness. If she'd have *told* me, I could have helped her. But she chose to keep it from me. I suddenly feel very alone, realizing how much of my life I have spent in the dark. With my parents' deaths, I may never have answers…unless I join Abbot Whiting in his quest. Is that what my mother wanted me to do? Or had she waited to tell me because she, too, was unsure? I try to make good decisions without her here, but I suddenly feel young again, and in need of a parent's guidance.

Would she be disappointed in me, if I refuse? How much had she found out—are we *really* connected to the great King Arthur? The idea, preposterous as it is, warms me, as though I can feel a glowing lifeline spreading from my core and out, beyond my body and across the many years, connecting me to something bigger than myself. I am small, but not unimportant. My decision now will not be unimportant, either. I want to know if this connection is real—but just how much would I be agreeing to? Doing research is one thing. Perhaps I could pick up where my mother had left off. Hadn't the abbot implied that was part of why he'd given me the position?

But I can hardly forget the rest of his plan…the plan to protect King Arthur's remains from near-certain destruction. The plan to commit treason.

"I…need some time. To think," I hear myself say faintly. What will he think, when I keep running out the door every time he tries to have a serious conversation? How far will his patience extend? It doesn't matter, though. I *do* need time. Of course, that's the one thing we both know is running out.

When I get home, I go straight to my parents' old room. Unexpectedly, my eyes well up with tears, and I kick their old bed frame in frustration. As much as I miss them, I am angry, too, at the years filled with lies and half-truths. Why would they do that to me? Actually, why would *she* do that to me? Did my father—assuming he *is* my father—even know? Why does everything have to be so hard, so confusing?

I sink down on the mattress, folding my arms over my knees and resting my head. I need to collect myself. I breathe slowly, until the whirling emotions that threatened to overwhelm me begin to dissipate. I take another breath, and sniff. The air is stale and musty from being closed up so long. I must remember to air out the unused rooms, or everything will go to rot.

Eventually, I push myself up. Long bouts of self pity won't gain me any answers.

The pendant is exactly where I expect to find it, in a little velvet pouch tucked into the seam of the mattress. When I shake the contents into my hand, it falls out first, followed by an ornamental comb and a pearl ring. I glance at the other items, but discard them quickly. They may have value, but they bear no apparent relationship to the heavy, ancient pendant.

I kneel, turning the object over and over in my hands, barely aware of the dust collecting on my skirts. The silver seems to warm quickly to my touch. There is no doubt the design matches the one worn by Abbot Whiting. The pattern reminds me of symbols I've seen carved into old tombstones, though I can't recall ever seeing its exact match—until yesterday.

Would my mother have wanted me to continue her work? Would she have wanted me to go even further—spiriting away the contents of Arthur's tomb and guarding it in secret? Did she think it her destiny and, by the blood we shared, my destiny too?

I know one thing. She wanted me to protect Sam. The abbot's words come back to me. *A quiet, peaceful little manor, tucked away inconspicuously in the countryside. You can keep taking care of your brother.* I know it won't be that simple.

As I sit there, turning the pendant over and over in my hands, another piece of the final conversation with my mother comes back to me. *Be good, and take care of Sam.* She'd paused, gathering strength. *It's up to you, now. Listen to Abbot Whiting.*

I'd forgotten the last part. She'd slipped away so quickly after that. *What's up to me?* I should have asked. But honestly, I thought she was just telling me to mind my employer. After all, I would need my position more than ever, to keep the roof over our heads and food on the table—to take care of Sam.

Now, like so many other things, I remember the words in a new light, and suspect they meant more. *Listen to Abbot Whiting.* If I do, it might be my only chance to learn my true heritage, and fulfill my promise as well. My mother is gone, and as frustrated as I am by her secrets, I don't want to lose her altogether. In choosing this path, I feel as though I can gain back a part of that loss—that I can re-forge a bond grown weak.

I wish I could ask someone for advice, but the abbot's warning—*speak of this to no one*—echoes all too clearly in my mind.

Before I know it, I am back in the abbot's study. Sam was none too happy about the idea of returning to the abbey this evening, so I left him home after we ate. He'd given me a look when I'd told him I was going back. "You're behaving oddly."

I'd cringed, knowing it was true. But I'd also known I wouldn't get a wink of sleep if I didn't come back here and get answers. I gave Sam some lame excuse about having forgotten to finish a letter that needed to go out the next morning. I could tell he didn't buy it, but from the speculative gleam in his eye, I'd guess he thought I was slipping out to meet a boy. Which would also be odd, for me, but far easier to imagine than my true purpose.

When I enter the study, Abbot Whiting just gives me a patient look. He'd known I would return. The thought is humbling.

I put out my fist, slowly unclenching my fingers, to reveal my mother's pendant.

He arches an eyebrow. "That wasn't a lot of time for thinking."

"My thoughts are all jumbled. I need to know more."

"There is little more to know. And, unless you decide to accept your role in this, you know too much already. You have to make a decision."

I fold my fingers back around the pendant, dropping my hand. I'd told him I feared I would fail all of England, should this charge be entrusted to me. But there's one thing that would be worse. If I turn it down, I might fail my mother.

"Is this the only way?" I whisper.

He takes his time in answering. "It is not the only way. I believe, though, that it is the way that is meant to be."

"I need to know more," I insist. "I…I'll do it. Though I may not succeed."

"Failure is a risk we must both accept."

I worry the pendant between my fingers. No wonder it is so worn, if everyone who has carried it has had such things asked of them.

"Audrey."

I look up at his use of my given name.

"Even now, this mission stands on the brink of extinction. Only two known protectors remain. One who did not know her role until just now, and one who is very old. Though I carry my pendant with pride, I have no progeny to whom I can pass it down. Whether by natural causes or other, it is likely I shall meet my maker before long."

The word "progeny" resonates with me. I think of Henry Bledsoe. If this mission rests with me, it will also die with me, unless I bear daughters of my own. I have a hard time seeing the patient, unobtrusive farmer as a partner in this venture. But I don't want a marriage shuttered by secrets. I want to honor my heritage *and* my husband. I can't live the way my mother did. If I see this through, it may well rob me of my potential marriage.

I expect to feel sad. I *should* feel sad. But I only feel empty.

If I don't marry Henry, how am I to have children?

It hits me that—for me—that is a strange thought. Perhaps I have already accepted my new fate, for suddenly it is important to have children, when before, I was perfectly content with the prospect of entering a convent and forgoing the possibility of children. More than ever, that future is lost to me.

"If you die…"

"I do not expect you to undertake this task alone. Indeed, that would only set you up for failure—and contrary to your fears, that is not my intent. Like it or not, you will need a man's protection, Miss Thorndale. I have an excellent partner in mind. Someone who will balance your strengths and weaknesses perfectly."

In spite of myself, I'm curious. "Who?"

"Tobias Seybourne."

I almost laugh. "But…but Master Seybourne is so…so very opposite of me."

"Exactly. But he is a good man, don't you think?"

"He is," I affirm. There is no question of that. But 'good' and 'good for me' are two different things. "Wait. Is he a…I don't know. What are we called? Does he know the song? Or have the third pendant?"

"No, my child."

My hopes fall. "But you told him about this?"

"I did. I have known young Master Seybourne since he was in skirts, and I suppose you could say I trust him like a son. With no children of my own, I chose an alternate to safeguard my small piece in this legacy."

Interesting. Of all the men the abbot could choose from, that he would pick Tobias as the son he never had. I would never have guessed it, but I have no trouble seeing how Tobias would embrace a task such as this. "So...that could have happened before, right? One of Arthur's daughters, or granddaughters, could have had no children, and chosen someone to take their place? So I might not be an *actual* descendant of the king?"

"Perhaps. Your mother had not yet exhausted her efforts to trace her family's lineage."

Strangely, I find the idea of *not* being related to King Arthur disappointing. In the space of two days, I've gone from being quiet, meticulous Audrey who knew exactly who she was, to a woman I barely recognize—one considering dangerous deeds, plunging into the unknown.

Doing so with Tobias Seybourne at my side makes the idea slightly less frightening. "If Master Seybourne is to be a...my...partner, why isn't he here?"

"He was, just a short time ago. He and I have already discussed the plan, or most of it, and he is committed. However, we thought it best that I approach you privately, first. Give you time to consider the idea."

"Coward," I mutter.

The abbot gives a startled laugh. "Now, my child..."

"I didn't mean it," I hastily apologize.

"You and Master Seybourne are friends?" he asks.

That give me pause. Is Tobias a friend? A couple months ago, I would have said we were only acquaintances. But lately..."I suppose you could say we are friends, and neighbors as well, when he is in town."

"Good. It will work better if you are friends."

"What will?"

"The rest of the plan." Abbot Whiting has the grace to look slightly apologetic as he utters his next words. "My dear child, you're going to have to marry him."

CHAPTER SIX

"But…but…" Once again, I am stupefied. This is happening lately with frightening regularity. Why would Tobias want to marry such a dim-witted girl? I give voice—sort of—to the question. "Why would he marry me?"

"Never sell yourself short, Audrey Thorndale," the abbot says, which is not really an answer. "Even now he has gone off to find your uncle, to ask his permission. I, of course, have already given mine."

I frown. With my father deceased, my uncle *is* the next closest male. I just feel a twinge of annoyance that, in spite of the abbot giving me time to think, the decision is already made. My destiny *and* my mate. The "time" is just a kind way of letting me come to terms with it.

Not to mention—the idea of Tobias Seybourne having to ask permission is laughable. His family could purchase mine thrice over, and have money left. Once, perhaps, we were of more equal position. My uncle will be only too glad to give permission. Heavens, he'll likely be beside himself, or think

Tobias is jesting. Or—worse, but likely—he'll think Tobias is entirely serious, and that we've been caught fooling around. He'll think the marriage a matter of necessity.

I hate to think of my reputation being bandied about like that. I've always taken care to be above reproach. I've never fooled around. Now everyone will wonder.

"Assuming your uncle consents," the abbot continues, "we should hold a betrothal immediately. I would be honored to be present for your vows."

Looking at him, and realizing Tobias has already committed to this plan, I know the matter is all but settled—which leaves me feeling quite *unsettled*. Am I not to be consulted in the matter of my own marriage?

It appears I am not.

"Sam could be my partner," I offer half-heartedly.

"Sam has a good heart," he acknowledges. "But he is just a boy. You need a man, and preferably a well-connected one."

I am somewhat mollified by the fact that he does not cite Sam's leg as the reason my brother is not a suitable partner.

"Besides, you did say you and Master Seybourne are friends."

"True."

"Do you have some other objection to the match?"

"Um…" *No.*

He ducks his head. "Of course, there is also the matter of passing the legacy on. It appears to have passed from daughter to daughter, over the centuries. Unless the time for King Arthur to rise comes within your lifetime, you may be called to pass it on as well. I have no daughter, nor a son, to teach. But you, Miss Thorndale, are young and healthy and may very well bring daughters into the world who will carry on this work."

My cheeks will burst into flame if they get any hotter. It didn't matter that I'd had these same thoughts. Hearing the abbot speak them aloud is plain mortifying. "Only a few months ago you were willing to let me join a convent."

"True, true. You are intelligent enough to understand that choices are not always clear. I am a man of God. How could I deny that path to someone else who felt the calling? And yet, you chose to stay, as I suspected you would. Knowing what I knew, I wondered if it were divine intervention, God's will, that kept you here."

I truly don't know what to say. In the span of one conversation, I am gone from a maiden to a married woman with multiple daughters. And it is God's will. It is more than my mind can take in.

I just blink back at him. At least I know from the tightness in my jaw that I am not gaping like a fish.

He appears to take my silence as assent. "When would you like to hold the betrothal? It should be soon, I think."

Tobias

Marriage was not a part of my plan. To be fair, it was not the idea of my soon-to-be-betrothed, either. The best part of being a second son is facing freedom to seek adventure, wherever it may come. In my limited observation, marriage and adventure do not mix well.

But that is what makes Abbot Whiting's proposal so intriguing—intriguing enough that I find myself mounted up, mentally composing the words with which I will ask Audrey's uncles for her hand in marriage. Yes, Abbot Whiting's idea requires commitment, both to a marriage and to a cause greater than myself. But in exchange for that commitment…an adventure of staggering proportion. I can think of nothing else.

My time at court, intriguing though it is—at least when I am not composing foolish poems for barren widows—has little purpose beyond personal gain. And while some people find great purpose in the Church, I must confess, it does not hold that power over me. King Arthur, on the other hand…I grew up playing at knights and battles, mythical quests and fair women. Now I have been presented with just such a quest, complete with secrecy and a fair woman.

As for the fair woman, there is no denying Audrey is lovely. Those big green eyes reach out to you, and her mourning clothes—which it is surely time she shed—do little to hide the trim curves of her figure.

But, God's blood, the maid wanted to become a nun. Who wants to marry a nun? I am learning, though, that things are not always what they appear on the surface. I learned it when I first went to court, but never realized it could also be true so close to home. I have been watching Audrey, getting to know her day by day. She says she values peace and quiet reflection. That may be true, but those are not her only values. If they were, she would have turned Sam and the house over to her uncles and left for a convent in France. If she couldn't bear to abandon Sam, she could at least have succumbed to marriage already—found a man to ease her burden. I suspect she has the strength of iron at her core, for she has done neither.

There is merit in the abbot's plan. I cannot say what marriage will hold—only that life will never be dull. The thought of missing out on the opportunity to be the one to save King Arthur is enough to seal my fate. For better or worse, I'm in.

CHAPTER SEVEN

Audrey

The next time I see Tobias, I am utterly tongue-tied.

We're standing in the abbot's outer rooms, waiting for him to emerge from his private chamber. He requested both of us meet him that morning. Both of us are too nervous to sit. Or at least I am. Maybe Tobias is just being polite.

I'd taken my time getting ready, and walked extra slowly on the way to the abbey, knowing what awaited me. In the wee hours of the morning, a cold wind had blown in, blanketing everything in a fine layer of snow. Sam, who'd suspected I was going out to meet a boy last night, kept elbowing me, teasing that I mustn't appear tired after my late evening, and that we'd freeze to death if I didn't put a spring in my step.

He'll be convinced he was right, that I *did* sneak out for illicit purposes, if I tell him of a sudden betrothal. I'll never live down his teasing. A gurgle of laughter bubbles up in my throat, and I realize I am on the verge of hysterics. Stay calm, I tell myself. Deep breaths. It's not easy.

As always, he finds a way to put me at ease. I'm staring out the window, trying not to make obvious eye contact with him, but watching him all the same, and I see him extract a small wooden object from his ever-present satchel. He turns it over in his hands a few times.

Since it seems like a safe topic, I ask, "What is it?"

He comes over and shows it to me. "A whistle. It blows two notes—one high, one low. I thought I could show Sam how to make one."

"He'd enjoy that, certes."

"So...I hear there's more to you than meets the eye, Miss Thorndale."

I give him a weak smile. "Abbot Whiting thinks I am a long-lost descendant of King Arthur. Of a daughter who lived quietly and stayed out of the annals of history, and whose descendants are destined to guard his legacy." We speak quietly, even though there's no one else around.

He gives a low whistle. "That's some secret society," he jokes. "So secret its own members don't know they belong."

I smile a little more. "Do you know why he chose you?"

"Proximity?" he quips.

"He thinks of you as the son he never had."

It's gratifying to see the way his eyes widen. Even Tobias, who never takes anything seriously, cannot help but feel honored. "That's...I shall endeavor to be worthy." He stands a bit straighter.

Neither of us mentions marriage.

I don't want him thinking I have gotten too big a sense of my own importance. "The stories of Arthur are near a thousand years old. Even if they are true, and even if the maternal line from this daughter remained unbroken for generation upon generation, it has just been so long. An awful lot of water will have leaked into that wine."

"True enough." Abbot Whiting comes from his private rooms, startling me even though we've been expecting him. "The question, then, is whether the wine still holds the potency to do the job."

They both look at me. Right. I am the wine. I don't feel potent at all.

As the abbot ushers us into his study, I can tell from the doubtful lift of Tobias's eyebrows that he's not entirely convinced of my lofty ancestry, either.

"The difference between you and I, Master Seybourne," says the abbot, "is that I am a man of faith. My life's work is built on believing that which cannot be proven by sight or speech, and which may even depend on miracles."

I think of the task before us—one so great it may depend on a miracle. The idea makes me feel very small.

It seems to have the opposite effect on Tobias, though, for the usual jaunty look returns to my new partner's features. "I can't speak to miracles, but I find Miss Thorndale very potent. Indeed, 'twas only the other evening I walked home beside her, and found my mind as muddled as though I'd drunk a full flagon of wine."

My cheeks grow warm, but knowing Tobias, he's just in this for the adventure of it all.

Abbot Whiting watches our interaction, and I think I detect a gleam of approval at Tobias's flirting.

"A long-lost descendant of King Arthur," Tobias muses. ""That would be quite a heritage. King Henry—the elder, not our king now—spent a hefty purse full trying to prove he descended from that bloodline. Why, if the current King

Henry knew, he might just propose marriage himself, so that he might strengthen his own ties."

He's joking, but I suppress a shudder at the thought. The king is said to be an intimidating figure. I've only seen him from a distance, but I know fate has not been kind to his last three queens.

"Speaking of marriage…"

Ah. Here it comes. My gaze locks on Tobias, and his on me. I am certain I cannot entirely hide my trepidation.

Marrying Tobias Seybourne. The prospect is at once both frightening and exhilarating. I do need to marry, but I hadn't thought to reach so high.

What if he resents having to marry down? I would hate that. I don't want to spend the rest of my years feeling unworthy and burdensome.

I wish I had been present when the abbot suggested it to him, so I could have seen his face, tried to discern how he felt. Does he think this a duty? Just one more way he serves England? Or is there a spark of something more? When Sam asked if Tobias was courting me, is it because my little brother saw something I did not? I am afraid to hope for this, but I do.

If I am to be carried along like a leaf in a current, I should at least like for the waters to be warm.

"Are you both willing?"

Panic flares in my chest. "Wait." I squeak. "You mean to do this now? The betrothal?"

The abbot looks surprised. "Oh. No, though I suppose the words did come out that way. I want to be certain you both understand the commitment you are making."

The panic subsides, but I am still tingling with nervousness.

Abbot Whiting gives Tobias a slow, measuring look. "She is pure."

I can see his throat bob as he swallows. "Yes, Father."

"And a little too trusting, in spite of all she has lost. She will need you."

In spite of the chill in the room, I can see a fine sheen of perspiration break out on his forehead. It occurs to me that, as a second son, he is unused to having anyone truly need him. I like to have people need me. It helps me know my place—even if sometimes I long for freedom from the responsibilities. Just one taste of that freedom—that's all I want. Tobias has feasted upon it for years.

"Do you feel as though I am saddling you with a burden to bear?"

I'm glad it was the abbot who asked, rather than me.

"No, no," he protests. "I do not. Audrey—Miss Thorndale—is very comely."

The abbot's gaze narrows. "But you have some reservations."

"I would be honored to marry Miss Thorndale. I only wonder if…she deserves better than what I have to offer. I live by sword and horse. She longs for home and hearth."

The abbot's stern countenance relaxes, and I find myself breathing easier, too. "Every good man thinks his wife deserves better than he can offer. You need a hearth to come home to, do you not? A place to tie up your horse?"

"Every man does. And 'tis a lucky man indeed who will call Miss Thorndale's hearth his home. But what of the times I am away? I would not wish to subject her to danger or loneliness, yet I fear I would do both."

I know my place among men, but I'm starting to get annoyed. They're talking about this like I'm not even in the room, let alone have any say in the matter. Besides, I thought Tobias and the abbot had already discussed this, and Tobias was committed. Now, it sounds as though he isn't sold—

exactly what I was afraid of. When I think about it, though, do I really need to marry him? If we can find a safe place for the relics, then once they are hidden, what more is there to do? If Tobias will just help with the first part—the adventure of moving the relics without anyone noticing, then Sam and I can manage alone after that. I can find work somewhere, and if Sam can handle a fair-sized garden, we'll get by.

I straighten my spine, about to speak up for myself, but Abbot Whiting chuckles. "Ah, the folly of youth. Master Seybourne, if you look deeper than Miss Thorndale's face, you will uncover a depth beyond that loveliness. She has a different kind of strength…not to battle, but to endure. I have faith in you, too—that you will become the man she deserves."

Tobias thinks about that. "What do you expect we will be called upon to endure?"

"That, I do not know. For centuries the relics have rested safely within the halls of Glastonbury. But if I look back further, I know that holy relics rarely change hands without some element of bloodshed."

"But the whole idea here is to avoid that, is it not?" I ask.

"If we can. Yet I doubt the road you travel will be an easy journey. I suspect that, bloodshed or not, it will test you to the very foundations of your strength and your faith."

It is not a reassuring thought.

"I'm ready," I say quietly. "With or without Master Seybourne. After all, whether by blood or by choice, I am a daughter of King Arthur. Even if I did not know it until now."

Tobias blinks, then steps forward and clasps my hand in both of his. "Forgive me. I did not mean to come off as such a heel. Of course you won't have to do this alone."

"It's understandable," I allow. "The idea does take some getting used to."

"The idea of marrying you takes only a little getting used to, for me. The timing is the only surprise. I've often thought, once I'd won my fortune, I should return home and ask for your hand. I didn't know if you would wait, of course. I could hardly ask that of you."

"So the blackberry tarts…and stoking the fire…you weren't simply being neighborly?"

"Maybe on the first. But the second?" He smiles, and when our eyes meet I know the answer.

Warmth spreads through me. I see the abbot retreat to his desk, though I'm sure he is only pretending to be absorbed in the papers he has spread out. He's just giving us a moment. It's possible Tobias is just charming me, easing my fears so he does not get left out of the protectorship, but I let myself believe it's more. Maybe Sam has been right all along.

"It's because I care for you that I don't want to take risks with you," Tobias continues. "That's the only reason."

He looks earnest enough. I should be honest, too. "I suppose I share your fears, in a way. I like who you are, and I fear that by marrying me, you will feel trapped, tied down before you finished your adventuring."

"Audrey, I thought of marrying you well before I knew anything about your ties to King Arthur. But now that I do, and I see your willingness to accept your destiny, I admire you even more. If you'll have me, my adventuring days are hardly over. In fact, they may have just begun."

"'Tis an adventure unlikely to win you a fortune," I warn.

He nods, sober again. "I shall have to find a way to do both. I shan't have us living as wards of the church for long."

He gives my hand a squeeze. "I know I haven't followed convention entirely, but I *did* receive your uncle's permission for the betrothal. So, Audrey Thorndale, will you be my wife?"

The last of my resistance breaks away. There's really no choice here—other than to abandon this plan, and Tobias, entirely. I can't do that. The idea of a life with Tobias at my side…I want that so much more than I ever wanted a life with Henry Bledsoe. Maybe even more than I wanted the convent life. I squeeze back. "I will."

❧ ❧

After Tobias takes his leave, I prepare to settle in to my daily tasks.

Abbot Whiting stops me. "Never mind that. Your education begins today."

"Today?" So much is happening, so fast. I long for my old routine.

"You will continue as my assistant," Abbot Whiting says, "but I want you to devote your time to completing your mother's studies."

He hands me a stack of loose papers and bound volumes. I recognize my mother's handwriting on the top page and my eyes well up as I clutch the precious documents to me. This is what I wanted most—why I agreed to go along with any of this. Suddenly, the longing for my old routine disappears.

"What do I do with them? What needs completing?"

"Examine what has been done so far. When you have finished, we can discuss the next steps."

I nod and carry the stack to a little desk in the receiving area outside the abbot's study. This is where I usually write his letters, receive visitors, and carry out any other written tasks. Though the abbot's house is quieter of late, I am still nervous to look at the papers in a place where anyone might come upon me. I sit at the edge of my chair, hands ready to thrust the whole pile to the under shelf at the first hint of footsteps.

My nerves ease when I see that the first document is merely a family tree. The only unusual part is that it focuses on the maternal lineage, but there is nothing about it that would spell trouble for me. My name is at the bottom of the tree, with a thin little branch leading to my mother, Catherine. She had two sisters that died before the age of two. Their names, Mary and Anna, are written neatly on either side of my mother's name, with the dates of their brief lives beneath. My mother's name has only the date of her birth beneath it. I stare at it for a moment, then pick up a pen, dip it in ink, and—before my hand can start trembling—neatly fill in the date of her death.

The branches leading from my mother and her sisters converge at my grandmother, of course. Another Mary, followed by an Emma and before her, my great-great grandmother—another Audrey. I hadn't realized I'd been named for family. There are a few names beyond that, the oldest of which have dates with little squiggles next to them, which I take to mean the dates were my mother's best guess. The names of male parents and children are written in, but without even dates of birth or death. I take this to mean that, unlike Abbot Whiting's mother, who had no daughter with whom to share the secret, my own family did not pass their legacy on to the males.

Most interesting to me, though, are the names of my grandmother's sisters and their children, for it appears I may have relatives still alive.

Placing the family tree carefully to my left, I look at the papers beneath. Here, my mother has recorded more details. The names of the churches where she located the birth and death records, along with the parentage, of the names listed on the tree. Personal notes about those she knew of are written in beneath their vital information. Two of my grandmother's sisters died young, but the other two, Rose and Edith, married and moved to Kent. One was expecting at the time she moved, and the other had two children already.

Still living? my mother wrote next to their names.

Since my parents' deaths, I have always thought Sam and I were alone in this world. We had my uncles—my father's brothers—of course, but since their self-serving behavior knows no bounds, I hardly think of them as family.

My Great-Aunts Rose and Edith have likely passed on, but what if their children lived? And had children of their own? I wonder if I can find them…and even more, I wonder what they will know.

That evening after work, Tobias is once again waiting at the gate to walk home with Sam and I. This time, I expected him, but my heart still leaps into my throat at the sight of him. I stumble and my cheeks flare with heat. Sam gives me a curious look, but I don't offer any answers just yet. This is all so new. The man standing there waiting for us, the handsome one that Lowdie's younger sister just wiggled her fingers at as she passed…I am going to marry that man.

I really wish my mother were alive. She would be so happy for me, and she could give me advice—like on how to behave right now. Not to mention, she could spill a few of the secrets she'd harbored so well.

When we draw even with Tobias, his observant gaze takes us in. He catches my eye and I don't need to say anything, because immediately, his usual, easy demeanor drops into place. He makes small talk with Sam all the way home, and it isn't until we're within sight of the house that he says, "My goodness, Sam. You had me so caught up in telling tales that I hardly noticed the time pass. Might I have a word with your sister, so she does not fault me for paying her so little attention?"

"Sure." He grins. "I'll just…make myself scarce." He takes off for the house, swinging along on his crutch as fast as I've ever seen him go.

I turn to face him. "Well done, Master Seybourne."

"He's easy to talk to."

There's a moment of silence. Maybe I am not as easy to talk to as Sam.

"Can we just have the betrothal and be done with it?" I blurt. The mere thought of being the center of attention at a large gathering is enough to make me queasy.

He laughs. "I like you better every day, Audrey Thorndale. Any other maid would want to trot me out in front of every living soul in this town and the next five over as part of the ceremony."

"Is that a yes?"

He shakes his head regretfully. "Unfortunately, no. We should do this properly—a big celebration with many guests. Otherwise it appears as though we have something to hide."

My chin comes up. "But we don't."

"No?"

A flush creeps up my neck. "That is…we may be hiding something, but not *that*."

He laughs. "Your distress is charming, and I am all the more enamored of you for it. You needn't worry. The gossips will count the months afterward, whether you will it or not, just as they do with every marriage. When enough months go by, they'll lose interest."

I frown, still uncomfortable. I prefer to hover at the fringes of a crowd…involved, aware, but not what everyone is focused on.

He puts his hand to my cheek, and I let it rest there a minute. It feels good, which surprises me. It's been a long time since anyone has touched me…besides Sam and I jostling like siblings, or Henry taking my arm as we walked around the church yard. But no one's touched my face. I take an involuntary step forward, and his arms come around me. For an instant, I freeze. What if Sam is watching? I'm sure he is.

Then again, he'll know soon enough—about Tobias and I, at least. Pushing my worries aside, I rest my forehead against his chest. It feels solid and warm. Unfamiliar, and yet comforting.

"It will be all right, you know," he murmurs.

I want to believe him…but I am no child to be comforted. I've seen too many times that things do not turn out all right. "How can you know that?"

He is quiet a moment. "I can't *know*. But I believe it to be true. One way or another, things will turn out all right. I've been thinking of it all afternoon. Now that we have chosen our path forward, my mind is at ease, even knowing challenges lie ahead. I suppose Abbot Whiting would call it faith."

I look up at him. *Faith.* I've always found faith before. Why does it seem so hard now? I wasn't lying when I told Abbot Whiting I was ready, with or without Master Seybourne. I am ready. I'm just not as convinced that everything will actually turn out well. Tobias isn't the most pious of men—but he is brave. I am glad for him, and for his faith. Thank heaven I do not have to face this journey alone.

"As for the wedding…maybe a quiet betrothal, and a larger wedding feast?" he suggests. "That will give you more time to get used to the idea."

Finally, I give him a nod. He is too good for me, truly.

He gives me a little squeeze and lets me go. I like it when he does that…like the way he squeezed my hand when we were in the abbot's study. Like we truly are partners. I suppose, from here on out, we truly are.

Then I think of something else. "Should we tell Sam?"

"Uh." He waggles his brows. "My sweet, I think Sam will notice if we get married. We may as well tell him."

I giggle. I can't help it. Sometimes he can be so funny. Maybe the abbot hasn't entirely lost his mind in pairing us together. Tobias does have a way of adding levity to a situation. "You know that's not what I meant."

"I know." He cocks his head. "Do you want to tell Sam?"

I think about that. I *don't* want to tell Sam—I want to protect him. But isn't that just what my mother did to me? In the end, it made things harder. "I think we have to, Tobias. Wherever we end up, he's got to come with us. I can't leave him behind, and it will be easier if he understands why we have to leave. I know he's…not as independent as other boys." I hate apologizing for Sam.

"He's fine. And of course he's coming with us. He may even prove useful…as a lookout, or something."

My heart warms a little more toward this man who has suddenly gone from friend to future husband. "He doesn't need to know *everything*. 'Tis safer for him if he doesn't. Perhaps we just tell him there are certain church records that the abbot has asked us to safeguard in our new home. Taking some records, some old parchments…that wouldn't be so bad, would it? If they were of no value to the king?"

"Not *as* bad. I'm sure there is still some law that forbids it— or the king could invent one, if he thought there was reason. We just won't give him a reason."

"Sam won't tell anyone. You needn't worry about that," I say. *He hasn't got all that many friends.*

"I do not worry that he would intentionally tell anything. There's nothing wrong—that I've observed—with his mind. But he is merely a boy. There are men who would not hesitate to put pressure on him if they thought it necessary. The less he knows, the better."

"True." I do not like the thought of these ruthless men he speaks of. I want to protect Sam from them, but I don't feel any more capable of doing so than he would be.

Take care of Sam. Now *take care of the relics* is added to my burden. But who will take care of me?

I lift my eyes to Tobias, and pray I am looking at the answer.

CHAPTER EIGHT

"I'm getting married."

Sam lifts his head from the mattress. I don't think I was outside talking to Tobias for *that* long, but maybe he's just tired. "Excellent. When?"

He doesn't sound surprised at all. How can he not be surprised, when I still am? "When? Not 'to whom'?"

He plops his head back down, but his eyes stay open, alert now. "Well, of course you're marrying Master Seybourne."

I peer at him. "But I've been courting Henry Bledsoe."

"Pah." He scoffs. "That was never going to happen."

It's true Henry is a placid soul, but I didn't think our cause was that hopeless. Sometimes I think Sam knows more than he should. "Did Tobias speak with you? Or did Henry?"

"No. Not exactly. I just…well, I live with you, right? So I can tell. You've always had an eye for him."

"You're an eleven-year-old boy. You're supposed to be oblivious to me having an eye for anyone."

He shrugs. "Nearly twelve. And I don't have many friends to run off and play with, now, do I? So I notice things. Anyway, when are you getting married? Is he going to come live here? You shouldn't live with John. And you should tell Henry yourself, so he doesn't find out from someone else."

I suppress a smile at the unsolicited advice. "The betrothal will be soon. I'm not certain of the rest, yet. Though I doubt we would live with John."

"Good. He's all right, you know. Just—you know."

I do know. Tobias has to make his own way, without his older brother lurking or giving direction. I wonder if Sam feels that way, or if he will someday.

Tobias says Sam might prove useful, but I wonder if enlisting his help in protecting the relics is doing him a disservice—whether it will tie his fate to mine forever. For now, I limit my announcement to the topic of my engagement.

We begin holding council regularly—a small, secret council. So far, only the abbot, Tobias, and myself are members. We meet early in the mornings, before the abbot's usual stream of appointments takes over. When Sam grumbles at the longer days in the kitchens, I tell him only that the abbot needs more assistance than usual because he is busy making plans for the disposition of the abbey.

That silences him quickly enough. Tobias and I agreed to tell Sam, eventually, but not until we have a plan in place—not until there is need. Until then, we are a council of three.

"I had hoped that other members—other protectors—might come forward," Abbot Whiting says. "Especially now, when it is apparent that so many of England's treasures are threatened. Everyone knows that Glastonbury houses Arthur's tomb. If there *are* others who carry the song or the pendant, it makes sense they would be nearby."

"My grandmother had two sisters who moved to Kent," I venture.

"I remember your mother mentioning that. She wrote to find out if there were any living descendants, but if she received an answer, I did not hear of it."

I frown. A letter could so easily go amiss, especially if the recipients had moved. Tracing relatives through the maternal line is challenging—for although parentage is unlikely to be called into question, women change households and names as they marry. I'd planned on writing a letter myself, but now I wonder if I will have to travel to Kent and ask questions or search parish registers until I find my answers. No wonder my mother did not have them all.

"But you think there may be yet others, outside of Miss Thorndale's relatives?" Tobias asks.

Oh, if only it were true. I think of all the people I know in Glastonbury. If I didn't even know my own mother was involved, how would I know of any others? Anyone could be a descendant of Arthur. "But, Father Abbot, how could they come forward? How would they know with whom they could share their story?"

"I had hoped that by keeping a close watch over my flock, I might discern who among them shared this history—the same as I did your mother."

"'Twas good fortune that you heard my mother humming that day. To have such luck again would be like hoping for lightning to strike twice in the same place."

"Perhaps. There might be other protectors whose knowledge of their history is not as diluted. If they already knew their calling, they might share our concern for the abbey's fate and, possibly, approach me about it." His forehead furrows. "A thin hope, admittedly, but I always nurture hope."

"You are a great and powerful man in the eyes of many," I tell him respectfully. "Perhaps they are shy and fear to approach you with ideas that could consign them to a hangman's noose."

"And perhaps, like Miss Thorndale," Tobias puts in, "they do not realize their unique heritage, nor the responsibility that comes with it."

"Quite likely. I cannot wear my pendant openly to help bring them forward. I had hoped, Miss Thorndale, that if we repaired yours, you might consider wearing it occasionally."

My fingers rise, and I uncertainly touch my throat. "You want me to draw out the others? If there even are any others?"

"Won't that put her in danger?" Tobias takes half a step in front of me, already my protector.

I shoot him a grateful look.

"Think about it. If you didn't know what it meant, who else would? You might receive a few questions, and you can simply say it is an heirloom passed down from your mother—which is true."

"That doesn't sound so dangerous," I admit. "If someone asks more questions, or thinks they have seen another like it, I shall direct them to you."

"Good, good. Now, I think the big challenge, aside from moving the relics without drawing attention, is selecting their new resting place."

Tobias rocks back and forth on his heels, and I can't tell if he's nervous or excited. He shoots a quick glance at me. Nervous. "Father Abbot, are there not certain…groups in existence that might be very interested in hiding these objects?"

"There are. But, Master Seybourne, surely you are familiar with the expression that it is unwise to place all one's eggs in a single basket?"

We both nod.

"The group you refer to has, shall we say, a basket already near to overflowing. In addition, their history makes them subject to scrutiny at the merest whisper."

It dawns on me that they're talking about the Knights Templar—the group that was disbanded two centuries ago, yet rumors of their continued existence have never died out. Some of their members were absorbed into the Knights Hospitaller, but even that group is under pressure from the king now.

"I understand. What do you suggest?" Tobias asks.

"As the monasteries are dissolved, King Henry is granting lands that once belonged to the Church to those that follow him now. Master Seybourne, you have had some favor at court. You should pay attention to this practice. If you become a favorite, you could win some land of your own."

"Ill-gotten gain." He scrubs a hand over his jaw. He has forgotten to shave this morning—or has not yet been home to do so. I try not to wonder.

"'Tis only ill-gotten if you do not believe the king's actions to be God's will."

Tobias contemplates that, never breaking the abbot's gaze. "I did not mean to suggest that."

"Of course not."

I am getting the headache, listening to them speak. Tobias says that at court, every conversation is thus—filled with unspoken meanings. I hope I never have to go there.

"Indeed, I would be hard-pressed to turn down an offer of ."

"The farmhouse?" I ask. "'Tis too big for Sam and I, as it is."

He shakes his head slowly. "Only as a last resort. I would prefer something further from town, so that any comings and goings will not draw undue attention. Also, you will need a secure place to hide the relics. They cannot simply be stashed in the root cellar where any scullery maid might stumble across them."

We don't have a scullery maid, but I keep quiet, knowing that he is correct in principle.

"My family has land already," Tobias offers. "It belongs to my brother, of course, but we could find a spot…"

"If you do this thing, you will most certainly be guilty of deceiving the king. I am already asking much of you. I would not have you endanger your family as well."

Tobias rubs his jaw again. "'Tis true, Father Abbot, that my brother has enough burden to bear already. How much time do you suppose we have? Though I'd prefer to make my own fortune, I could borrow money from John and procure some land immediately. He'll understand if I tell him I wish to marry."

Abbot Whiting grimaces. "We must keep that in mind, but let us not resort to borrowing just yet. There are some, ah, discretionary funds belonging to the abbey that I can contribute to our effort. Unfortunately, the coffers of Glastonbury are well accounted for. The king's men know the largest accounts and holdings already, so the funds with which we support this quest will be meager. And when the abbey falls, they will stop coming. My sources in London tell me that the king has other matters on his mind at present, and Lord Cromwell's eye is not yet fixed on Glastonbury. I cannot say when this will change, but we have *some* time before the abbey is taken."

"You speak as though that is a forgone conclusion, Father Abbot." Perhaps it is. Has the word already come down? Is he, even now, protecting us from the full burden of knowledge? "Is there no chance at all that a few of the great abbeys will be preserved?"

He inclines his head. "I do not mean to give you cause for despair, child. I place my faith in God, as always. But I think we have reached the point where clinging to those particular hopes will not serve us well. We have days, perhaps months, but 'tis unlikely we have years until our time runs out."

"I understand." I know this already—I *do*—but it is still so hard to believe.

"It would be wise, as well, for both of you to begin attending services at a new church. The Church of England."

Tobias's eyes widen. "But, sir—you want me to stray from the fold?"

Abbot Whiting gives a wry laugh. "Soon enough, all my lambs will be set astray. I place my faith in our heavenly Father. I believe him wise enough to know those that are faithful, regardless of the services they attend. When at court, especially, you must embrace the new faith."

"Oh, my." Who am I, if I profess one faith but practice another? Are they very different? I worry my bottom lip between my teeth.

"Many of the services are nearly the same as those to which you are accustomed, my child," the abbot says to me. "After all, where do you think the pastors were trained?"

Tobias turns to me. "You asked me once, which master I serve. Do you remember my answer?"

"You serve England."

"Always and ever. And especially now. Always remember that, and it will seem easier to stay true to yourself." He glances at Abbot Whiting. "I have been making some inquiries on behalf of the abbot. Without using his name, of course, or even hinting at any details. Here is the trouble. Until the king's men arrive to dissolve the abbey, Glastonbury will continue to hold services, correct?"

"To the very last day."

"Then we cannot simply hide the relics—they are too well known, and those that are on display would be missed. If we wait, there is a chance we could collect the relics during the chaos of the destruction—much as the local villagers helped themselves to the spoils of Reading Abbey. But that leaves too much to chance. Lord Cromwell will demand an accounting, and who's to say where he will stop? Can we trust he will focus *only* on gold and silver?"

"We cannot trust him at all," I spit out, then clap my hand over my mouth.

The men have the grace not to comment on my outburst, but I see the hint of a smirk at the corner of Tobias's lips. My sudden show of spirit doesn't bother him.

"Exactly. Instead, I would suggest we commission replicas of certain key items, such as the lead cross, while spiriting the true relics away for safekeeping."

"Spirit away…" My chest constricts. I try to breathe slowly, but I can barely inhale. For some reason I'd imagined we would wait until the destruction, and quietly stow away the Arthurian items while the king's men focused on items for the royal treasury. We would keep them from being lost or destroyed—but now we're planning to steal them from under the king's nose. "This is…this is treason we speak of."

The abbot lets out a slow breath, as though contemplating how to answer. He won't lie to me. I know him to be an honest man.

"It has always been treason. However, I prefer to think of it as protecting the country's assets."

"From the king?" I drop my head into my hands as the reality hits me. All I ever wanted was an orderly, peaceful life among women of the church. So how have I come to be in a conversation with two powerful men who are calmly plotting treason? And why, oh why, do they insist they need *me* to help? Because I know a certain song? Because my mother had an old and broken pendant?

"For a time, yes, the assets must be protected from the king. There may come a day, God willing, when the king is at peace with religion, and is able to turn his mind to preservation, rather than destruction and reformation."

"And there may not." I'm not going to be placated with pleasant, but unlikely, possibilities. *Remember the little house in the country.* I focus on that image. I *will* have the peaceful, quiet life I long for—though not in the halls of a convent. The plan has its merits. I'll have a home, and I'll be able to take care of Sam—without marrying the butcher's son. Or Henry Bledsoe, either—unless I abandon this madness now and forget I ever considered it. But as wildly as I waver between fear and determination, I do not want to give up. I want to marry Tobias, and I want to know what my mother knew.

"There may not," the abbot acknowledges. He does not look afraid. His expression is…resolute. "In truth, I expect to be charged for treason. Not because of the relics. That will remain a secret—again, God willing. But Glastonbury is too great a power for them to let it fall quietly. I have prayed over this matter for many hours. Glastonbury will fall, and those in power here will fall with it. I know this in my very bones. There will be no pension for me. If I am to be charged, I may as well be guilty."

CHAPTER NINE

"I will take thee to wed."

Tobias speaks the words quietly, but they sound like a thunderclap in my head, and the echo of that thunder is me, repeating the words back to him.

The ceremony is small, just like I'd requested. We hold it in late February, before the beginning of Lent, and after Tobias returns from another month at court. The abbot is there, of course, since the presence of a priest is required to bless the betrothal—and he has a particular interest in this betrothal. Tobias's mother and John, his brother, are present. Sam, of course, and my father's eldest brother, who probably attends only to be sure we actually go through with it. It will absolve him of all responsibility for me—but it will also mean there is no hope of the property being passed to him. That is the total of our party.

Tobias's mother keeps glancing between the two of us. It's making me nervous. I'm not sure what she thinks of this sudden betrothal. She isn't scowling, at least. John looks mildly amused by the whole thing, and Sam is eager.

Most importantly, Tobias looks sincere. We have a secret, now, and it has done more to bond us than the actual betrothal ceremony.

"May I present you with a gift—a token of my affection?" he asks, holding up a small ring.

The gold band is heavy as he slides it onto my finger. An emerald winks at me from the center, set into the thick band. Initials from several other couples have been engraved inside the band. The oldest ones have faded away, and now ours have joined them.

I present him with a gift as well—a single silk stocking, carefully laundered and folded. It is an intimate gift, meant as a promise of things to come. My everyday stockings are far more practical. These were tucked away with the items my mother had set aside for just such an occasion. Not a full dowry, but a few special things I would have to start my own marriage and household.

My stomach flutters when I present it to Tobias—especially when I see his eyes darken with desire. The gift is a traditional one, given by thousands of brides-to-be to their grooms, but that does not diminish its impact now that *I* am the bride-to-be.

Abbot Whiting gives us his blessing, and then Tobias leans forward. The betrothal contract must be sealed with a kiss.

I close my eyes, partly in anticipation, partly to avoid having to see everyone watching us. The touch of his lips is firm—not the chaste, featherlight kiss I expected. He draws me closer and lets the kiss linger for a moment, until I almost forget we are being watched. When he lets go, I have to blink a couple times to recover myself.

It is done. Somehow I am still on my feet. John and Sam are both grinning.

My uncle departs immediately.

The abbot also bids us farewell. The rest of us stand uncertainly, slower to disperse. I can tell Lady Seybourne is anxious to grill us with questions, for she only arrived in time for the betrothal, and has not yet had the opportunity.

"Shall we take dinner at my home?" John offers.

"Nay. Let us eat at the inn," Tobias suggests. "To celebrate."

I quickly weigh the options in my mind. If we eat at the inn, everyone will notice the ring on my finger and the gossip will spread like fire. But if we retreat to John's estate, I will be subject to much closer scrutiny.

I do what a wife should, and support my almost-husband. I clasp my hands and smile. "Lovely—a celebration."

He smiles back, and I suspect he knows the root of my enthusiasm.

The rest of the group traipses off, but he puts a hand on my elbow. "Wait. I have something else for you." He reaches into his satchel and pulls out a small pouch.

"You are always giving me things. You have given me too much already," I protest.

"Nay, for this is already yours. 'Tis only that you have never before claimed it." He lifts my hand and empties the pouch, revealing my mother's pendant. The symbol of Arthur's daughters. It has been freshly polished and attached to a new, thicker silver chain. I run my thumb over the intertwined triangles. Like before, the metal feels warm to the touch.

"Will you wear it?"

I nod, not trusting my voice. Somehow this means as much to me—perhaps more—than the betrothal ring he placed on my finger.

I turn and lift my hair from where it spills out beneath my hood. Tobias takes the pendant and moves behind me. My breath catches at the brush of his fingers upon my neck. The weight of the pendant settles just above my breasts, a silent beacon to summon any who might remember and share in the duty to protect.

We follow the others to the inn, and I resign myself to spending the next week—at least—answering to the curiosity of Glastonbury's townspeople.

I can't stop thinking about Tobias kissing me, and wondering when he will do it again. Although the betrothal is as good as the marriage itself in the eyes of many, Tobias and I will not live together until after the wedding. This was my request, at first, to give me time to get used to the idea of becoming a wife. Now, I find myself wondering if I was wrong—though I am still nervous about, well, everything. But I do want to be kissed again, and I don't want to wait until our wedding day for *that*. I am turning into a silly girl, obsessing over a boy. It's the worst possible time to do so, for we have much darker deeds to plan.

The first thing that must be done is to commission a replica of the leaden cross and a few other articles found in the tomb. The cross is the trickiest, though, for it normally sits on display on a velvet tuft off to the side of the tomb. Also, Abbot Whiting wants the work done well away from the abbey, so that it won't draw notice.

Instead of waiting for me at the gates, Tobias now comes all the way into the abbot's quarters to meet me after work. Since news of the betrothal is all over town, it is an easy excuse that gives the three of us a few moments each afternoon to conspire. If we linger particularly long, I can always say we are seeking spiritual guidance so that our marriage will be blessed from the beginning.

What we really are doing, of course, is conspiring.

"You need someone with the talent to make the replica look just the same as the original" Tobias mutters. "Same color—same weight, too. Not to mention someone who would never, ever betray us to the king. A private forge, where there is no risk of being observed. Who can be trusted to do something like this?"

I lift a shoulder in question. Though I have agreed to be a part of this, I still don't feel as though I have much to offer. Half-forgotten song lyrics and an old pendant. Tobias had the chain repaired for me when he took my betrothal ring to be engraved. I've begun to wear it, but thus far, everyone is too interested in the ring to ask about the pendant. Abbot Whiting has promised to fill me in on my mother's research, and I am anxious to learn more about that, but we must focus on the relics first.

I try to drag my focus back to the conversation, instead of admiring the way my betrothed's features light up when he is intrigued by something, as he is now.

"The cross itself is not terribly intricate," I say. I've seen it many times, sitting on its squab of velvet on the pedestal in the alcove where it is displayed. "Perhaps in its time…but now, the work could be done by most skilled metalworkers, as long as they take care to *not* make the piece too fine."

"True. But most skilled metalworkers in England have either been in the employ of the king at one time or another, or would gladly rat us out for the opportunity. Most men fear him. A few well-placed questions or threats…who can we trust not to crumble?"

Abbot Whiting looks at us through hooded eyes. "I have in mind an old acquaintance. A Frenchman. Interesting background…he is a member of a rather obscure order of knighthood, the Ordre de Saint-Lazare. A learned man, with a keen interest in history and no particular love for England's reigning monarch."

"He is skilled in metals?"

"Skilled enough."

Knowing how clever the abbot is, I have to ask. "Is there any chance this Frenchman also carries a pendant that resembles yours or mine?"

"Not to my knowledge—though I will add that to the list of miracles for which I pray." He lifts a thick paper from his desk. The wax seal has already been broken. "I took the liberty of writing to him already, inviting him for a visit. Of course I could not specify my true purpose, but I offered up that Glastonbury houses a great deal of history that might pique his interest, and hoped he would find an opportunity to appreciate it while time permits."

"Nicely put," I murmur.

The abbot gives me a small smile. "He is understandably concerned about his safety. I might be able to convince him if you, Master Seybourne, acted as his escort. I understand you have gained some skill at arms."

My heart makes a sudden leap into my throat. If the Frenchman requires an armed escort, things must be tenuous indeed.

Tobias's brow furrows. "I have some skill, Father Abbot, but I cannot promise how long my services will be available. I am, after all, on leave from the king's service. He could summon me back at any time."

"You think he will summon you during Lent?"

"Quite possibly. I've stayed away far too long. Henry will wish to gather his court for the spring season, before the heat of summer enters the city."

It's hard to think of summer heat when a thick layer of frost still coats the grass and the windowpanes. I know I should be paying attention, but my mind drifts away as the low murmur of their voices continues, sorting out all the possible "what ifs" of the mission we will undertake.

I need something to do with my hands. I pick up my dusting cloth, lifting the inkpot, the quill, the candle holders, and wiping clean the surface beneath them while my betrothed and my employer work out the details of their crimes.

I see a letter that the abbot must have begun writing, for the script leaves off halfway down the page, and it is not yet signed. I'm not trying to spy, but my eyes are drawn to the words:

Dear Edward, it says, *I have selected the perfect pair with which to entrust this mission. I am sure of it.*

I quickly move on, lest they notice my snooping, but my head is spinning. I thought we were the only three people in the world—as yet—aware of this mission. Edward is not the name of a Frenchman—at least, not as he has spelled it—so 'tis unlikely a letter to the man who will replicate the relics. No, what this letter means is that Abbot Whiting has secrets of his own—and whoever Edward is, he's about to know ours.

CHAPTER TEN

"You're so lucky," Lowdie murmurs enviously.

"Hmm?"

It's Thursday morning, and Lowdie and I are mopping the polished stone floor of the Lady Chapel. Normally one of the lay monks does it, but there were fewer of them now. Many have transitioned to secular life, or to a country with a more friendly attitude toward the Catholic Church. There's some sort of ague afflicting several of the remaining monks, so the chore fell to Lowdie. I don't have to help, but, like the day I swept with her, sometimes I get to feeling cooped up in the abbot's rooms. Putting my body to work lets my mind relax. Today's chore is no easy one, either.

Yesterday's rain made the ground soggy, so people tracked mud in during the evening service. In spite of—or perhaps because of—the turmoil over the fate of England's abbeys, the services at Glastonbury are still well-attended. The floor is an absolute mess, and the mop water dirties so quickly we must run back and forth to the well to refresh it. The clouds haven't cleared, leaving a chill in the air. The cold water is only making it worse. My fingers are numb and achy at the same time. This is going to take hours. I can't imagine why Lowdie thinks I am lucky.

"Marrying a Seybourne. Imagine," she says dreamily.

"Oh. That." I smile, like I am supposed to. "Yes, I am lucky." Privately, I have my doubts.

"He's such a fine looking man. You'll never want for anything."

I just keep smiling. What else can I do? To Lowdie—to nearly everyone, for that matter—my betrothal is the talk of the town, a dream come true. Poor, orphaned Audrey, receiving an offer of marriage from one of the best families in the area. It must be a love match. With Tobias's charm, he could have any woman he wanted. Even if I'd been foolish enough to let him under my skirts and gotten myself with child, I have no father of my own to hold Tobias accountable and insist on a wedding. So it must be real.

The town is convinced the pair of us must have fallen madly in love, and I am smart enough not about to disabuse them of that notion. I keep myself grounded though, remembering that our marriage is arranged. Even if my betrothed does claim to be enamored of me, the fact remains that he was not prepared to propose marriage until the abbot intervened. Tobias and I have our friendship as a foundation, and I can only hope it is strong enough to build upon.

Whatever fears I have, it is better to hold them close. Lowdie, with her lazy eye and stringy hair, is never going to marry up. She has a good heart and a penchant for gossip. Truly, it is kinder to let her believe in the dream.

"He might even inherit, if his brother has no children. Or be knighted himself. D'you think he will?"

"He might." Tobias is gone most of the time these days, hoping to earn that very knighthood this spring—and doing whatever unspoken deeds he must do to protect the relics.

"He does go away a lot, though, doesn't he?" she asks, her questions echoing my thoughts.

"To London," I confirm. "He has done well for himself there, as one of the king's men."

"Mm-hmm. Do you suppose he visits the pleasure houses there?"

I trip over my mop in shock. "Hush, Lowdie."

I cast a glance at the ceiling, as though God might strike us down for speaking of such things—in a chapel, no less. "I'm sure I don't know," I whisper.

Lowdie shrugs. "Just curious. Don't you wonder about such things? I've heard some of them are quite elaborate. My brother went to one once. Not one of the fancy ones, though."

"Lowdie!" I hiss, more urgently this time.

She seems to take the hint. "Will you go to London with him, once you're married?"

"Perhaps." I really, really wish I could think of a way to change the subject. I'd like to go to London with Tobias—and not, as Lowdie might think, to keep him away from the pleasure houses. Not to visit the king's court, either—that terrifies me. I want to go simply because I believe a wife should be with her husband. Though, now that Lowdie has raised the question, I'd prefer if Tobias *didn't* visit the whores. If I'm not there to share his bed, isn't he more likely to seek someone warm and willing elsewhere? But I probably can't go with him—at least not until I am certain our secret is safe, and no one is after the relics. Since I can hardly explain all that, I stick with 'perhaps.'

"You should. I went to London once, did you know?"

I do remember. It was all Lowdie talked about for weeks. Finally, she's offered me the perfect opening. "Tell me."

Lowdie does, happily chattering on as we finish mopping. The inns they ate at, the alms houses, the sights they saw along the way... I breathe a sigh of relief. I have enough qualms already when it comes to marriage and my private life. Lowdie's scrutiny, no matter how well-meaning, is more than I am ready for. Thank heaven she is easily distracted.

Shortly after my uncomfortable conversation with Lowdie, Tobias does go away again. I'd known he would, but that doesn't make me like it any better. I'm not sure if he's returned to London and King Henry, or if he's gone to port to meet the Frenchman, or both. Just as we decided to limit how much we told Sam, Tobias warned me that he might not share every detail of his own taskings.

"But I'm your betrothed," I'd protested.

"Which means I must protect you," he'd answered firmly. "'Tis best if each of us knows only what is necessary to share, so that no one person, if caught, can jeopardize everything. You may have secrets from me, at times, as well."

I'd scowled. That didn't seem any way to build a trusting marriage. It's true that I've begun looking at my mother's notes, but so far, it's just tracing my family's ancestry. Nothing I would hesitate to share with Tobias.

He'd caught my chin and pressed a kiss to my lips. A promise. *We're in this together.* Not exactly the kiss I'd hoped for—the kind that makes me forget everything—but it did mollify me somewhat.

"Try not to worry. I am yours now, and will remain so, in all the ways that matter."

I remind myself that Tobias comes and goes like a summer breeze and always has. I hadn't expected that to change, exactly, now that we are to marry, but it still feels different after he leaves. Our futures are intertwined, now. I don't want to hold him back. It just…matters more.

Of course, Lowdie's question about whether or not Tobias visits the brothels hasn't helped at all. Curse her for asking such a thing and planting the idea in my head, where it has firmly taken root, no matter how I try to ignore it.

I hate thinking of him going to another woman for pleasure. It makes no sense at all, for I am terrified of being the one to give him that pleasure. I have never fooled around with the young men of Glastonbury. A few chaste kisses, perhaps, but no more. I know what marital relations entail, but not how to do them so as to please a man.

The very idea—that he will grow bored and turn elsewhere—feeds the doubts that have crept into my mind…that I am not worthy, that he is only marrying me out of some sense of duty to Abbot Whiting, or to England. That he will expect a marriage of convenience, but will not truly make a wife of me.

I can almost laugh at myself. My fear now—of *not* becoming a wife—is so opposite of what I feared just months ago, when I feared *having* to marry, and much preferred the option of taking the veil. The celibate life of a nun has begun to lose its appeal. I still long for peace and comfort, but I've begun to hope I might find it with Tobias Seybourne.

But not if he visits the whorehouses every time he can, anxious to be on the road and away from me so he may seek fulfillment elsewhere.

Ugh. Of course he will. What do I know about any of this? I'd never planned to marry. Even if he is fond of me now, how will I hold his interest in the years to come? Will we lead separate lives, married by name and partnered only by our vow to protect the relics? Never before have I considered the prospect of a peaceful, celibate life and found it so thoroughly depressing.

Tobias

My foot taps nervously as I wait at the dock. Noticing the movement, I rub the foot against the back of my other calf, as though easing an itch.

Abbot Whiting's colleague, the man whose support he hopes to enlist with replicating the relics, should be disembarking from the ferry that docked at Portsmouth earlier this March morning. Monsieur Lefèvre. I am to escort him overland to ensure safe arrival at Glastonbury. No one but the abbot knows I am here, least of all King Henry. I pray he doesn't summon me while I am away. Audrey likely thinks I am at court already.

Not telling her where I was going felt dishonest. I've never told her before, but now it's different. As my betrothed, she has more expectation of knowing my whereabouts. I don't like the guilty feeling, either. I've always come and gone freely, and suddenly I am worried about both King Henry and Audrey— let alone the task set before me.

That, at least, should be simple. But these days, things rarely are. The thing that set my foot to tapping in the first place was the soldiers. The ferry is being searched, the passengers waiting to disembark one by one, as their papers and belongings are checked by armed men. Tension between France and England means ships arriving from France are inspected most thoroughly, though we'd hoped the scrutiny would be lower than if the Frenchman had arrived in London's ports. No such luck.

Yards away, two guards have a man bound at the wrists. They lead him down the gangplank, swords drawn. Around me, men from fishing boats and other, local ferries have gathered to watch.

"What's happening?" I ask one of the observers.

"Smugglers."

I nod, uncertain whether this is just a guess or actual news. "Spirits?"

He shrugs. "Haven't heard. But they've confiscated three crates they brought off board." He indicates the offending items, which are stacked against the wall of a low building just off the docks. The guard standing near them looks tense. French cognac and armagnac is favored by a number of wealthy Englishmen who are willing to risk smuggling it in to keep their personal cellars well-stocked.

How Abbot Whiting's colleague had the bad fortune to book passage on the same ferry, I cannot say.

The next man in line to be checked before disembarking wears the garb of a cleric. I hope this is my man. He presents his papers, and I hold my breath, drifting as close as I can.

"State your purpose."

"I wish to pay a visit to an old friend."

"Says here that friend is the Abbot of Glastonbury."

Definitely my man. He sees me, too—we make eye contact briefly before he returns his attention to the guard. "Abbot Whiting, yes."

The guard frowns and mutters something to the second guard, which I cannot hear. He turns back to Lefèvre. "Purpose of the visit?"

"We wish to pray together," he answers calmly. I wonder if he's as tense on the inside as I am.

The guard scowls and signals another. "Go with him."

"I assure you, my papers are in order," he protests.

"Go with him."

There is really no option. At least they aren't leading him off the ship at sword point. As they step onto the main docks, I fall in line behind them and we trudge toward the low building where the crates are being guarded. The guard ushers Lefèvre inside, then notices I'm still there.

"You jus' gaping, or you know this man?"

"I am his escort," I reply evenly. "Sent by Abbot Whiting." I debate whether to say this last, as mention of the abbot seemed to be what triggered this scrutiny, but it's the truth, and I prefer to avoid lies until they become necessary.

An middle-aged man, older than the guards, sits inside the building at a wooden table. He too wears a uniform. I've never seen so much security at the docks. We are not invited to sit, nor does he provide his name.

"Papers."

Monsieur Lefèvre hands them over, and we wait while the man checks them against a long list on the table. My hand rests over the small purse concealed inside my coat. I am prepared to pay a bribe if needed. Much of the court and its surrounding administration works that way. A small fee for a small favor.

Finally, the uniformed man looks up. "Your name does not appear on this list, which is good for you, monsieur. How long do you intend to stay?"

"Three weeks," the monsieur answers.

"Point of departure also Portsmouth?"

Monsieur Lefèvre nods. I keep my face expressionless. I don't know if I'll be available to escort him back here in three weeks, but surely there are other men that could be trusted with that simple duty.

"You check back in here before you leave. Your belongings will be searched. If you fail to check in, your name will be added to this list." He indicates the one at his fingertips, which I assume is a list of persons not welcome in England. He gives a falsely apologetic smile. "I'm sure you understand. With the…state of the religious houses, Parliament has concerns about ensuring Church property remains where it belongs."

"I understand."

There is no mention of a fee, so I let my hand drop. Better not to muddy the waters by indicating I anticipated the need for a bribe.

He indicates the door, and as we exit, I draw the first full breath I've taken in several minutes. The air is full of the smells of salt and rot, but to me it is far fresher than the air inside the guard shack.

From the corner of my eye, I catch a hand signal between the man we just left, and the guard remaining outside. I don't know what it means, but I don't like it.

We don't speak much as we walk to where the horses are tied up. The monsieur travels light, like myself, which will aid our speed. We mount quickly and set off on a journey that should last no more than two days. We have the address of a retired monk with whom we may seek shelter for the night. Simple enough, and yet, I cannot dispel the prickle of unease that tells me our movements are being monitored.

Our first night on the road passes uneventfully. It's when we set out the next morning that we are ambushed.

We leave early, just after dawn, but make it no further than a mile down the road before an arrow whistles past my shoulder, narrowly missing the monsieur.

"Bloody Christ. Take cover!"

I yank the reins and send our horses plunging into the woods at the side of the road, praying the move isn't exactly what the archer on the other side intended. Another arrow zings past before the density of the woods gives us protection. Whoever our enemy is, he needs better aim.

No one attacks us in the woods, which I take to mean our enemy is alone. One versus two. He held the advantage of surprise, but that is wasted now. I dismount slowly, keeping my movements camouflaged as much as possible. I shoulder my own bow and quiver. My long dagger is already at my side.

I glance at Monsieur Lefèvre, who has also dismounted, but remains pressed against a tree. The horses snort nervously. "It's you he's after. Why?"

Lefèvre spreads his hands. "I am a man of religion, not of war."

Somehow, I doubt that. "At least half the wars I know of were fought over religion," I hiss.

It doesn't matter, though. I was sent as escort. Taking out this threat is my job, not his. "At least get the horses deeper into cover. I'll be back."

I edge back toward the road, squinting to try to see into the gloom on the other side. The road is the problem. Neither of us can cross it without exposing ourselves. I try to put myself in my enemy's head. What would he do? Having missed his first shots, would he give up?

Not likely…though it would help if I knew who he was, and why the arrows were aimed at the monsieur. Not a random attack from an outlaw. They usually traveled in small bands, and would have been indiscriminate in their attack. Someone from the docks, I suppose. The abbot swore no one else would know of Lefèvre's arrival. So…he recognized Lefèvre somehow, and either wants him dead, or wants something in his possession.

He'll have no choice but to follow us. We won't stay put forever. When we start to move forward, keeping close to the edge of the road so we can take cover again if needed, he'll circle back around, cross the road well out of sight, and sneak up behind us.

I will be waiting for him.

Audrey

Though Tobias has gone off to London—at least as far as anyone knows—he was not fooling when he said he wanted the wedding to be done the right way. We won't be able to wed until King Henry's court disbands for the summer. Some will follow him on progress about the country, but many will go to their own country estates to escape the heat and disease of the city. It seems like a long time, but before I know it, I am swept up in wedding plans beyond anything I'd ever dreamed.

Tobias and John's mother, the dowager Lady Seybourne, has bought into the love-match story with as much gusto as the rest of the town. I am surprised by this, admittedly, but it does make things much easier. I feared she would dislike me for grasping too high. Mothers never believe a woman is good enough to marry their son, and in this case, I feared Tobias's mother would be right. Perhaps it is because he is only her second son. Whatever the cause of her enthusiasm, I am most grateful.

For so long I have wanted the company of women. Their gazes gentle, arms comforting, voices soft—when they deign to speak at all. Instead it is men who surround me every day, and though they are as good as men can be, they cannot fill that void. My pending marriage has changed things, if temporarily. I only wish my own mother were here. Lady Seybourne must sense this, too, for she clucks over me and does her best to fill both roles. Not the same, but I try to count my good fortune.

"I worked with our cook all morning to come up with a menu for the wedding feast," she crows excitedly at tea on Saturday.

By "our" cook, she means John's cook. But since John's cook is the same one who served his parents before his father died and his mother moved away to live with her sister, I suppose she still thinks of him as the family cook. Perhaps even rightly, for the only time I've known John to put the man to solid work is when he knows his mother will be sharing a meal at his home.

"Peacock, as the center dish, done up fancy with the feathers, don't you think? Then plenty of mutton and quail to be sure all the guests have meat and fowl. Bread and sweetmeats, and platters of custards and tarts at the end. Oh, and wine, of course."

I blink. "Peacock?"

She gives me a sympathetic grimace. "I'm not terribly fond of it, either, but it shows so nicely. The guests will be expecting a show—especially with your betrothal having taken place nearly in secret."

It wasn't that I'm not fond of peacock…in truth, I have never tried it. I've only heard of such things, in the courts of the king. "Whatever you think best, Lady Seybourne," I say demurely. "It sounds lovely."

She looks satisfied, and makes a few notes to herself about the special items that will need to be ordered. It is a good thing we must wait forty days between the betrothal and the wedding, because she is intent on using every moment available to plan.

Besides having peacock, I am to have a new dress. Two, actually, and new shifts, but one gown in particular for the wedding day. I admit I am excited about this, for I have not dared to splurge on such luxuries since my parents' deaths. Even before that, my father believed wholeheartedly that a family would rise through hard work and good judgment. We indulged in frivolity on occasion, but rarely enough that I am still excited by the prospect of new gowns—especially when I run my finger along the finely spun cloth that Lady Seybourne has selected.

She gave word to her favorite cloth merchant, and sure enough, he must have made a trip to London just for her, because the lengths of cloth are more exotic than any I've seen in Glastonbury. My favorite is a smooth silk of pale green, but of course it is entirely impractical, and I try not to keep looking at it. I've never had a garment of silk, which is usually reserved for the nobility, or those in service at the king's court.

Lady Seybourne, having married a knight, wears silk. But I am only marrying a man who *hopes* to be knighted. I don't want his mother to think I am presumptuous. It doesn't matter, though, because Lady Seybourne snatches up the green silk and holds it against me.

"It brings out the color of your eyes," she says in a dreamy voice.

"Thank you." Unable to quell my practical nature, I point out, "The yellow wool is lovely, too, and it looks very soft. Like sunshine on a spring day. It might wear longer."

"It might," she agrees, "but if you are to accompany Tobias when he travels with the king's court—which you should do, at least for a short spell, as soon as you are married—you must have at least one silk dress." There is iron beneath the soft cadence of her words. She doesn't say the next words, but I can almost hear her thinking them. *Otherwise you will be labeled a nobody. My son is a man on the rise, and must have a wife befitting his station.*

She is right, but so am I. The yellow *will* wear longer.

She casts a glance at the dress I have on. It is of decent enough quality, but the black—I had it dyed after Mother's death—has faded.

Lady Seybourne is inscrutably polite, but I know what she must think by the fact that we end up with both the green and the yellow—and, though the warm season is quickly approaching, she also commissions a fur-lined hood and several linen undergarments.

I leave the Seybourne Manor that afternoon feeling like I am floating. The gold band and tiny emerald of my betrothal ring sparkles at me in the sunlight.

Thus far, I can hardly believe my turn of fortune. This mad plan of the abbot's does have some benefits—though I know the dangers associated with it still lie ahead.

CHAPTER ELEVEN

My heart pounds in morning mass a week later, when I notice the velvet squab where the leaden cross normally rests is bare.

So, it has been done.

The Frenchman must have arrived. My heart pounds harder—did Tobias escort him, as planned? Surely he would not have come and gone without at least saying hello?

Sam nudges me. Startled, I meet his gaze, and he rolls his eyes toward the priest performing the mass. Usually it is the other way around and I must keep Sam from fidgeting too much during services. I try to pull my attention back to the priest, but it inevitably slides back to the empty pedestal.

A little card has been propped up, sitting conspicuously in place of the cross. My gaze keeps drifting toward it, and it is only the movement of people around me—and the occasional poke of Sam's bony elbow—that signals me to the flow of the service.

After mass ends, I make a point of drifting past the velvet pad, trying to see what it says without lingering too long. My Latin is rudimentary—Sam and I only had a tutor in the good years. Behind me, someone whispers a translation. "The item on display has been temporarily removed for cleaning."

My whole body sizzles with awareness. *Tobias.* I *knew* he wouldn't leave without saying hello.

"Keep moving," he whispers, now at my side and taking my arm.

He's right. As much as I want to stop and greet him, we are standing in too conspicuous of a place.

I raise my brows just the tiniest bit and we share a half-smirk as we whisk on by, the happy betrothed couple with nary a care in the world.

"I cannot stay long. Meet me at noon—by the large hawthorn near where the lane splits."

I nod quickly, knowing exactly which tree he refers to. Where the lane splits between Seybourne Manor and our little farmhouse, just to the right—on my family's side—stands an enormous hawthorn tree that must be hundreds of years old. There are hawthorns aplenty all over Glastonbury, but aside from the famous one on the abbey grounds, there are few, if any, as towering as the one at the edge of our land.

The rest of the morning passes in nervous anticipation. Sam, for once, asks no questions when I leave the house just before noon, for he is on his way out as well. He has plans to fish the stream with a couple of the serving lads from the abbey's kitchens. Fishing is an activity where he can keep up, as long as he leaves for the stream earlier than the boys who can run. "Catch a big one," I tell him.

He just shoots me an impish grin. "I'll try. Hard to compete with the one you've caught."

I gasp in laughter as the tips of my ears heat up. "Who says it was me, and not Master Seybourne, doing the fishing? Go on, then." I shoo him out the door. At least he's trying to make friends.

I hurry to the hawthorn, hoping my flushed cheeks will fade before Tobias arrives, but he is already standing there, waiting. I hurry faster, and he pulls me to him—not so much as a "hello" before his lips land on mine.

This is the kiss I'd been waiting for.

His lips brush mine, and his hand cups the back of my head as he holds me tightly to him—much closer than the kiss at our betrothal. The whole length of me is pressed against him, my head tilting back to meet with his. He is gentle, but I can feel the tautness in his muscles, as though he does not *want* to restrain himself. He drags his lips from mine and trails kisses along my jaw, stopping to nip at the underside of my earlobe. The onslaught of sensation startles me, the tickle of his beard stubble in that sensitive spot. Without thinking, I wriggle closer. Tobias laughs and kisses my lips again.

He pulls away much too soon, and from the glance he casts down the road, I can sense his restlessness.

"When do you leave?"

He presses a kiss to the top of my head. "Today. Now."

I swallow hard. I'd expected as much.

"Be brave, Audrey."

"I'm not brave."

"You are. Braver than you know. Sam says so, too."

I smile at that. What could Sam know of bravery?

I wish Tobias didn't have to leave. I try to think of something else. What comes to mind is the empty display pedestal with the "removed for cleaning" sign, and the curiosity gets to me. "Where is the cross, really?"

"Moved to a small chamber, where Monsieur Lefèvre can weigh it, take measurements, and make the drawings he'll need for his…work. He'll return it soon."

"I'm sure he'll clean it as well, for good measure," I say, making Tobias laugh.

"I daresay he will."

Tobias surprises me by returning a scant two days later. Not coincidentally, I am sure, the leaden cross is back in its usual resting place. The original, as far as I can tell. The replica could not possibly be done already.

"Is the monsieur gone?" I whisper to Tobias. We are sitting on the bench in the back garden of Seybourne Manor. I can see Sam, who is poking around a felled tree, picking up and examining bits of wood. Tobias gave Sam a knife as a gift when the two of us got betrothed, and now Sam has a mind to carve little boats and whistles and such.

Tobias's brother is hosting a small dinner tonight—his mother's idea, really. We escaped to the garden to steal a few moments alone. Just in case, though, I keep my voice hushed. They say the king has eyes and ears everywhere.

Tobias does likewise. "Gone to the forge, for now."

"I never even saw him."

"'Tis just as well. Monsieur Lefèvre is no friend of the king, and 'twere better you not be associated with him."

"Is he safe in England?"

"Safe enough where he is. The forge is all but abandoned."

I picture a man working alone in the near-wilderness, building up the fires and hammering the metal into place, forging an item that could get him killed—all as a favor to Abbot Whiting?

"What ties him to our cause? Why is he willing to help us?"

"I don't know. He has some history with the abbot. Neither man chose to elaborate."

"You think he's trustworthy?"

"I don't think anyone is trustworthy. Except, perhaps, you." He folds my hand into his.

We sit quietly until we are called in for the meal. An older couple and their spinster daughter from a neighboring estate have joined us, but besides them it is just Lady Seybourne, John, Tobias, Sam, and myself.

The conversation is pleasant, but dull. The neighbors have questions about the betrothal and pending wedding, and they are the same questions Tobias and I have answered dozens of times. There is some discussion of whether it is more profitable to grow crops or raise sheep, with the price of wool on the rise. In the northern climates, sheep are clearly the answer, but we are far enough south to have a better growing season, if the weather cooperates.

"Someone's coming." Sam, usually quiet at the table, speaks up. He has a view out the window and down the lane.

We all turn, and sure enough, a single rider is approaching the house.

Tobias's body shifts, suddenly alert. "I know him. If you all will excuse me, please…" He pushes back his chair and exits to greet the man.

We are all curious, of course. Perhaps it is someone of import, if Tobias felt the need to meet him personally, rather than letting the servants handle it. Or perhaps it is someone he does not want us to see. Though we make a pretense at carrying on the meal, most of us are watching out the window, even though we cannot hear what words are spoken.

The quality of the rider's horse and gear make it clear he is person of wealth. Tobias greets the man, then takes him around the side of the house, presumably to put up his horse.

A few minutes later, they appear in the doorway of the dining room. We all rise.

"Mr. Moyle, may I present my mother, Lady Seybourne, my brother, John Seybourne, and my betrothed, Miss Audrey Thorndale." To us, he says, "I am delighted to introduce the Honorable Thomas Moyle, member of Parliament and acquaintance of mine in London."

Thomas Moyle. I've heard his name bandied about, usually in conjunction with that of Lord Cromwell.

"An honor indeed, Mr. Speaker," John says.

Oh. The full import of the name registers at John's words. Speaker of the House of Commons. Well-known agent of the king. And he's here, in Seybourne Manor.

"How terribly rude of me. I've interrupted your meal. I only meant to deliver some news and be on my way."

"We were just finishing," Lady Seybourne says diplomatically. I can see her swell with importance—a key member of Parliament has arrived, and in front of the neighbors, too. Her second son must be moving up in the world, indeed. This will increase the family standing among the locals. "Rivers, please take a tray to Tobias and our guest in the sitting room, and the rest of us will join him shortly."

After that, we all finish quickly, curiosity superseding our hunger. The neighbors, of course, are looking at John and his mother, and even me, with new respect. I am terrified, but I do my best to share their enthusiasm. What has Tobias been doing, to merit a visit from someone so high up?

When we enter the sitting room, Tobias is asking much the same question.

"Since when has the king made you his messenger boy?" His jovial tone makes it clear he speaks in jest and not with any intent to slight the man.

Moyle shrugs. "I was headed out near Bath anyhow, to visit kin. Glastonbury is a convenient stop along the way. Though I cannot stop here for long. Your hospitality is beyond reproach, but I have other visits to make as well."

"Yes, Your Honor. We won't keep you."

Moyle hands over a small scroll, and Tobias scans it quickly, then looks up. "I am wanted back at court."

A royal summons.

"Indeed," says the king's agent. "It seems you are in high favor these days. He says he misses your wit, and the brightness you bring to a court too often solemn."

Tobias inclines his head, acknowledging the compliment, but protests, "I told King Henry, I was leaving for my betrothal."

"I know. He says, 'bring the…bring her, too.'"

King Henry is known for his appetites, including his appetite for women, and I suspect his original words were less fit for polite company.

We all blink. Or at least I do.

"Bring Audrey?" Tobias questions.

"That's what he said."

And just like that, the whole household is turned upside down.

The Honorable Thomas Moyle, Speaker of the House of Commons, bids me farewell. Me, Audrey Thorndale, a nobody.

"Good luck in London," he says. "You'll be meeting King Henry before you know it. I suspect he wants to see the girl who has brought a confirmed bachelor to his knees."

My face is hot, knowing I've done no such thing, but I manage a bobbling curtsy as he departs.

Tobias stares after the messenger. Lady Seybourne is sizing me up, while John and Sam simply stare at me, then Tobias, then me again. The neighbors make some hasty excuses and depart for the evening, though I suspect they will be chattering avidly the whole way back.

Sam has disappeared—whisked off to the kitchen, most likely, upon the intrusion of our unexpected guest. It could have been due to his age, but I suspect his obvious deformity also played a role. Keep the cripple out of sight. He'll be grumpy later, no doubt.

"And here I thought *I* was the confirmed bachelor," John jokes. He slumps into a chair with obvious relief. He's been holding his posture as rigidly upright as possible.

I appreciate his attempt at levity, especially since he is so often somber, but I am too stunned to offer more than a weak smile.

Slowly, Tobias turns back to us. "Right. Actually, my previous state of bachelorhood presents a problem. I haven't got a house in London. I board with the other men."

That will hardly work, if he is to bring me along. He and John blink at one another. "There are the Seybourne cousins," John volunteers. "You can crowd in with them while you arrange to rent a place."

Tobias nods, but then his glance flicks between his mother and I.

"We aren't married yet," I murmur.

"A betrothal is nearly as good as marriage," Tobias offers.

"Nonsense," his mother disagrees. "I'll come with you, as Audrey's chaperone. You'll have to hurry and find a house for rent, though. I've lost track of how many babies Mary

Seybourne has put out, but the cousins' house has little room to spare. Once you have us settled, though, we'll have good fun. Audrey and I can plan the wedding while you entertain the king. "

"The king will want to meet Audrey, as well, if Mr. Moyle is correct."

That brings me back down to earth. I give him a quick shake of my head, but I know there is no point. If King Henry wants to meet me, then meet me he shall. "I've never been trained in court manners."

Lady Seybourne brightens. "All the more reason for me to come with. I shall be happy to instruct you. You do have excellent manners. Court manners are just …an added layer. You can't be seen at court until at least one of your new dresses is finished, anyhow. Tobias, how soon are you needed?"

Tobias flicks a hand in a noncommittal gesture. He's trying to keep his mother happy, but I can see the answer in his eyes—when Henry summons, you don't waste time in obeying that summons.

"It's all right, dear," Lady Seybourne says. "The seamstress should have the bulk of it done by now, and my maid is good with a needle, if there are any adjustments to be done."

"I can stitch a hem and manage a bit of embroidery as well," I offer.

"Good. You can embroider the sleeves while Tobias or I tell you what you need to know. Being at court means everything has an edge. Everyone has a purpose, and that purpose often lies beneath the surface of what they say."

I drop my head into my hands.

"You don't have to play those games," Tobias says quickly.

His mother disagrees. "Everyone plays those games. It is expected—a mark of one's intelligence. If Audrey does not, then how shall we present her?" One finger taps at the edge of her jaw. She is giving this the attention of a commander planning his battle strategy.

"She's charming just the way she is," Tobias defends me. I give him a grateful smile.

"Indeed. Don't try to play games of wit, Audrey," John says. "'Tis no slight on your intelligence, but I think you will go further at court by simply being sweet and demure. Compliant."

Lady Seybourne looks at her eldest with an expression that says her estimate of *his* intelligence has just risen a notch. A slow smile lifts her features. "I completely agree. She'll remind him of Queen Jane."

Tobias scowls. "She better not remind him *too* much of Queen Jane."

Everyone knows King Henry was fond of his deceased third wife, Jane Seymour. With the way he cast off his first wife to acquire his second, and then his haste in marrying the third just as soon as he'd dispatched with the second…well, it's come as a surprise that he hasn't yet taken a fourth. At any rate, I don't want to remind him of the unfortunate Jane.

"I don't think we even look alike," I say, though I only ever saw her from afar, and before she married the king—meaning that I didn't pay that close of attention, for she was merely a lady in waiting.

"You don't resemble her," Tobias assures me. "Mother just meant that if you behave thus, he will be pleased with your manner, as he was with Queen Jane."

"Of course," Lady Seybourne says.

We all relax slightly, though I have a feeling that Lady Seybourne has aspirations for at least one of her sons to rise at court, and if I can help him do it, she will have me presented however she thinks the king will best be pleased.

"What about Sam?" I ask. It seems to be a question I ask often.

The Seybournes all glance at one another, and I know they are thinking that this cousins' house of theirs, whom we will impose upon, is going to be spilling out the rafters.

"He can stay here," John suggests. "That way he can keep an eye on your home while you are away."

I'm beginning to really like John. For all his reclusive ways, he has a good heart if you get past the barriers. I think of Sam's recommendation, upon learning of my betrothal, that we not live with John. I bet he never suspected Tobias and I would go off, and leave *him* with John instead.

"Thank you. If you truly don't mind, I think that would be best."

"I don't mind at all."

We set about planning, and the evening passes quickly.

"Is there time for this trip to London? I mean, with everything else that must be done?" I whisper to Tobias on the way home. Sam has gone on ahead of us, rolling his eyes at the lovebirds that dawdled so much we fell behind a boy with a crutch. We are alone, but these days, even the reeds growing in the ditch might have ears.

"Sweet Audrey. It doesn't matter if there is time. A summons is just that. We must go."

"I know. I just… Why us? Why you? I had not realized your importance."

"That's just it. I am not important. I haven't a single drop of royal blood in me—and that may actually be King Henry's favorite thing about me."

"I don't understand."

"Audrey, every man with royal blood is a man who might purport to have some claim—no matter how distant—to the throne." He drops his voice even further. "Henry *must* keep the noble families close, so that his spies can observe and report as to which of them may be plotting against him. I, on the other hand, am too lowly to have such ambition. I amuse the king, and am no threat to him, so my favor grows."

"You are a likeable sort," I admit. "Everyone in Glastonbury thinks so, too."

"You, in particular, I hope."

"Aye." A smile steals across my face, and my thoughts drift off. I will have to get Abbot Whiting's permission to leave Glastonbury tomorrow—though Tobias gently reminds me there is no "permission" about it. My name might not have been on the king's scroll, but I am summoned just as surely as my betrothed.

"Don't worry. I'm going to get you away from the court as quickly as I can. You truly are sweet and demure, and I pray God will keep you that way. The other women at court—no matter how sweet they may seem—are ambitious, striving creatures. I would not keep you there long enough to let them taint you."

I smile in the dark, warmed by how he thinks of me.

We have reached my home, and I offer my lips for a kiss. He presses his lips to mine, warm and firm. The scent of wine mingles with the scent of *him*. He cups the side of my face in a strong hand as he lets the kiss linger, brushing his lips over mine. My breath hitches and my heart starts to hammer. Slowly, he pulls away.

"Sweet," he repeats.

He opens the door for me, then closes it with a final "good night"—seemingly unaware of the windstorm that has swept up and jumbled all my thoughts.

I might be falling in love with Tobias Seybourne. That isn't so bad. After all, we are promised to marry.

I am going to London, and I am going to be presented to the very king against whom my betrothed and I have conspired. That is very bad.

CHAPTER TWELVE

London is teeming with people when we arrive. I've been to the city before, but that was years ago and only for a stay with an elderly aunt on the fringe of the city. I don't remember the awe-inspiring size and the constant bustle. King Henry is in residence at Hampton Court, which is even more awe-inspiring—but thankfully we pass it by. I am not ready yet.

Tobias leaves his mother and I at his cousins' house while he sets about finding lodgings. They are a busy family, and full of questions for me. I let Lady Seybourne take the lead, smiling demurely and putting in soft answers when I can. Good practice for when I must go to court. "Yes, I am delighted about the betrothal," and "yes, it is very much a love match," and "yes, how exciting to be summoned by the king himself."

Lady Seybourne plays up the whole story as though Tobias and I are practically a noble couple and amongst the king's closest circle. I go along with it, trying not to think of how many of the king's inner circle have ended up losing their heads.

Fortunately, Tobias returns quickly, having found good lodging not too far from the palace. One of the other courtiers' wives is heavy with child. She expects the baby to be born in early summer, and the couple decided to leave for the countryside early, so that she might spend her confinement there, where at least the air will be fresh, rather than shut up in a dark room in London during the summer heat.

The rooms are decidedly less grand than I expected, and I wonder if I am becoming spoiled already.

My expression must give me away. "We've done well, to get rooms here," Tobias says. "Proximity to the king is the measure of luxury, and we are not far at all from the palace."

"The rooms are perfect," I tell him. "'Twas only that I am unused to the closeness of the city air." 'Tis true enough. It is a damp spring day—still, with low-hanging clouds. No breeze to blow away the stench of the river, or the smoke from the many hearths.

"Oh, that." He grins. "You'll get used to it, my country wife. And soon enough you'll be back where you can breathe."

We get settled quickly, with Lady Seybourne's maid, Binnie, seeing to most of the mundane chores, then pulling out my half-finished dresses to stitch the remaining seams. I *am* getting spoiled. But I am hardly lounging about, for Lady Seybourne keeps up a running commentary of all the important people at court that I must know, or at least know *of*. I write notes to help me remember. There is Thomas Cromwell, of course, and Thomas Howard, the Duke of Norfolk. Then there is Thomas Cranmer, the Archbishop of Canterbury.

By early afternoon my head is spinning. There are too many Thomases, and I know with a certainty that I will never keep them straight. Too bad I cannot simply pull out my notes during a face to face encounter.

I must know their official position, but I must also suspect where their true allegiances lie, and then *further* guess at whether the king is aware of their true allegiances, and whether he is sympathetic to them. The whole idea of it is exhausting, but Lady Seybourne is full of energy, thrilled at the prospect of gaining entry into such exclusive company. I have come to understand that my husband's family has done well, and while their fortunes have continued to rise, their political climb has been stalled since the death of John and Tobias's father nearly a decade ago.

To be honest, I don't really understand the desire to grasp power, to seize hold of it and shake it like a dog with prey. In my limited observation, power makes for dangerous prey—it seems to turn and bite back.

When Tobias tells me we are to attend a feast the following week, I feel like I, too, am prey—only I will not bite back. I am terrified of our king. What if he knows at once—what if he can sense my guilty conscience? It is one thing to agree to hide in the country with a cellar full of stolen relics. It is another to plot such things, then break bread with the man you are plotting against.

It is a week before I see the king. It feels like a week until I see Tobias, too, for his hours are nearly all spent at court, while mine are spent in the confines of our rooms, working feverishly with Lady Seybourne and her maid to become the fashionable, savvy young woman that has won the heart of a charming adventurer—a daunting task, indeed.

The evening of the feast arrives just as Binnie and I have finished the last details of my yellow dress. I wanted to finish that one first, so that I might save the green silk for my wedding—though if we stay long at court, I suspect I shall need it before then. The yellow wool is lovely, with a closely-fitted bodice that rises just above the swell of my breasts. I am quite scandalized when I realize the expanse of skin above the bodice is far greater than I am accustomed to revealing, but Lady Seybourne assures me that I am at the fashionable court of King Henry now, with summer nigh approaching, and not in the chilly halls of an abbey. The gown is entirely appropriate, she claims. The lower part of the bodice is stiff, with a thin panel of wood inserted between the layers of fabric that end in a V at my waist. My mother had bodices like this, but I have never had one quite so stiff—especially once Binnie laces me in. The effect, once I catch my breath, is quite fetching.

I never thought myself vain, but I cannot help but stare at my reflection in the small looking glass Lady Seybourne has propped above the dressing table. The wide skirts are not as heavy as I feared, in spite of the yards and yards of fabric that disappeared in their making. Binnie has even used scraps of the fabric to fashion a new hood for me, in the French style, to attach to the simple linen coif I usually wear over my hair. We sat long into the evening as she used paste to stiffen the fabric, then rolled and trimmed it to fit the shape of my head exactly. At the upper edge of the hood and at the front where my hair is exposed, we stitched a border of thin, braided ribbon. The noble women will have decorated theirs with beads and jewels, but this is by far the fanciest head covering I have worn in years.

I've only had time to finish embroidering a small border of flowers on the sleeves of the gown, and that will have to be enough. We have spent nearly the entire week working on this—not to mention the hours spent by the seamstress in cutting and assembling the initial pieces of the dress before we took over. Though it was a week of women's company, it was not quite as peaceful as I once imagined—not with the endless stream of court gossip and advice coming from my well-intentioned companions.

When I am finally dressed for the feast, Lady Seybourne fastens a chain with a gold cross around my neck. "Just to borrow," she says when I start to protest. "The king is of a devout mindset these days, I am told. The cross has been in my family for ages, but it hardly gets worn. Its simplicity is perfect with your fresh, youthful look."

Again I feel like there is more going on to her scheme besides dressing me appropriately, though it's beyond me to guess what, exactly, she hopes to achieve.

Still, when Tobias arrives to fetch me—he has spent his day at court, as usual—I allow the weeklong effort may have been worth it. He literally stops in his tracks at the sight of me, and the way his eyes drink me in make me feel desirable. Cherished. Almost even powerful.

"Audrey," he breathes.

The fact that he can come up with no more of a compliment is a compliment in itself. From the corner of my eye, I see Lady Seybourne nudge her maid and mouth the words "well done."

Finally Tobias recovers himself. "Miss Thorndale, I always knew you were beautiful. But tonight, I shall need a sword in each hand to fend off the suitors who will surely attempt to steal you from me."

"They will never succeed," I reply, and it is true. Tobias is altogether dashing himself, with a deep burgundy brocade doublet and smoky gray breeches. His short cape is of simple wool, in deference to the sumptuary laws which proclaim only those with the rank of knight or better may wear velvet for their capes. Like as not he'll look to discard it at the first opportunity anyway, for the evening is still warm as we set off for the feast.

We arrive at the palace amidst many others. I am grateful to be lost in the crowd. I am even more grateful when we arrive in the great hall, and I realize we are seated at one of the lower tables, far from the king and his closest courtiers. With any luck, I won't have to speak to him at all.

The feast is quite impressive, and the din in the hall swells until I have to lean close to Tobias for him to hear me.

"Your mother would love this," I say, as servers bearing great trays of jellied fruits and carved ham pass by, followed by a platter so enormous it takes four kitchen boys to hoist it and keep it level. The palace cook must have quite an imagination, for it holds a creature too fantastical to believe…it appears a lamb, a boar, and a peacock got into a tangle and came out as one. Each dish is presented to the king before it is served. Most of them he simply nods. Some he will taste, or have those closest to him taste, before it passes on. This one, though—the lamb-boar-peacock—gets a pass for its theatrical merit alone. The king gets a serving that includes a bit of each kind of meat, and begins eating in earnest. He is a large man, King Henry, and eats with an enthusiasm which makes me uncomfortable.

"My mother *would* love this," Tobias agrees. "It's just as well she is not here to get any ideas."

"She has them already. We're going to have peacock for the wedding," I reply, unable to keep the smirk from my lips.

"No," he deadpans.

"Oh, yes. Yes, indeed. Peacock for certain."

He passes his hand over his eyes, then raises his gaze dramatically to the ceiling. "Are you sure you wish to marry?"

"It wasn't my idea in the first place." I match his teasing tone, surprised how natural it is to flirt with him.

"I know. I'm just giving you the chance to run while you can. Soon she'll be your family, too."

I kick him under the table. "She's not so bad. She only wants the best for you."

"Then I wish King Henry would decide 'the best' was fresh venison and good ale, and we could leave it at that."

I study the king for a while. "He doesn't seem a man given to simple tastes," I murmur, anxious to keep others from hearing.

Tobias considers. "Simple in some ways. A desire to win, to never seem weak. Easily attracted by a pretty young face…some things you can always predict with him. Others, you cannot."

I think of the weeks, the months, Tobias has spent in the man's presence. He must be very perceptive, always gauging the mood of the king, and of anyone else important, before allowing himself to react. I am impressed with him, truly, for that level of skill is needed to survive in this world. He can change himself on a whim, becoming the person the king, or Abbot Whiting, desires him to be. The very idea is exhausting.

After the feast, the king pushes himself up. He is tall as well as broad—a formidable presence. Immediately, the din dies down.

"We have an announcement," he calls. The way his voice fills the large space, winding into corners and sailing up into rafters, is as powerful as his use of the royal "we."

"Our Parliament has, today, passed An Act Abolishing Diversity of Opinions. With this act, we have confirmed the six articles of faith upon which Our Church is formed."

I look at Tobias for explanation, but his gaze is focused on the king.

King Henry continues by reciting the newly confirmed articles, which include the belief that transubstantiation is real and not symbolic, that priests may not marry after becoming priests, and that vows of chastity ought to be observed, among other things. "Our Church" is the Church of England, but these sound like Catholic beliefs.

I listen intently, but I am soon confused. Most of what he says sounds no different than the church I have known since childhood. So what is all the fuss over? Is the break with Rome really about nothing more than a powerful man's fit over not being granted an annulment?

I have heard whisperings of more radical ideas for the new church—ideas such as justification through faith alone, and of women taking an active role—but these are not the ideas the king proclaims. They are only whispered in corners, by people who profess that *they* don't believe in such heresy, but speculate as to which of their peers might.

"He's trying to quell the rebellions," the woman at my side murmurs. Mary someone-or-other. There are so many Marys. Her husband is another of the king's men. Probably named Thomas. "He's trying to show that the new religion isn't really all that different from the old. There's enough threat of invasion from the outside. Spain, or even France. Our king needs loyalty from within."

I just nod.

She drops her voice even lower, so I have to lean close to hear. "Of course, those who *want* reform won't be happy. They'll view this as the king going backward."

"Do you think the dissolution of the monasteries will end?" I whisper back. If only that could happen…I could have a normal life with Tobias. I would still watch over Arthur's tomb—it's odd, I would never have guessed that to be my destiny, but now that I know, I feel it in my blood. But if Glastonbury were saved, I could watch over the relics without actually stealing them.

Mary flattens my hopes. "Oh, no. I very much doubt it. Eliminating the monasteries is about politics and control, more than religion." She gives me an apologetic look. "At least, that's what my husband says. I wouldn't profess to know."

I smile uneasily, then straighten and refocus my attention on our king. It's hard to imagine a man of his influence feeling threatened by priests. But it is so much more than that, and Mary is right, even if she is quick to attribute the words to someone other than herself. She could be dangerous, I note to myself.

As a fresh face at court, everyone is anxious to gossip with me…to feel me out, see where my thoughts lie. I try to excuse myself from those whispered conversations. I no longer know where my thoughts lie—but I do know that being seen whispering can lead to nothing good.

CHAPTER THIRTEEN

The following day, the castle is in a panic. Last night's feast is all but forgotten, for there are rumors of an outbreak of plague in London, and those rumors have reached the king's ears. It is early, not yet truly summer, but the king takes no chances. He will start his summer progress early, traveling through the countryside.

"Does King Henry fear death, do you think?" I ask Tobias, when we are safely back at our own lodgings.

"Not death, exactly—at least no more than any man harbors such fears. But he is a king, with only one son, and a small boy at that. If he or the prince were to die now, who knows what would happen?"

"Of course." When he says it, it makes perfect sense. I do not think the way a king thinks, but all of England remembers the strife before King Henry's father, Henry VII, took the throne. The Wars of the Roses happened before either Tobias or I were born, but we have been raised on the tales of turmoil and angst. A boy king must be guided by a regent until he reaches the age of majority—but rarely does the Regent have only the boy's interests in mind. It would be only too easy, if King Henry were to die now, for someone else to lay claim to the throne. His fear of disease is understandable.

"We leave tomorrow. The king is shut in with his closest advisors today."

"You mean we can go home?" I perk up, nearly as excited as the king himself about the prospect of getting out of the city. Glastonbury is no tiny village, true, and I, of all people, know how quickly disease can spread. But Glastonbury is home, and London is not.

He looks uneasy. "Soon. The king wishes us to accompany him."

My enthusiasm flags at this announcement. "All summer?"

"No. I did remind him of our impending nuptials. He says we shall accompany him for as long as our paths travel the same direction, and then we may divert. He even gave hint that he could make it well worth my while."

A thought occurs to me. "Do you think he suspects…our other purpose? Do you think he's trying to keep you away from the abbey?"

He smiles. "Poor Audrey. You are not accustomed to living in a world where everyone suspects everyone else of conspiring against them. But no, actually, I do not think he suspects anything. I think, in fact, that is why he favors me—he believes me a jovial fellow without any duplicitous purposes."

I nod, only slightly relieved. That is how I always thought of Tobias, too. Very likely it was an accurate perception, until recent months.

"Very well," I sigh. It is only a minor annoyance, after all. The king could very well have ordered Tobias to hold the marriage here, or wherever the king deemed convenient, and we would have no choice but to obey.

"How quickly you learn, my sweet." His tone is teasing. "You'll become a trained courtier yet."

I give a mock shudder.

He laughs and pulls me in for a squeeze, planting a kiss on my lips. No one is about, so I kiss him back. The kiss quickly turns heated, and I grasp the shoulders of his doublet, hanging on for balance as the world shrinks to the tiny space we consume—the press and heat of our bodies, the gasp of breath when we finally pull back.

How is it that this man can make me lose my head with the merest touch? I am lucky to be betrothed to a man I find attractive. A few days at court has been more than enough to remind me how many women marry for position, and how few of them are happy.

Tobias and I will be happy, I think—as long as word of our treasonous deceit never reaches the always-listening ears of the king.

"But what of the relics?" I whisper. "What if we run out of time? Just because the king has decided to go on progress does not mean Lord Cromwell will also tell his men to go on holiday." That group is bent on a path of destruction, and will not easily be swayed.

"I know."

I can see a crease between Tobias's brows, which is unusual for him. He is quick-witted and fearless—not often given to worry.

"The documents I was studying…Abbot Whiting was helping me to translate some of them…what if the abbey falls before we can return?"

"I'm sure he'll store them safely for you."

I'm sure he'll try, but who knows how much warning he will have. I would feel much better if I were back in Glastonbury, preparing for my new role under his tutorage whilst such a thing is still possible.

What I want, let alone what I wish, is not to be. The king's wishes must always come first——at least in the words and behavior we portray outwardly.

The next morning's procession out of London is more organized than I would have thought possible. We will go first to Richmond Palace, well upstream from Westminster. It is a lofty goal for one day's travel, but the king will rest easier with distance between himself and the possibility of disease. Richmond is one of the royal palaces. With it being so early in the season, the court has not yet published the list of noble residences to be visited on progress, so Henry will start with one of his own. Richmond is a huge palace, and since some of the king's retinue has dispersed to their own country residences, Tobias and I will be able to stay at the palace. I admit I am excited when I hear this. I have never stayed at a palace, nor even dreamed of doing so.

The servants leave very early. Their laden carts and slow workhorses will take much longer to reach our destination. We hear the rumble and clatter as they stream from the castle gates. The men and women of this group look weary, true, but apparently they are used to the king's sudden decisions. Some will stay behind to do additional packing, and fewer still will stay on permanently, looking after the palace while the king is away.

Tobias and I, having few possessions in the city, are easily enough packed. We ride toward the rear of the king's procession. Lady Seybourne is just ahead of us, riding beside another widow who knew her late husband, and with whom she has struck up a friendship. This is her rightful place in the procession—behind the nobility but ahead of the rest of us—but I have noticed that, in other group settings, she is careful to defer to Tobias, as though he already bears the rank she hopes he will someday earn. It is clever of her, I think, for although she does not overtly state her ambitions, others unconsciously follow her lead, asking Tobias for his advice and opinions, then listening with respect to his answers. King Henry already thinks well of Tobias. Soon, it will seem like no more than a natural conclusion to grant him a knighthood, or better.

The rise and fall of families and titles is the bread and butter, the sustenance that feeds the ambitious minds of the court. "Just look at Lord Cromwell," the people say. "Son of a blacksmith and cloth merchant. A nobody. And look at him now."

Yes, look at him now.

Others mutter things less flattering—especially those born to high rank. They do not like the threat of a base-born nobody rising to become their equal. As for me, I fear Lord Cromwell, but I must not let on. I only hope that Lady Seybourne's ambitions for her son do not reach so high. This is a court full of possibility, but I suspect it is those with few ambitions and even fewer opinions who end up living the longest.

The whole court is weary and tired of one another's company by the time we arrive at Richmond Palace. The servants put out dinner, but the king does not appear. Most of the rest of us eat quickly and retreat to our rooms, which are less well-appointed than I had imagined. We have a small suite—basically just two rooms connected by a door. One for

Lady Seybourne and I, and the other for Tobias. Binnie makes up a pallet beneath the window.

I suppose the castle does sit empty most of the year, which may account for the sparse furnishings. Perhaps the rooms allotted to the nobility are more lavish. I don't know. I have not been invited into those hallowed halls—and while a part of me would like to look upon them, just to see, I know that rooms like the one assigned to Lady Seybourne and I are safer rooms.

The following morning is cool, but the sun shines brightly. I have been eyeing the palace gardens from a distance. They are just visible, if I lean the right way, from the window in our room. On the way here, everyone spoke enthusiastically of the extensive hunting grounds at Richmond, but I was happy to see there are cultivated gardens as well. My legs are stiff from the long day of riding, and I long to stretch them.

"May we go walking this morning? Or must you attend the king?" I ask Tobias.

"We have time for a walk. The king has not summoned any but a few close advisors this morning. I expect he'll organize a hunting party later, but I may or may not be included."

I pause. Something in his tone was...different. "Does it bother you?"

"To be excluded? Or to be included?"

"To not know on any given day, which it will be."

He shrugs. "Only in that it limits the promises I may make to you, my sweet. But I am long used to the life of an adventurer. You stay open to opportunity, and take what comes."

"It sounds frightening," I mumble.

His arms come around me as he chuckles and kisses the top of my head. "You have nothing to be frightened of, silly girl. Now, are you ready to explore those gardens?"

He takes my hand and leads me outdoors. We walk and walk, and the gardens are just as wonderful as can be—nicer, in my opinion, than the interior of the palace. Row after row of hedges trimmed into artistic patterns, and flowers of every color bursting into bloom. Some are in carefully arranged beds, while others spill over ornamental pots and hanging baskets. Faded blooms have been carefully snipped, leaving only those that flourish. The gardener must understand the king well, for it reminds me that the king is quick to eradicate decay or corruption when it crops up in other aspects of life, as well.

Past the flower gardens are the orchards. We take a turn through the trees, where the blossoms have finished and tiny fruits are just beginning to form. Pears and plums, mostly, which will someday make their way to the king's table in the form of jellies and tarts.

When we reach the hedges once more, Tobias slows me, turning me in for a kiss. His lips move over mine slowly, making me yearn for more. I am not as shy as I once was.

"I hope our marriage will prove as fruitful as this orchard, my plum," he murmurs.

I choke out a laugh and swat his arm. "Tobias. You are too bad, really."

"Not at all," he protests. "A marriage is supposed to be fruitful."

"Yes, but…" My face heats as I think of the acts that make a marriage fruitful. I suspect he has them in mind, too, for he laughs and kisses me again, and then I am not thinking of anything.

We are walking back toward the palace when we hear voices a hedge or two over.

"I don't like it. The factions are grumbling again."

"Your Highness, all the known faction leaders have been…removed."

Tobias pulls me to a sudden stop. *The king*, he mouths. I catch a glimpse of King Henry, accompanied by a black-garbed scholar with ink-stained fingers, hardly more than a boy, just before Tobias pulls me down so that the tops of our heads cannot be seen. The thick hedge hides us from view, but the voices of the king and his companion carry.

I want to ask Tobias why we have stopped, why we are hiding, but I know better than to make a sound. Whoever the king is speaking with, it is not someone Tobias wants to interrupt, nor even let his presence be known. What strange games we play, my betrothed and I. He is favored by the king, yet hides from him.

"Maybe," the king says, "but others will rise to take their place."

"What grumbling have you heard?" his companion asks cautiously.

The king makes a weary noise. "The usual. They question my supremacy over the church, among other things."

The scholar is quiet for a moment.

"Speak plainly, Hutton. I would know what you have heard."

"Yes, Your Highness," Hutton says. He sounds uncomfortable. I would be, too. Who is this young man that he holds the ear of the king? One of his many spies, most likely. They say the king has men in his pay everywhere. The name sounds familiar, but I can't place him.

"There are those with whom the break with Rome still does not sit comfortably," Hutton admits. "They fear the power of a king with both religious and military might. They look to discredit you. I have heard the rumors of which you speak, and others as well. They point to your father's efforts to trace the family lineage back to King Arthur, and thus establish the Tudor family as the rightful heirs. They said he had the documents forged—that no real proof existed. They say you are king, but that does not make you the one, true king."

I can almost feel Henry's glower through the shrubbery. "I am the one, true king."

"Of course, Your Grace."

I dare not breathe. My legs cramp from hovering low to the ground. Tobias sees, and settles himself to the ground, pulling me atop him. We move quietly, eavesdropping openly now. The mention of King Arthur has both of our attention.

"Who says this? I'll have the head of any man that would dare speak thus."

Hutton is silent, and again I wonder at his background. "I only know the rumors exist. I could not say from whence they came."

I imagine that the King's glower is turned on his advisor as he stares him down, trying to decide if the man speaks the truth, or is protecting someone. His next words confirm this impression. "You can do better than that. Why do you think your priory still stands, Hutton, when greater ones have already fallen? It is because you are useful. You should consider how best to remain useful."

"If I may, Your Grace?" Hutton's voice has gone timid, and no wonder.

"Go ahead." The king's mood has turned sour, and his words are riddled with impatience.

"If you could produce proof…"

"Bah. You think my father did not already commission the best of scholars? You think I have evidence that he did not?" The king, dismissing this idea, moves to stand.

"Nay, Your Highness. I am certain your father's documents are of the best possible quality. I was thinking of…something else." He emphasizes his last words, then pauses, and I admire the way he knows when to speak, and when to wait. The king settles back on the bench, focused once more on this meek advisor.

"Such as?"

"There are other rumors, you know—not about you, but which may be of benefit to you. There are some who say the Templar knights were not all caught. That those who lived after the order disbanded continued to operate in secret. Their diligence in protecting certain secrets will not be shaken by fear of death."

I can almost hear our king thinking, as he tries to piece together what new threat this underground group of knights poses to him.

"You want me to rout them?"

"No. I want to unlock the secret of the treasure they have so long guarded. Your Majesty, you need a way to regain the people's faith—not in the church, but in you, their rightful ruler. A symbol—something more powerful than words."

"For the past several years we've been telling people *not* to worship relics and false idols. Now you advise me to reverse course?"

"I'm not talking about just any symbol." He sounds excited. "Your Highness, I would not suggest you reverse course. But I think you could safely say there are *some* relics of such holy significance that they should be protected, rather than destroyed. And there is one, in particular, which would prove beyond all doubt that you are not only the descendant of King Arthur, but are favored by God himself. A beacon of light which, when held in your hands, even Rome could not deny."

I can hear the king's breath as he grows excited by this lofty idea. "Go on."

"Your Grace, this is no mean feat of which I speak. But if you could manage it…"

"Manage what?"

"To bring forth the Holy Grail."

CHAPTER FOURTEEN

The Holy Grail. Tobias goes still beneath me—so still I think he must have stopped breathing.

Even the king is silent for longer than is characteristic of him. Finally, he says, in a voice lacking the bluster of moments before, "If you jest, I will have your head."

"I would not dare jest about such a thing, Your Highness."

"I suspect that is true, which is the only reason we are still talking. These Templar knights. You can name them?"

"A few."

"The grail would be a closely-guarded secret. No mere initiate would do."

"No."

I can hear both fear and determination in the scholar's voice. He wants to be done with this conversation, away from the powerful king who could end his life with a single order. But even more, he wants King Henry to believe him. Why? What does he stand to gain? The favor of the king? The glory of having been the one to lead the king to the one treasure that has eluded all kings before him? Somehow, those ideas do not ring true. Hutton gives off the impression of a meek man, one who would be more at home surrounded by books and scrolls than questing for glory. I recall the ink stains on his fingers. Perhaps it is knowledge he seeks. He wants to know if he is right—but he knows he alone does not have the wherewithal to extract it from the clutches of those who protect it.

"You have my attention, Hutton. But we have sat too long in an open space. Such things must be discussed with caution."

"Yes, Sire."

"You will await my summons. In the meantime, you speak to no one."

"Yes, Sire."

We wait until we are certain both of them are gone. I am stiff and horribly uncomfortable by the time I peel myself off my betrothed. He has fared the worst, though, for in addition to having my weight atop him for so long, the morning dew has thoroughly soaked the back side of his clothing. I brush him off as best I can, but I can't brush off the telltale grass stains.

"We should hurry back before someone sees us," I say. "How would we explain?"

A smile tugs at his lips, and he taps a finger to his chin in a mockery of deep contemplation. "Hmm. How *would* I explain that I went walking alone with a beautiful girl, and somehow the back of my shirt got grass-stained?"

My mouth falls open. As I snap it shut, he darts forward and steals a kiss. "I do so love your innocence, my sweet. I think you needn't worry about explaining."

My cheeks are on fire. "People will assume…"

"Is that such a bad thing?"

Now a matching smile tugs at my lips. "I suppose not."

Let them think my betrothed cannot keep his hands off me, nor I him. It is close enough to the truth—and it will keep us safe. I lift my chin as a more selfish reason occurs to me—that other women will be less likely to throw themselves in my husband's path if they know he is content with the woman he has. I will not always be with him. I trust him, but I am no fool. He would be a tempting conquest for many a woman of the court who has found herself tied to an aging, incapable man.

My, how I have changed. I used to want no man. Now I want no one other woman to have my man.

I smile up at him as he tucks my hand in the crook of his elbow and we set off through the grass.

It isn't until we reach the privacy of our room and I put my hand to my heart to catch my breath, accidentally brushing my fingertips on the heirloom pendant, that the memory hits me. Suddenly, I am whisked back to a time nearly three years ago, when I stood at the fringes of Abbot Whiting's office, quiet as a mouse, while he spoke with a prior in traveling robes. That was back in the days when I was a nobody, and men did not think to ensure I left the room before holding their conversations.

"Do you have a plan?" the prior asked.

"I do."

I remember the flash of a square cross sewn into an under sleeve. Inconspicuous, and yet branded in my mind.

Templars.

King Arthur.

The Holy Grail.

I need to sit down.

I gingerly make my way to the stool near the fireplace. The thin tuft of the cushion is no cushion at all from the assault of memories, the questions that pierce me like arrows.

"Audrey? Are you all right?"

I rub the sides of my head with my fingers. "Tobias, I just realized…the Templars. King Arthur."

He flicks a glance around the room. His mother, whose room adjoins ours, is out and about. He comes close, taking a knee at my side. "What do you mean?"

"Hutton, and the king. You heard what they said. The Templars have the grail."

"Yes. Such rumors have existed for centuries. Do you think Hutton really knows anything more than the legions who have come before?"

I shake my head as my thoughts try to drift. I feel like I *almost* can grasp the connection I believe is there, but not quite. "Maybe. I don't know. But with all the monasteries and abbeys being destroyed, if the grail was hidden at one of them, wouldn't they *have* to move it now, or risk it being lost? Or even destroyed?"

"They would—*if* its hiding place is in England, and *if* it is threatened by this turn of events. Do you think, though, they would have done it already?"

"I don't know what to think, honestly, Tobias. When this first began, we all thought the larger abbeys would be spared. But now…"

"All right. Let's suppose, for a moment, that the grail *is* here, and its keepers believe it is no longer safe." He nods to himself. "Not too different from our own circumstances with…you know. If Hutton could tell King Henry when it was going to be moved…and he were to intercept it in transit…"

A hysterical laugh bubbles up and escapes my throat. "Tobias...I think there's a chance Hutton does know something. The stories of the grail...they are so often linked with those of King Arthur. The legend we've sworn to protect."

His dark eyes are locked on mine, but I can see his curiosity is mixed with confusion.

"We've sworn to protect his mortal remains, and the cross that marks them as such. Nothing more."

"Nothing more," I repeat, willing it to be true. But so many things are not the way I once thought they were, that I cannot be certain of this, either. Not when I know what I have seen. "Tobias, the Templars do still exist."

He blinks. "My dear Audrey, I am already jealous that you are likely the long-lost descendant of King Arthur himself. Never tell me you are descended from a family of Templar knights as well."

He makes me smile. "No. But I have seen one."

"You have?" His lips quirk. "And here I thought myself the adventurer. Audrey Thorndale, for a small, soft-spoken girl, you are full of interesting secrets."

Only Tobias would see it that way, as though it's a good thing. But I know better. These secrets are dangerous.

"Do you know where I last saw a Templar knight?"

"Besides in a book?" he quips.

"At Glastonbury."

That sobers him up. Now Tobias is the one massaging his temples. "When was this? Do you remember his name, or from whence he came?"

"Two years ago." I squeeze my eyes shut, willing myself to remember more, but I cannot come up with a name. There are so many visitors to Glastonbury. If it hadn't been for the pattern sewn into that one's sleeve, I doubt I would have remembered him at all.

"He was a prior. An older man, though not as old as Abbot Whiting. I cannot remember hearing his name, or the location of his priory."

I tell Tobias the rest of what I remember—that the two men were wary, even then, of what the future might hold for the religious houses, and that they'd spoken of a plan.

"Tobias, do you think…" I can barely give voice to the words. "Do you think the grail is at Glastonbury?"

He just holds up his hands, palms up. He doesn't know any more than I do. Only Abbot Whiting could say.

"We need to go back."

"I cannot just leave—not when the king specifically requested my presence."

"But the Templars have a spy in their midst. Should we not warn them—or at least warn Abbot Whiting?"

"If we run off now, we risk giving our own position away. First, we must learn what we can while following the king's court. Just as Hutton is useful to the king, so we may prove useful to the abbot."

I sigh, but I know there is little choice. I don't feel useful at all—I feel trapped, as though my feet are following a path that leads over the edge of a cliff, and yet I cannot change course.

"Will you speak with the king this morning?" I couldn't sleep at all last night, with so many thoughts tossing around in my head. Then, my monthly courses arrived, leaving me sore and entirely out of sorts this morning. In spite of our decision to make ourselves "useful," the first words out of my mouth today were a plea for home.

"I will speak with him, certainly," Tobias says agreeably. "But I doubt I will get the opportunity to broach the topic of leaving, for I am to officiate this morning's tennis match."

"You, officiate? I didn't even know you were familiar with the game."

He gives me a courtly bow. "I am a man of many talents."

"Does that mean you basically call the game so as to be sure King Henry wins?"

"Sometimes," Tobias says sagely. "First, I will try to ascertain his mood. Most days, he prefers to win. Occasionally, though, he likes to be made to feel as though he is a regular man, against whom other men will honestly compete. He has to lose just often enough to keep up the farce of legitimate competition. But mostly, yes, he prefers to win."

"Who is his opponent?"

"The new Earl of Bath."

"Is he talented?"

"Reasonably so. He is a few years younger than the king, and still fit. He understands the game." He gives me a wry smile and amends, "Both games, that is. You should attend."

"Oh, I don't think so."

"The king thinks you are shy."

"I am shy."

"You can stay toward the back if you wish."

I probably should go, since Tobias is officiating, but I am tired and my head aches. "Next time?"

He brushes his knuckles against my cheek. "All right. Try to get some rest. You look pale."

After he leaves, I push the room's only comfortable seat, a padded bench, up against the wall and pick up my embroidery. My back and head still ache, and Tobias's recommendation to rest is tempting, but I feel as though crawling back into bed would be akin to admitting defeat.

Being on progress feels like long stretches of inactivity interspersed with brief spurts of activity. I miss my work at the abbey—especially now that I know the real reason the abbot selected my mother and I to work for him. I was just starting to understand things—or at least to understand what research had been done, and what remained for me to do. That research has come to a standstill, but there are still so many things I haven't worked out in my mind.

While on progress, I carry a copy of Malory's *Le Morte d'Artur*, but reading it does a better job of improving my French than teaching me about King Arthur.

For one thing, the legends are unclear as to what happened when Arthur died. Some even say he didn't die, but was carried to the island of Avalon to where he lies in a magical sleep, to be cured when the world is ready. I enjoy a fanciful tale as much as the next person, but since we have his tomb at Glastonbury, I must assume he did actually die—unless Glastonbury *is* Avalon, and Arthur lies asleep in his tomb. That idea is just too unnerving to consider.

There are other tales I remember, saying that Arthur waits under a mountain, but that seems rather implausible. The Welsh say that Arthur has gone to lead the Wild Hunt—a group of spectral huntsmen that can sometimes be seen rushing madly across the countryside, horses and hounds at full speed. I don't know what to make of that, or how one would return from it.

That's the part that bothers me most—the matter of his return.

How will it happen? And when? It's one thing to believe in the possibility—after all, if God could send his own son to live amongst us, then surely He could send Arthur back as well. It's another thing entirely, though, to be charged with the actual duty of ensuring that, when the time is right, Arthur's remains are…what? Ready? Will he rise from bones and dust? Or has he shed that body like a snake sheds its skin? Perhaps he will not need it at all. How am I to know?

Embroidery lets my mind wander, but today it is wandering too much. I am making a diamond-patterned border at the hem of each sleeve on the yellow wool, adding to the flowers I'd already finished. I'm certain I've miscounted between diamonds, and am recounting my stitches for the third time when a hand claps over my mouth.

I jab myself with my needle and cry out, but the sound is muffled by flesh. The hand belongs to a man. I start to struggle, but another hand wraps around my throat. Not a large man. His flesh is soft, but I can feel the bones of his wrist pressing into my windpipe. Tears spring to my eyes.

"Don't speak."

I nod, indicating compliance. I know that voice. That, and the smell of ink on his hands.

"You were in the garden yesterday, weren't you?"

His question confirms my suspicions. *Hutton.* I nod again.

The pressure on my windpipe increases. "What did you hear?"

I can't possibly answer. My vision is getting fuzzy and sparks of light dance in front of my eyes.

He gives me a little shake. "If you cry out, I will kill you. You understand?"

I'm petrified, but somehow manage to move my chin just the tiniest bit.

Hutton takes it as acknowledgment, and the pressure slowly decreases. "Now. What did you hear?"

"I—I—what do you mean?"

"You were sent to spy on me, weren't you?"

"Me? No!" My surprise is real.

"I saw you sneak from between the hedges."

I picture the scene from yesterday, and I know what I must do. "Th-then you…that is, did you see anyone else? With me?" I try to sound worried that *I* am the one whose illicit behavior has been found out.

"Your husband."

"He's not—I mean, that is, we'll be married soon enough. I promise, I won't do it again."

"Do what again?" He's starting to sound confused.

"Lure him out there." I hang my head like I'm ashamed, yet still desirous. "I couldn't help myself. He's just so…charming. He makes me forget…but his mother's always here, always watching. I thought, if we could be alone…Oh, no. How much did you see?"

He gives me a shove. "Stupid girl. Did you see anyone else out there? Hear anyone else?"

I pretend to think. "Um. Were you out there? Is that what worried you—that I might have seen? I swear, if you have a lover, I won't tell a soul. Not one."

He gives me another shove. "I wasn't out there. And you shouldn't have been either. You should be more careful with your person."

"Yes, yes. I'll be more discreet. We shouldn't have…"

"I wasn't here this morning, either. Remember that, or you will surely come to regret it."

"I'll remember."

I am staring vacantly out the window when Tobias returns, my embroidery forgotten in my lap.

"Are you feeling better, my sweet?"

I turn my head at his voice, but I cannot find my own voice to respond.

At my silence he hurries over. "Audrey, what's wrong?" He glances down at my needlework. "Did you jab yourself?"

A drop of blood has fallen on the yellow wool, staining my newly-stitched border. I shall have to soak it in vinegar to get it out.

"I guess I did," I murmur.

"Audrey?"

I need to tell him what happened. But Hutton's threat still lingers in my ears. If he believed that I was no more than a foolish, desire-ridden girl who expected everyone who hid between hedges did so to meet a lover, then Tobias is safe.

But he definitely won't be safe, the minute he starts asking questions. I have to tell him.

He shakes his head and clasps me to him when he hears why my sleeve hem is stained. "From now on, you stay by my side."

"Tobias, you can't always be with me."

"Yes, I can. At least until we get you out of this place."

CHAPTER FIFTEEN

Tobias

I try to remain calm for Audrey's sake, but inside I am seething. I cannot wait to get my hands on that weasel of a scholar and issue a few threats of my own. Unfortunately, I do have to wait—at least until night.

For the first time, I am glad of my mother's overly strict sense of propriety—the sense that dictates that a betrothal is not as good as a marriage, which means she and Audrey share a bed, with the maid on a nearby pallet, while I sleep in a separate room. I am glad, because it makes it much easier for me to slip from the room in the dead of night and pad silently down the corridors and out to the low building that adjoins the chapel—the rooms where clerics, scholars, and other religious men are housed. The rooms are sparse and unguarded, but the windows are small. The corridors have no windows at all. Once I am in, I pause to let my eyes adjust, which hardly helps.

I keep one hand on the right side of the wall, counting the number of doors as I pass by.

When I find the chamber, I am able to slip in easily. Hutton is a fool. If I were conducting the sort of business in which he is engaged, I would be sure to bar my doors at night. I blink at the sudden steam of moonlight, which now seems overbright.

Hutton's form is still in the bed.

A sense of foreboding washes over me.

I creep closer, my hand on the hilt of my dagger. I am not a violent man, but I will do what is necessary. My plan is to spring upon him, frighten him near to death, and see what information I can extract. But there are plenty of men who sleep with a weapon at hand—I can't rule out that Hutton is one of them.

I pounce, clapping my hand over his mouth to keep him from crying out—but there is no reaction at all, and I spring back just as quickly. Something is very, very wrong.

The only sound of breath in the room is my own—harsher now as my blood races.

I am too late. Hutton is dead.

My gaze lands on a pillow, lying discarded on the floor, and I know in my gut that he did not die of natural causes. Hutton was small of stature—it wouldn't have been difficult to overpower him, hold him down, smothering the breath from his body. I'd planned to overpower him myself. Only, my plans stopped short of murder.

My first instinct is to get out, and fast. I am Tobias Seybourne, charming courtier and aspiring nobleman. I cannot have my name mixed with these dark and deadly deeds. I should slip away, go back to my room, and pretend this never happened. Hutton can be of no more danger to my betrothed.

But whoever killed him might. I cannot leave just yet. This is my last and only chance to find out what he was up to—if he left anything behind to reveal those plans…and if his killer did not already find them.

The room is sparsely furnished, even more so than the chambers assigned to my family. A small writing desk with a single drawer yields only a bible, writing utensils, and a few sheets of thick, blank writing paper. Whoever was here before me probably took everything else.

I tuck the bible under my arm, in case it has any notes inside. I feel for any false backing or depth to the drawer, but it is simply made. Of course. The room was not furnished with the intent of housing spies.

A shelf above the desk holds a few bound volumes…religious and philosophical treatises of the type one would expect a scholar to have. I thumb through each—it's too dark to read, but I check if any loose papers have been slipped inside the covers. There are none.

His cloak hangs on a hook, his boots placed neatly beneath. These, also, give up no secrets.

There is no wardrobe. Only a small stand next to the bed, the lower shelf of which holds a few undergarments and personal items. Hutton traveled with little. I pace the room slowly, wiggling my feet to see if any floorboards are loose. No.

That leaves the mattress, and Hutton himself.

A sweep beneath the bed yields dust, and a discarded pair of hose. I run my hands carefully along the seams of the mattress and underneath…and finally I am rewarded. Hutton was intelligent enough not to tuck his things beneath the mattress, but not intelligent enough to avoid the next most obvious spot…a slit in the seam of the mattress, no longer than my thumb. I slip my fingers inside and extract a single, rolled scroll.

This whole time I am aware that the hour grows late…or rather, early. I don't have long before the other scholars and clergy rise and begin to move about.

To be sure, I still have to check the body.

I set down the bible and the scroll to run my hands over the corpse. For the first time, I realize he is still—other than the cloak and boots—fully clothed. I don't know what that means. Did his killer arrive while he was still awake and outman him? Or did he go to bed this way, in anticipation of his own night wanderings, not realizing they would never come to be?

I need to hurry. I cannot say who else might come looking for this man. Even the king has met with him in secret.

His eyes are still open, his expression fixed forever in a horrific grimace. I dare not close them. Whoever finds him next must believe he is the first to do so.

God's blood, this is disgusting. Give me a bloody wound or a broken bone any day…but something about handling Hutton's fresh corpse makes my skin crawl. Maybe it's not the body so much as my distaste for the man who formerly inhabited it.

I pat him down thoroughly, testing for any hidden pockets in his clothing. I retrieve one small, folded note, but that is all.

Just before I leave, I turn back and retrieve the offending pillow from the floor and tuck it beneath the scholar's prone form. He'll be found by daylight. But who's to say how he met his end?

I make it back to my chamber just as the early servants begin to stir. In the kitchens and bake house they will have been up for hours already, but not in the general living quarters. With any luck, I have not been seen.

I light a brazier to examine my findings. By now I am just reacting without thinking, doing what needs to be done. I cannot say if Hutton's death has freed Audrey and I from his suspicion, or placed us in even greater danger from an unknown foe. If I dwell on the thought, I might give in to fear or uncertainty and lose the ability to act. That cannot happen.

The folded note I found on Hutton's person turns out to be nothing more than a physician's note, meant to be carried to an apothecary, recommending a mixture of herbs to aid in digestive problems. I don't doubt Hutton suffered from indigestion, given what he was up to, but I doubt the herbs could have cured that, and they certainly won't help him now. I toss the note into the banked fire. It lands on one of the coals and settles, until the heat catches it and it goes up in a brief burst of flame.

The scroll from the mattress is more promising.

I have word that the matter of final disposition is to be decided by October. Glastonbury and Waltham are standing by. RW will know before the others. Recommend preemptive action.

Veritas Sanctitas

Foreboding, no doubt. But what exactly does it mean? There is no addressee, and the only signature is Veritas Sanctitas. Truth and holiness. Not a name. Someone's initials? A motto? Clearly, the cryptic nature was intentional. Even the wax used to seal the scroll had no insignia pressed into it. RW is almost certainly Richard Whiting. But what is it the abbot will know before others? And what is to be decided before October? The abbey's fate? Unless I miss my guess, that decision has long since been made, despite being kept close. But if they are talking about the final disposition of the grail, then there is much at stake…

I keep coming back to the Latin phrase at the end. Veritas Sanctitas. I feel like it should mean something to me, but I come up with nothing. Then again, I am no scholar. I took my education seriously enough to keep my parents from despair, but I'll admit I was usually out the door and into the woods before the tutor had even finished packing up his books.

I'll have to ask Audrey—though I don't look forward to explaining how I came by this note.

Audrey

All the following day, Tobias hovers at my side like a mother hen, and I think he is taking this protectiveness a bit too far. The king had planned on hunting today, but the hunt was delayed when it was discovered that the king's favorite mount was favoring his right foreleg. Instead, Henry calls for tennis matches, which are hastily arranged and mean that instead of having several hours to myself, I must go with the others to cheer.

Tobias does not seem disappointed by the change of plans. The only time I am allowed to leave his side is during the king's first tennis match, which Tobias officiates. Still, I have to sit with Lady Seybourne, always within sight of him. In the afternoon, the role is bestowed on another, so Tobias and I watch together as the king soundly defeats his inexplicably clumsy opponent.

"This morning's match was much closer," Tobias confides. "To win a second match the same day proves he is a man of stamina."

The king is sweating profusely and limps off the court, but he is the victor. No one wants to best the king today—at least not in this forum.

"Congratulations, Your Highness," I murmur, curtsying and dropping my gaze as he passes. "Well played."

He pauses, looking me over, and I try not to squirm.

"Why, thank you." He gives Tobias a nudge. "Though perhaps it is I who should offer my congratulations to your betrothed, for winning himself such a sweet and lovely maiden."

"Oh." I bring my fingertips to cover my mouth and hope I am blushing. I'm certainly embarrassed enough.

"Long have I admired her from afar," Tobias says, as gallantly as any knight in a romance. "Fortune truly has favored me—though I fear I shall never develop the skill Your Highness exhibits on the court."

"Heh." The king gives a grunt of laughter and moves along, no stranger to flattery, but not immune to it, either.

When he is out of earshot, Tobias whispers, "Very nice. You made him feel strong, potent. It's important to him. He'll hold himself high until he reaches the privacy of his chambers. He doesn't want everyone to know he will collapse as soon as he is out of view."

I look around uncertainly. Everyone is laughing and chatting, and an informal tennis match has been struck up between two of the former ladies in waiting. With no queen, they have no one upon whom to wait, but they linger at court nonetheless. After all, the last two queens came from the entourage of a prior queen, so I suppose the remaining ladies think their chances good. Catherine Howard gazes after the king, as do a few others, but they don't follow him.

"They already know."

"They do. But it doesn't matter. He's the most powerful man in England."

Tobias draws me to a corner alcove, standing just a bit closer than is seemly. From the sudden soberness in his eyes, I realize there is more to his hovering than I know. Fortunately, anyone watching will think we just want a lovers' moment. It fits right in with my new love-enfeebled act.

"We have a problem. The king won't be getting any more ideas out of Hutton…and neither will we."

"He left?"

"No. Found dead this morning."

Dead. Not "Hutton's too careful with his secrets to say anything else," or "he departed at first light." I swallow. "Did he die…of natural causes?"

He fixes me with a look. "No."

I don't ask for details. Only, please God, I pray, don't let Tobias have been involved. "Who else knows?"

"I don't think word has gotten out…he's not the sort who attracts much attention, so few are likely to have missed his presence thus far."

My heart is beating in triple time. "How do you know?"

He pauses, releases a pent-up breath. "I found him."

"You found him," I repeat stupidly.

He looks down. "When you told me how he threatened you…I thought to issue a few threats of my own. There was no need."

The air around me grows heavy, and I struggle to drag in a breath.

"Audrey."

The intensity of his gaze burns through me, bringing me back to the moment.

"It's imperative you stay in my sight, at all times. Think about it. Hutton knew you were in the garden, and he let you live. Whoever knew of Hutton's deeds was not so merciful."

"You think he was killed because of…what we heard in the garden?"

"Yes, I think it does seem too coincidental that he should meet his end so soon after that conversation. Though I don't know the full extent of Hutton's dealings. He could have a host of enemies."

I'm having trouble drawing breath. I try, again and again, but all I get are shallow little gasps of air. Little flecks of light dance in front of my eyes.

"Audrey?" Tobias's voice seems far away. "Audrey, come sit down."

He pulls me further into the alcove and down to a marble bench that was surely intended for decoration more than actual sitting. I bend my head and manage a real breath. Tobias stands in front of me, doing his best to shield me from the others' view. He casts a quick glance behind him.

"Audrey, my sweet, I don't mean to be rude, but if you are able, please sit up. Now that the king has gone, the others are looking for a new subject of gossip."

"All right. I'm all right." I manage a couple more deep breaths, and straighten. *Hutton, murdered.* I send up a prayer of thanks that Tobias had the instinct to bar our doors last night. "Hutton certainly made no friends with me. But how would anyone…*oh.* What if someone else was there, hiding as we were, and overheard what was said?"

"Overheard, and then killed Hutton to prevent his plan from going any further." He scrunches up his face, then quickly schools his expression as he realizes the alcove in which we stand does not shield us entirely from sight. Instead, he gazes at me tenderly, and I wish this really were a stolen moment between lovers instead of the terrifying conversation that it is.

"Who would have wanted him dead? That conversation outed him as an agent of the king, but he gave up no specific names—just his idea about the grail. Who would kill to protect…" I trail off, knowing the answer already. *The Templars.* No question—they would kill to protect their secrets. But that would mean there is one of them among us.

I look around as though the courtyard full of people would present an obvious answer—a sinister, lone character lurking at the fringes of the crowd. But of course there is no such person. Brightly attired, laughing people mingle and converse like any other day—and knowing this court, every one of them has secrets. Occasionally one of them will glance at us with a knowing smirk. I reposition myself into a coquettish stance.

Our eyes meet, and I know he has reached the same conclusion. It could be anyone. "I don't know—but I will keep my ears open, and you by my side. Audrey, whoever killed Hutton wanted to silence him. Who else, besides the king, knows what was said in that garden?"

My heart turns to lead. "We do."

"Hutton knew we were there. Whoever killed him might have heard or seen us, too. We can't be sure."

"There's more."

I try not to cringe.

"When I found…the body, I also…found something else. A note."

He tells me what it says, and that he has Hutton's bible as well, but all I can think is that if Tobias is caught with Hutton's belongings, he'll be accused of murder. I could be a widow before my wedding.

"We have to get rid of it," I whisper urgently.

"It could be important," he argues.

I'm scared. Tears start to well in my eyes, and I turn away from the view of those still in the courtyard. Now they will think this a lovers' quarrel. It is exhausting.

"I couldn't let them fall into other hands," he says. "No one will think to search me—you alone know of my connection to that little weasel. Audrey, please, just think. If we can figure out the meaning, I will burn the note, I swear."

"Veritas Sanctitas?" I repeat, trying to force my mind to work in spite of my fear.

"Truth and holiness. Common enough words, but the way they are used in place of a signature…It seems like a code, or a motto…some kind of salutation exchanged within a brotherhood," he muses.

"Or an inscription," I offer. "It sounds like the sort of thing carved above the entry to a church."

He claps a hand to his forehead. "You're right. I hadn't thought of it, but now that you've said it, I know I've seen *Veritas* above the entry to Blackfriars."

"Just *Veritas*? No *Sanctitas*?"

His excitement wanes. "No. I suppose it doesn't mean much, by itself. Have you seen the whole phrase somewhere?"

The images of Glastonbury Abbey flash through my mind's eye. "Nooo," I say slowly, "but Glastonbury is the only church I know well, and I don't think it is there. It could be anywhere."

"Waltham?"

"Maybe. I've never heard of Waltham in the grail stories, though." I suck in a breath. "Maybe that is the intention. Move the grail somewhere no one would think to look for it."

"Seems like a dangerous plan, with the dissolution."

"True," I admit. Thinking of our own involvement—getting the Arthurian relics well away from the church until this madness is finished, it doesn't make sense they would move the grail to an abbey.

"What about the Templars? Was *veritas sanctitas* their motto?"

I frown. Until the day before last, I'd never had cause to pay much attention to the Templar stories. After all, the order was disbanded over two centuries ago—recent history compared to the death of King Arthur, but long enough ago to have fallen out of the common people's realm of thoughts. Still, I should know more than most, having worked at an abbey so long. That is where their influence lingered longest…in the churches they once frequented. "They had an emblem, I think, of two knights riding atop the same horse. A symbol of poverty."

He looks up, recognition dawning. "I remember that. Some people thought it hypocritical, since the order eventually became so wealthy."

"They claimed it was because of their faithfulness to their vows, their service before God, that they were so blessed."

Tobias quirks a brow. "Apparently the Pope disagreed."

I shrug. I'm certain there were all kinds of power and politics at play, but I don't pretend to understand them. I cannot even keep up with the politics of my own time. "I cannot remember a motto, though. There must be records somewhere."

"My dearest betrothed, you do realize that a mere mention of the Templars and their possible link to the grail was enough to get Hutton killed. You cannot possibly think it wise to suddenly ask about, as though reading up on such things were simply a pastime."

I scowl at him. "I may not be brave like you, but I am no fool either. There is a very particular person I thought to ask."

He brushes his knuckles across my cheek. "'RW will know before the others,'" he says, repeating the words in Hutton's scroll. "Of course you are not a fool, Audrey. You want to ask Abbot Whiting."

I do. I close my eyes and lean back against the sun-warmed stone of the alcove. But more than that, I simply want to go home. I wish I had never heard of the Templars, or King Arthur, or the Holy Grail. And, though I will never, ever admit it aloud, I wish I had never heard of King Henry.

CHAPTER SIXTEEN

That night, we bar the doors.

"But what has happened?" Lady Seybourne asks.

"No cause for alarm, Mother. 'Tis only a precaution."

She frowns. "You haven't gotten involved in anything untoward, have you?"

"Of course not. 'Tis only that I sense some in this court are…unsettled. The recent acts of parliament, and the sudden departure from London have people on edge. I remain friendly with everyone, but there are those who think I reach above myself."

"Likely they do the same."

"Likely," he agrees, choosing not to mention anything about Hutton's intrusion earlier. "And there are some who are unable to bear the idea of another succeeding when they may not. Anyway, as I said, 'tis only a precaution. I value you both too much to risk your safety."

"Thank you, son. This is not the same court as when your father was alive. That was a happier time."

I hear the wistful note in her voice, and wonder if it is Tobias's father, or the happier times, that she misses most. When Sir Seybourne was alive, Henry was a younger king, still happily married to Catherine. There was no talk of a break with Catholicism, and while there may have been military campaigns, they were against other nations—not this internal strife, where men and women can fall from grace in the blink of an eye, and be dragged to the Tower whilst most of the court is fast asleep.

With the doors barred, I am able to sleep—at least more so than the night before, though my dreams are riddled by anxious, nameless monarchs, searching for lost treasure. It is the grail they seek, but in my dream the grail becomes my pendant, and I am eager to part with it—if only I knew which of the phantom monarchs had the rightful claim.

After Hutton's death, each day we spend with the court seems interminably long. Tobias remains protective, to the extent that I long for moments alone. I have never spent so long in another's company. Working for Abbot Whiting used to afford me so many quiet hours that my voice would grow rusty from disuse, but now I miss those days.

The only times Tobias leaves me are when he goes into the next room over at bedtime, or when the king invites him on a hunt, and he never leaves without ensuring his mother and Binnie are both present. We continue to bar the doors at night. Word of Hutton's death is out, and while it bears no seeming relation to us, it is cause enough that Lady Seybourne and Binnie no longer question the extra precaution.

During the day, being with Tobias means I am constantly on display—so much so that Lady Seybourne, sensing the rising tide, had Binnie to alter one of her own dresses so that I might have another in which to be seen. I am not skilled in courtly pastimes such as writing amusing poetry or playing board games, but I bring my embroidery and stitch until my fingers ache, smiling sweetly up at Tobias whenever I have the chance.

More uncomfortable than being on display, though, is the growing understanding I have of why Tobias is favored by all—and with whom he must consort in order to remain so. Richard Pollard is my least favorite. One of Cromwell's men, he is the sort who measures his own importance by his power to crush others, and he leers at me when he thinks I am not aware.

But Lady Seybourne says everything is going according to plan—whose plan, I'm not sure, but I am not given to argument. Good thing, because after the next hunt, Tobias proves her right.

"I have good news," he announces as he strides into the room, smelling of horses and sweat. He walks tall, his shoulders thrown back and his chin lifted.

"You have?" Immediately I have guessed what happened, but I won't spoil it for him.

"Indeed. Beginning tomorrow, you may address me as 'Sir' Seybourne." He grins.

"You did it!" I jump up and, impulsively, hug him. He hugs me back, a happy squeeze, and then suddenly we both spring backward, laughing in embarrassment.

His mother doesn't seem to mind, though. She's risen to her feet as well, and when I move away, she clasps Tobias by the shoulders. "A knighthood, just like your father, and his before him. Well done, Sir Seybourne."

"Yes, well done, Sir Seybourne." I lean toward him again, lowering my voice. "Though I would prefer to address you as 'husband.'"

He laughs again. I am getting better at flirting, and he likes it. "And so you shall, very soon."

Lady Seybourne is moved to tears at the ceremony the following day, and I am happy for her—for all of us.

We travel with King Henry's court a few weeks more, but eventually the large progress disbands. The king must go south to inspect the military fortifications in progress, while our route continues to the west.

Henry had told Tobias that when our paths diverged, we were free to go. But when the time comes, he is displeased. "I've just made a knight of you, and you wish to leave?"

Tobias bows deeply. "I am honored beyond measure, Your Highness. But I've a wedding awaiting me, and thanks to your generosity, new land to tend."

"Yes, yes. I cannot fault a man for wanting to sow his seed."

I lower my gaze demurely. I've picked up enough of the court's double entendres to know the king isn't referring to plowing the fields.

"You'll come back in the fall, though." It isn't a question. For whatever reason, he finds my betrothed entertaining, and does not wish to part with him. Courtiers exist for his delight alone.

"It would be my honor." After all, what else is he to say?

The journey home is no trouble at all. It's when we arrive that everything goes wrong.

It is well-on evening by the time we reach Glastonbury, but none of us wanted to spend another night on the road. My heart warms as first the roads become familiar, then the trees and farmhouses dotting the land, and finally the tall outline of the abbey itself, black against the twilight sky.

"John won't be expecting us tonight, and I've a mind to catch up on any news," Tobias says. "Shall we take dinner at the inn?"

The question is directed at his mother, who purses her lips before saying, "Very well."

We are all looking a bit worse for wear after being on the road, and I know she is concerned about appearances—especially as we have news of our own, and she wants to make a good impression.

"We needn't linger long," he promises. "Truly, the innkeeper has based his business upon providing food and shelter for those coming off the roads, and has met me many a time in just such a state. He'll not bat an eye."

The aroma of ale, meat pies, and leek soup assaults our nostrils as we walk in, and my stomach growls in anticipation.

A group of locals recognize Tobias and greet him with enthusiasm, offering up a coveted table and chairs as they depart. We accept gratefully, and my weary bones protest as I ease down onto a chair, though their complaint is quickly overcome by the promise of a good, hot meal.

Scattered about the room, I notice several men I've never seen before. Not unusual, for Glastonbury has always attracted visitors, but these mean don't wear the clothes of travelers. They aren't all together, though. Only two sit at a small table, while another stands near the bar, and a fourth perches on a stool near the hearth. One, the man leaning on the bar, stares at me. At least I think he does. Maybe he recognizes me from London? I have been introduced to so many people, I cannot remember them all, but I don't think I recognize him. When I dare to meet his gaze, he looks away.

I nudge Tobias and point the strangers out. "Who are they, do you think?"

He considers them for a moment, without making it too obvious. "I don't know." After the soup is served, Tobias excuses himself to stand near the bar and catch up on news, as he'd wanted to do. I am anxious to hear the news as well, but must act the part of a lady and wait until he tells me later—which he does, as soon as we are out of the inn and on the way to John's house.

"Foreigners," he says. "Two from France, another from Wales, and a fourth from parts unknown."

"Their business?"

"Nothing official, at least according to the innkeeper. Rumor is, they've got an interest in the abbey's goods, but Abbot Whiting will hear no talk of sales or trades, so they wait—believing that sooner or later, the abbey's time will come. They've done this before—camped out near their prey, waiting to swoop in and make off with what they can carry. You heard what happened at Reading Abbey—the villagers were blamed, but they weren't the only ones sharing in the plunder."

Of course I'd heard of Reading Abbey. No sooner had the abbey surrendered to the king's men, than locals and other observers looted the grounds for anything of value. Violence broke out, but many were never caught.

"Carrion birds." I nearly spit the words, such is my disgust.

Tobias is amused. I wrinkle my nose at him, but he just shrugs. "I like it when you show spirit. And you, Mother," he says, "I am quite impressed you managed to keep my secret, back there."

"I decided there is merit in your approach," she says loftily, as if it had been her idea all along. "Those who saw you tonight will later realize what you kept hidden, and will credit you for not rising above yourself."

"I haven't risen above myself," he protests.

"Exactly."

He just shakes his head. Eventually, Lady Seybourne's horse drops back a few paces from ours, and I see she is nodding in the saddle, keeping herself just awake enough to keep her seat. Since her maid is even further behind, I don't worry too much. The horse knows the way, and he is a gentle creature.

As we get closer to Seybourne Manor, I sense Tobias growing pensive beside me. "What are you thinking?"

"Only that I hope John is not upset."

I place a hand on his arm, briefly—my mount doesn't like being so close to another and shies a few steps away when I ride too close to Tobias.

Some men would enjoy nothing better than to tell the tale of their triumph three times over, but Tobias isn't one of them. He's never been a braggart. It has always been the adventure and excitement he loves best, and that he managed to make something of it is a credit to him. "John will be happy for you. Even if it pains him to know you have accomplished that which he could not, he would never wish it away from you."

"I hope so."

When we reach the house, Tobias's mother suddenly perks up, dismounting and heading straight inside.

By the time Tobias and I put up the horses and enter the house, John is there to greet us with an arch brow and open arms. "So, *Sir* Seybourne, is it?"

Tobias couldn't help grinning. "Indeed. I suppose Mother had to be first to tell someone."

Sam stands behind him, looking up at Tobias with even greater hero adoration than before. "A knight," he murmurs in awe. "What did you do? A feat of bravery? Did you win in the lists?"

"I simply served my country, and my king, to the best of my ability."

"Oh, come off it, tell us more," Sam begs, certain there is a feat of heroism somewhere in the tale.

Tobias obliges, though the only adventurous parts of the story that took place this summer are his tales of the hunt. His earlier service included missions to France, and any number of messages transported. I never heard some of these things before—though I remember teasing Tobias, months ago, about being a messenger boy, and I feel badly for it now.

When Sam's curiosity has been satisfied, John jumps in. "So, Sir Seybourne, have you been granted land of your own? Or shall I continue to have a runabout brother who leeches off of me—but now expects me to address him by a title?"

His tone is a teasing one. In truth, I've never seen him in such a good mood.

"Are you looking to disinherit me, dearest brother?"

"Only if I have a son of my own," John retorts.

We all stop as Tobias, his mother, myself, and even Sam exchange looks.

Sam blurts, "But you're not married." The same thing all of us were thinking.

"True. But I am considering marriage."

No wonder he is in a good mood.

"Are you jesting?" his mother asks. She's half-risen from her seat, her hands clasped and an expression that says she is afraid to hope.

"Nay, no jest. I may marry. Eventually. I have my eye on a quiet young miss from Bath. Good family."

"Does she know you have your eye on her?" Tobias asks. John is reclusive in general, but particularly so with women.

"We've spoken a few times. As I said, she is quiet, and very unassuming. But I do know her family, and I believe if I spoke to her father…"

Tobias chuckles. "I wish you the best of luck, then, brother. If you end up with a son someday, I shall consider that an excellent reason for disinheriting me." He gives John a brotherly half-nudge, half-shove. "In fact, I would consider it the *only* good reason for disinheriting me."

"Fair enough," John agrees.

"Not to worry, though. My leeching days are over. The king did indeed grant me a plot of land," Tobias announces proudly.

"Excellent."

"Where? Where?" Sam asks eagerly.

"Well, at first he offered me the land that once belonged to the nuns of Godstow, in Lincolnshire—"

Tobias hadn't mentioned that part to me before—that Henry had originally planned to give him church lands. Most of the lands distributed by the king lately once belonged to the Catholic Church, but am glad Tobias came up with an excuse for something different. I have a hard time swallowing the idea of staking claim to an abandoned convent. But he doesn't get very far in his explanation before his mother interrupts, her eyes narrowed at John. "If you think you will succeed in changing the topic now that you have expressed an interest in someday achieving the state of holy matrimony, I assure you, my son, you are mistaken."

"Enough, enough, Mother. There is little enough to say on the matter, as yet. Let Tobias tell us of his land."

"I told His Highness," Tobias continues, "very humbly, of course, that I had in mind something closer to home. John, please forgive me—but I might have implied your health was failing, and I wanted to be nearby."

"Bastard."

Tobias shrugs good-naturedly at his brother's insult. "You should choose your insults more carefully in front of our mother."

"Oh, damn. Forgive me, Mother. You know I never meant it."

"I'll forgive you, but when I question you later about the girl you have your eye on, I expect you shall be gushing forth every detail."

John's shoulders slump. "Yes, Mother."

Tobias smirks as though to say *She bested you on that one.* "Anyhow, Glastonbury has always been home, and I *did* wish to remain nearby. Fortunately, the king was in a jovial mood. He is most generous when he is happy. So he asked his steward if there was any parcel near here that could be granted. As I expected, that good man pointed out the old king's forest—the section that runs into the marsh, which the king hasn't hunted on for years. Henry was quite happy to turn it over to my keeping."

"A patch of swamp?" John questions. "Has your brain become addled?"

"There is forest and dry land as well. No big game for the king's hunting, but plenty of small game, and the land should be fine for farming. No shortage of water."

I have learned enough about the ways of the court to suspect the king's steward received a coin purse on the sly to ensure his knowledgeable response. But there is no harm in it—the other honorees had probably done the same. No one served in King Henry's court without some eye for gain.

"That sounds promising," John admits. "'Tis over near Bridgewater, no? When will you move?"

"Yes, near Bridgewater. We'll not be moving just yet. Part of the reason the king was happy to grant that particular land is that it is, after all, just a little-used hunting ground. There is no manor house—just a hunting lodge of sorts that will require some repair before we can live there."

"We have my parents' home until then," I say. It's risky, for it means transporting the relics twice—or finding a hiding spot so secure they can be left unguarded on the new land until we are ready to occupy it. But I don't want to spoil the celebratory mood, so I change the topic, asking my husband-to-be what sorts of crops he wishes to plant, or whether we will keep grazing animals.

He picks up on my lead, philosophizing over the merits of the wool business and the uncertainties of edible crops, as though neither of us had any plans grander than becoming a gentleman farmer and his wife.

The conversation ebbs and flows, and I am lulled into such a state that I drift along with it, a toy boat in the current. I hardly realize I am nodding off, and I wish this moment of peace could last.

❧ ❧

By the time Tobias walks us home that evening, Sam is ready to drop. Like me, he'd been half-asleep at John's house, and would've likely stayed on another night if we hadn't roused him. He falls into bed without even removing the outer layer of his clothing.

The air in the farmhouse is stale and dusty, though I can see evidence that Sam and Old Megs have kept the place up during our absence.

Tobias seems in no hurry to leave. "We can stay here for a short while after the wedding, but I shall begin the repairs to the property immediately. I'll feel more comfortable knowing you are settled in a permanent home. I must also hire someone to dig out a large cellar. The existing lodgings were never a permanent home, so none exists."

"We must have a cellar, indeed," I agree. "One with adequate…storage."

He grows sober. "I can expand and secure it later. I doubt you'll wish to pay your respects to the king of old each and every time you go down there to fetch a basket of root vegetables."

I shudder at the thought. "I shan't mind if we must do so at first, but it seems disrespectful to house King Arthur amongst the onions and ale barrels."

Tobias draws me over to the far corner of the sitting room, speaking low in case Sam isn't entirely asleep.

"I didn't want to spoil a good evening, but, Audrey, you need to hear this. We're running out of time."

I draw a shaky breath. "I knew there was something. Some bad news to temper the good. It's been weighing on you since we left court. Is that why we stopped for dinner at the inn?"

He looks worried. "Did I say something? How did I give it away? Tell me. Before this year, I've never been a secretive man. But now it is crucial that I learn. Great harm could come to both of us if I don't."

I give him what I hope is a gentle smile. "Relax. I doubt anyone but myself—and *maybe* your brother—would have noticed anything at all. Abbot Whiting tells me I am very observant. It's why he had me to assist him. I have known you for years, Tobias. I know when your smile holds the slightest tension at the corners."

"That's it? My smile?"

"That, and the fact that you repeatedly rub your thumb over the seam of your chausses, as though rubbing at a sore spot." Not that I'd been eyeing his legs. Well, maybe a little. He is a finely built man. And he *is* to be my husband. I'd never paid too much attention to such things before, knowing how easily the other girls got caught up in the sins of lust. But now that I am to marry…

With effort, I drag my mind back to the topic at hand. "We're running out of time?"

He glances at his seam. "Thank you for telling me that. I'll be more careful." He pauses, glancing toward Sam, whose mouth has fallen open in sleep. He checks the other corners of the room, too, as if to make sure no one else had snuck in to eavesdrop. "Yes. Glastonbury is now the last abbey in Somerset. I fear it will not hold much longer. You remember Richard Pollard from the court?"

"I do." I wrinkle my nose.

"I have…well, I wouldn't say *befriended*, exactly, but I have gained his trust. He's been working for Lord Cromwell—he's been among the men who go about the country, taking stock of the assets of the religious houses, and supposedly assessing their corruption or loyalty to the king."

"Sounds like a pleasant man," Sam says.

Tobias and I both jump. Sam's eyes are still closed, but he is clearly *not* asleep.

"Sarcasm is unbecoming," Tobias retorts.

Sam just shrugs. He props himself up on one elbow. "The air is thick as thieves with you two whispering. How could a body sleep?"

Tobias rolls his eyes. "You're a better sneak than I thought."

"No one ever credits the cripple," Sam quips.

I narrow my eyes at him. "You are wise beyond your years. I don't know whether to congratulate you or give you a good whipping," I threaten.

Sam looks to Tobias, his eyes pleading for help.

"Oh, fine. You get off this time." Tobias draws me back toward the warmth of the hearth now that there is no point in keeping quiet for Sam's sake. "Anyhow, Pollard takes pleasure in reporting back the work he has done. Hasn't got an original thought in his head, but is quite gleeful about executing the ideas of his master. He told me that King Henry has grown increasingly uncomfortable with the idea of allowing any of the Catholic houses to remain standing, even if they have been cut off from Rome."

"Any at all?" I whisper. The news confirms what we've long suspected, but that doesn't make it easier to hear.

"Mind you, this is all third- and fourth-hand information. The king has spoken with Lord Cromwell, his advisor, who in turn spoke to Pollard, who in turn spoke to me."

"But you have no reason to distrust him."

"On the contrary, I rarely trust anyone—least of all Pollard. But I cannot think of any reason he would lie about this," Tobias admits.

"What else did he say?"

"That Cromwell is drawing up a list. That none are to be spared. It is summer now, so most of the court is away in the country, and such efforts are more difficult to coordinate. But he expects things will move quickly once the weather cools."

I have to ask. I force my mouth to form the words, though my lips and teeth balk at such treachery. "And Glastonbury? Where are we on this list?"

"I dared not ask specifically." He clears his throat. "Pollard knows where I'm from. He asked if I wanted to join him, when it came time to tear down Glastonbury. I wanted to punch him."

"I wish you had," Sam growls.

"I'd love to meet him in the lists. Unfortunately, that is not his style. He prefers to attack those who dare not fight back."

I can see his muscles tremble, his jaw clench, as recounting the conversation makes his fury fresh.

"I told him that although the king's mission was certainly a worthy one, I thought it best left to those already well-versed in the procedure."

"A worthy mission?" Sam echoes.

"Hush, Sam," I chide. "You know he doesn't mean it."

"I had to tell him something."

"I know. You did well."

"Pollard just laughed. Said it would come soon enough, with or without my help."

"How long do you think we have?"

"A month. Two if we're lucky. No more."

CHAPTER SEVENTEEN

We go to the abbey the following morning, walking Sam—who is full of questions about our travels—to the kitchens before heading to the abbot's house. When we enter, I see one of the other monks sitting at the small desk where I used to pen correspondence for the abbot. It feels strange not to work here anymore.

We make an appointment to see Abbot Whiting, ostensibly because he is to perform our wedding. When we enter his study, he looks up with a smile, and I must quickly hide my dismay at how old and weak he has grown. It is as though we have been gone years rather than mere weeks.

"Come walk with me. My old bones need to move, lest they decide to settle in one position evermore."

We walk with him to the main chapel, our pace excruciatingly slow. I hear the rattle of each breath as he struggles to fill his body with breath.

Light filters through the tall windows of the empty nave, making the dust motes sparkle in the air. Absent the shuffle of the congregation and the chanting tones of the priests, the chapel is mysterious and awe-inspiring. I have seen it hundreds of times, but it is always so. Abbot Whiting leads us to the alcove where King Arthur's cross rests in its usual place.

"Is that…the replica?" Tobias whispers.

"No."

Alarm shoots through me. Surely it is complete by now. The look on Abbot Whiting's face tells me to wait.

"What happened?"

He draws a shuddery breath. "Trouble at the forge. We found the body of Monsieur Lefèvre last month, hanging from a crudely erected cross."

"We?"

"Myself, and one other. A man I trust implicitly."

A Templar. I'd bet my life on it.

"When he didn't return in a timely fashion, I suspected something had gone amiss. A colleague and I went to investigate. I am deeply saddened that Monsieur Lefèvre lost his life on account of a request made by myself."

"Was our mission compromised?" Tobias asks.

"I cannot say with absolute certainty, but I think not. Monsieur Lefèvre may have been no friend of the English crown, but he was a man of integrity, and his work was well-hidden."

"But how did they find him?" Tobias frowns.

"I do not even know who committed this atrocity. There was no note, no warning left by the body. It may have been someone serving the crown—and it may not. We live in dark times, when one cannot even identify one's enemies from amongst the many possibilities."

Tobias speaks up. "I cannot say how they found him, but his arrival in England did not go unnoticed. When I first escorted him from the docks, we were followed."

Abbot Whiting narrows his eyes. "You did not mention this before."

"I did not think any threat remained, as I had…dispatched the problem." He glances apologetically at me.

I understand what he is saying. Hutton was not the first to lose his life in this tangle of deceit. But I also have questions. Were they attacked, and Tobias killed the man in defense? Or did he sense they were being followed, and hunt the man down? Does it even make a difference? I cannot say.

"His pursuer was a mere dock guard. No one of import."

The abbot gives him a stern look. "Maybe, maybe not."

Tobias looks appropriately chastised. "True, Father Abbot. I know little of him—nor do I know to whom he may have mentioned the monsieur's presence. I thought him a low criminal, the sort who supplements his meager wages by accosting travelers on the road. I should not have dismissed him so readily."

I ponder that for a minute. The surprise of Monsieur Lefèvre's death has distracted me from the reason for our meeting. We may not know all our enemies, but neither do we know all our friends. If the Templars are protecting relics, too, then they are friends of a sort, are they not? Or at least co-conspirators.

"Father Abbot, may I ask a question?"

"Of course, my child."

I frown, trying to think how to ask. After all we've conspired to do, this shouldn't be so hard. But it is. I don't want to sound like a fool. After all, this is the holy grail I mean to bring up.

I begin with what I know—or think I know.

"In our travels with the court, we met some…interesting characters. One, a scholar by the name of Hutton. Have you heard of him?"

"Not that I recall."

"He…well, I cannot say how we heard this, but he advised the king to seek out a particular relic—one that no one has laid eyes on for centuries."

"The grail."

"You know?" I'm astonished. I've always known Abbot Whiting was a man of great knowledge and many connections, but how could he know this?

He smiles gently. "My child, it was but a guess. Between your words and your dire tone, I knew it would be no small thing."

"Indeed, he spoke of the grail," Tobias confirms. "Hutton implied he had evidence to make such a feat—bringing forth the grail, that is—possible. He implied that the grail's location was known, but protected by an order that disbanded long ago. Unfortunately, he died before we could learn exactly what he meant."

The abbot is alert, but his expression gives little away.

"Father Abbot," I ask, "could he have been talking about Glastonbury? Do our relics have anything to do with…"

"The grail is not among the relics with which you two have been entrusted. Of that you may be certain."

Tobias and I glance at one another, and I know we both heard what he *didn't* say.

Suddenly the abbot winces, hunching forward in his seat, bracing his hands against his knees.

Panicked, I rush to him, but a flick of his hand tells me to stay back. I don't know what to do, so I wait, my fingers twisted together until they lose color. The abbot wheezes, struggling to draw breath, but finally he straightens.

We're running out of time, Tobias said last night. But I worry that the abbot might be running out of time even faster. I cannot imagine the pressure he must feel. I try to comfort him. "Perhaps this is too much, Father Abbot. You've served long and well. You could retire."

"In another day and age, that might have been possible. But there will be no pension for me, and there is no one to take my place." His eyes are weary, but there is dignity in his tone. "I am the last abbot of Glastonbury. All I must do now is hold on long enough that I do not fall before my abbey does."

Tobias comes to stand by my side. I feel his hand at my back, a reassuring presence. "Father Abbot, I know this is difficult, but we want to help. This scholar we mentioned…he left behind a note. It said 'Glastonbury and Waltham are standing by. RW will know before the others.'"

"I see. Do you have this note, perchance?"

Tobias retrieves it, checking first to ensure we are still alone, while I try not to scowl. I still think we should have burned it. The fact that Abbot Whiting wants to see it exonerates Tobias's decision to keep it somewhat, but it still makes me uncomfortable.

The abbot holds the note at arm's length, squinting as he reads. When he reaches the end, I see his brows shoot up in surprise, but he quickly schools his expression.

"This could have any number of meanings," he says.

"As I'm sure its originator intended," Tobias returns evenly. He, too, senses the abbot holding back. "Does *Veritas, Sanctitas* mean anything to you—beyond the literal translation?"

He frowns, but does not answer.

"We thought it sounded like a motto, or a password of some sort. The Templars, perhaps. I know you have contacts—at least one—among them," I admit. "I was here when he visited, nearly three years ago."

The corner of his lip quirks up. "You always were observant. Whom did you see? Can you describe him?"

"A large man. He was a prior, I recall. He had the square cross sewn into his under sleeves. I only noticed because it caught my eye when he waved his arm." I mimic the gesture. "He was very careful in his speech, but he asked if you had a plan—and you said you did."

"You have a good memory."

I lower my gaze. "I'm sorry. It was none of my business."

"Perhaps not," he says, still gentle. "But perhaps Providence had a hand in placing you in that room, that day."

Tobias smiles at me, too, and for a moment I allow the warmth of their approval to spread through me. That warmth will sustain me, I hope, in future moments of cold and doubt.

"But *Veritas, Sanctitas* is not a Templar motto," Abbot Whiting continues, dashing my hopes. "Their motto, if you can call it that, was *Non nobis, Domine, non nobis, sed nomine tuo da gloriam.* Nothing for us, Lord, nothing for us but for the glory of thy name."

"I've heard that before."

"I'm sure you have, clever girl. It comes from Psalm 113:9, and is used in a number of other places. For the Templars, it served as a reminder of their purpose and humble roots." He hands Hutton's note back to Tobias, who tucks it away.

My eyes follow the paper. Even if we were wrong about the *Veritas, Sanctitas*, I cannot imagine that we misinterpreted the 'RW will know before the others.'

Tobias straightens his shoulders. "What we're trying to say, sir, is that if the grail is here, or if you know who protects it, you must warn them. I do not know how much Hutton knew, or how much he revealed to the king before his death. Whoever killed him went through his things. I only found this note because it was well-hidden."

"I understand, though 'tis likely you worry overmuch. Groups like the Templars know that any man can be broken with enough pressure, so no one man is entrusted with more than a parcel of knowledge. That way, if that one man is compromised, he does not risk the whole group, nor that which they guard."

This reasoning makes sense, but what if Hutton spied on others until he gleaned their parcels as well as his own?

Tobias and I exchange glances, and I know he feels the same frustration I do. "Father Abbot…" he begins.

"My child, I hear what you have said, and I thank you for the warning. I will take time to consider, and pray, over the matter."

"Right, then," Tobias says slowly.

My mind is whirling. Has the grail already been moved? If it is safe, then no wonder Abbot Whiting is playing coy. But what if it isn't? I believe he knows *something*.

Not for the first time, the abbot seems to read my mind. He turns to me. "I suspect that you have not shared the full details of your responsibilities with your brother—am I correct?"

"Yes, Father Abbot—though I had to tell him a portion."

"Exactly. The abbey is full of secrets. Some, I have entrusted to those who will keep them, such as yourself. Others, I will carry to my grave." He pauses, staring out the window, across the lawn, to the rising arches of the main chapel. "Still others, if I had my guess, are locked within the walls of the abbey, entrusted to no one, and will there remain."

I feel a flicker of surprise. I always thought Abbot Whiting knew everything there was to know about the abbey. But

Glastonbury's walls have stood for many lifetimes, and have probably heard many whispered secrets.

He hasn't answered my question about the grail, and I don't suppose he ever shall.

For once, I am glad to be a part of this quest. At least one of Glastonbury's treasures, if not exactly its secrets, will not be lost when the walls crumble.

✍ Ͻ

"The man who followed you from the docks, when you escorted Monsieur Lefèvre. You killed him." It's been bothering me all day, and I feel compelled to bring it up once Tobias and I are alone. Sam is finishing his evening chores outside the house, so I keep my voice low. I am putting away the remains of our evening repast. It keeps my hands busy, so I can broach these topics without having to look at him directly.

"We were attacked. He hid in the forest with bow and arrow, knowing we would pass on the road."

I understand. Truly, I do. And yet… "Tell me honestly—did Hutton die at your hand as well?"

"Nay. I did not lie to you, Audrey."

My body trembles with shame. Here we are, not even married yet, and he thinks I am questioning him. "I'm sorry."

He sighs. "Killing him would have gained me nothing, other than satisfaction for the threats he issued you. But I am not so hot-headed as that. We stood to gain more by watching him, garnering his secrets."

Now that I have started down this path, as awful as it is, I cannot seem to let it go. "'Twas only the dock guard, then?"

"What do you mean?"

I swallow hard. "Have you killed other men?"

His face hardens, so unlike the laughing, clever courtier to which I am accustomed. "Audrey…"

193

"I'm sorry," I mumble again. My hands shake as I finish wrapping the cheese. "You needn't answer. I am just...uneasy, wondering how many enemies we may have."

He sighs again, and the hard look melts away. He touches my shoulder. "Yes, there are ugly men and devious plots in this world. If I kill, I do it not for sport, or for pay, but to protect myself or those whom I serve. I aim to lessen the ranks of our enemies, not strengthen them."

"All right." I let him put his arms around me. I feel very small. By now, I have learned that no courtier is what they seem on the surface, but it is still a struggle to reconcile the carefree Tobias I thought I knew —the man who spouts poems and pulls blackberry tarts from his satchel—with the reality. If what he has told me is true, it does not lessen his honor, but I wonder if he has confessed these sins. Is his soul washed clean, and that is why his heart often seems so light? But to whom would he confess? Who could be trusted? Abbot Whiting—but he had not known of the pursuer who'd attacked Tobias and Monsieur Lefèvre. In theory, he should be able to give confession to any priest of the true faith...but I am not naive enough to still believe that is true. Even good men of religion may crack under pressure, and we live in a time of great pressure.

Sam comes in, and Tobias bids me good night. I watch him amble down the road, darkness closing in around him. I watch for a few minutes' more, until I see a light flare up at the edge of the property. He is standing watch, just as he—perhaps spelled occasionally by his brother or one of the men from the abbey—has done each night since our return. I should not have questioned him. Whatever he has done, is done. I will do what I should as his betrothed. Trust him, and pray for him as well.

❧ ❧

Our trio of conspirators meets again the follow morning—though this time, we actually do discuss and confirm the details of the soon-to-be-held wedding. When those matters are settled, I depart, heading for home, even though it means I will have to make the walk a second time that day when Sam's shift is over. I need to prepare the farmhouse to be lived in again—fully lived in, that is, for although Sam and I never left, it feels as though we, and the house itself, have just been biding our time.

Tobias lingers, and I suspect he and the abbot intend to discuss new arrangements for replicating the lead cross. A tug of resentment settles in my gut, and I have to chide myself. A few months ago, I resented the abbot for dragging me into this mess. Now, I resent him for leaving me out?

It's true, though. My feelings have changed. I don't want them to protect me the way I protect Sam. I console myself with the reminder that even the abbot and Tobias don't know everything. Like the abbot said, no one man is entrusted with all.

While I am airing out the upstairs rooms of the house, my gaze keeps drifting back to the crevice at the back of the wardrobe where I have concealed the documents my mother was working on. I have neglected my own studies while traveling with the court.

Will they risk using the abbey's forge to finish it? I know there are many men loyal to the abbot who would never betray him, but the problem with a forge is that it is hot, noisy work—not something easily performed in secret. For that matter, I wonder about the cross itself. Why is it so important? It identifies the remains, of course, and thus authenticates the findings of that long-ago excavation, but the words on the cross have long ago been translated. If we lost it now, would a drawing or record not suffice? Our whole mission seems to hang in the balance of one poorly made lead cross.

Unless, of course, the cross is more than that.

The thought stops me in the tracks. I've seen it so many times. How could it be anything more than what it is? I close my eyes and try to picture it…the crude letters, the thickness of the lead. Roughly the length from my elbow to my fingers. Translated, the words say, "Here lies the renowned King Arthur, buried in the isle of Avalon." At least, that is what I think it says. One of the documents Abbot Whiting gave me to study was a copy of Gerald of Wales' *Liber de Principis instruction*, which he told me was written only a few years after King Arthur's grave was discovered. I'm not certain when the monk's copy was made, and my Latin is not the best, but Abbot Whiting pointed out the sections he thought most relevant, and when I study those, they appear to claim that the cross says, "Here lies buried the famous King Arthur with Guinevere his second wife in the isle of Avalon."

The only difference, of course, is the mention of Guinevere. What bothers me is that I have lived my whole life in the vicinity of this cross, and I cannot even be certain I know what it says. Perhaps the inscription regarding Guinevere is on the underside of the cross. I've never actually held it or turned it over. Tobias or the abbot could tell me for certain if Guinevere's name is plainly formed on the cross. But what if it's a matter of interpretation…knowing how to read the letters a certain way? What if there are other messages hidden in those same letters, or even in the lead itself? Could that be why Abbot Whiting is so set on protecting it?

I have an overwhelming urge to touch the object, as though the act of holding it could give me those answers. I shall have to be cautious, though, about believing such things, or people will start to wonder if I have lost my mind the same way my poor grandmother did. Her loose grip on reality goes a long way toward explaining my own mother's need for certainty…and yet, I still want to hold the cross.

I won't have time today, though, for the distant ringing of church bells, signaling the evening call to prayer, tells me I have lost track of time. I am late to retrieve Sam. Hastily, I recite the Lord's Prayer and half-walk, half-run toward the abbey. Surely Sam will have started home without me, as he's been doing the whole time Tobias and I were away. Still, for old times' sake I'd meant to meet him and walk home together.

Surprisingly, I don't run into Sam at all on the road. I start to wonder if he's gone off with friends, taking advantage of the long hours of daylight to fish or do whatever boys do. He would've said something, though, if that were the case. Perhaps he's had to work late—some new arrival of goods that must be put up, or the like.

All of my guesses are wrong.

I arrive at the abbey kitchens in the middle of a tense scene. Sam stands before Cook. His shoulders are up. His chin, too. Fear and determination vie for control of his facial features. My stomach turns to lead, but they haven't seen me yet.

"I'll do better. Work harder." It is a promise Sam has made before, though his body won't let him keep the promise.

"It's not that." Cook holds up his hands. "There are fewer people living and working at Glastonbury. People are leaving, and 'tis unlikely they will return. There are fewer bellies to feed, fewer chores to be done. I don't need an extra kitchen boy anymore."

My heart aches for Sam, even though I cannot argue with Cook. It is true there are fewer residents now. Soon enough, everyone at the abbey shall be out of work.

Still, I know why Sam is the first to go from the kitchens—and Sam knows it, too. He catches sight of me standing in the doorway and our eyes lock. His are filled with pain and shame.

"Here." Sounding almost apologetic, Cook hands him a large brown sack. "Take these. Dried apples." He shrugs. "I stocked more than we ended up needing."

Sam nods dully and hands the sack to me. There's nothing else to say. I help him gather his things, and we leave quietly. Sam's eyes are bright with unshed tears, and his spare frame vibrates with his frustration, but he does not break down on the way home. He has strength, this brother of mine, though most cannot see it.

It's not until we're home, and he goes out back to bring in the firewood, that I hear a garbled, choking yell burst from his chest. I run to the door, but he isn't hurt. He doesn't need me. He stands, shaking his fist at the sky. In sheer anger he flings his crutch away, heaving it with more force than I'd guessed possible.

I retreat back inside, giving him the time he needs. I can't fix what's wrong. He's shaking his fist at the only one who can. Instead, I focus on putting a small repast on the table. Thick bread and clotted cream. Even a bit of bacon I put in a pan over the fire. I tuck the dried apples away for another time. Cook meant well, in a way, but now is not the time for those.

Sam drags himself in, the anger gone, leaving defeat in its place. He goes through the motions of stoking the fire and adding wood before coming to the table.

I put a plate in front of him. He pushes his food around for a minute like he's too upset to eat, but I can tell his appetite will soon win out over his ill mood. He's twelve now, and always hungry. He won't let good food go to waste, no matter how rotten he feels. But he tries.

"I hate this," he mutters.

"The bacon? Well, then, give it over."

He looks up in surprise, defensively pulling his plate a little closer.

I take a quick bite to hide my smile. He narrows his eyes at me. "Not the bacon. No one hates bacon. If I were bacon, everyone would like me, too. It's being a cripple that I hate. I hate being the only one who's different."

A long speech for Sam. I have to swallow my mouthful before I can respond—this time with sympathy. "Oh, Sam. You're not the only one. There's John Seybourne, for one."

"Lord of the Manor?" he scoffs. "That alone ensures his place in society."

"True—but he still has few friends. What about Lowdie? Her lazy eye made her the subject of many a joke when we were younger, and will not make it easy for her to marry well. And Bert, the candle maker's son?"

Sam gives a reluctant laugh. We both know Bert is just plain stupid. Fit for tending the chickens, and not much else.

"All right," he mumbles. "You have me there."

I hate making Sam feel better at the expense of others, but right now, I just need him to know he isn't alone. Plenty of people have their troubles. Sam's are just…Sam's.

He's almost even smiling now, and he digs into his food as though the meal might be his last. Before long, he's using his bread to wipe up the last traces of cream.

"Seriously, though," he says. "If I had two good legs, you wouldn't have to worry about me so much. You're about to be married. You don't need me getting in the way."

I give him my exasperated-older-sister sigh. "Sam, even if you had *three* good legs, I would still worry about you. No decent family member would put a twelve-year-old boy out on his own, just because they were getting married."

"Maybe not out on his own, but they'd put him to foster, or apprenticeship," he points out.

I frown. Sam and I haven't really had a chance to catch up on all that happened while I was away. "Is there somewhere you want to be apprenticed?"

"Not particularly. I only thought about it, see, and I'm not opposed to the idea. I could learn a trade."

"You could," I acknowledge. Especially with Cook having just let him go, I don't want him to think that I look on him as incapable. "But for now, you're coming with me. I need your help, so you'll just have to get used to the idea."

For some reason, he takes it well when I give him a bit of attitude. Maybe because there's a certain comfort in knowing you can break down in front of a sibling, squabble with them for all you're worth, and still know that you have a place in their life that won't be revoked. At least that's how things work with Sam and I.

"It's true, Sam—we're going to need your help." Instinctively, I know this is the right time to tell him the truth. I take a deep breath. "Sam. What I'm about to tell you, you can't breath a word of it—not to anyone, all right?"

CHAPTER EIGHTEEN

When I finally get the chance to touch the burial cross, I am disappointed, for it does not offer up its secrets unto my hands. I don't know why I'd thought it would—I feel silly for indulging in such fantasy. Unlike my pendant, it is cool to the touch, closed to me.

Though I have seen it a thousand times or more, I study it again. At first glance, the letters appear crude—as though the blacksmith were unskilled, illiterate, or pressed for time—any of which may be true. Upon closer study, though, I wonder if some of the crudeness is by design. The "V" letters appear tilted, while the "S" forms are disproportionate in size. Not by much—as I said, the overall appearance is merely one of crude workmanship. My observations may mean nothing.

But that night, I have the most vivid dream—unusual for me. I rarely remember dreaming at all.

In this one, I stand at the edge of a battlefield on a misty morning. The battle is over, and it was a terrible one. People pick their way through the carnage in eerie silence, identifying those they have lost, and those who might still be saved.

A small cluster of knights hovers above one of the fallen. I move closer, until I am just behind the group. They don't seem to notice me. My chest constricts when I gaze down, and realize that the fallen man is their king. His wounds are grave, though his chest still rises and falls with shallow breath. Two of the knights weep openly, while a third kneels at the king's side, shaking his head as he does what he can to staunch the flow of blood.

"Treason," one man mutters. He does not weep, but shakes with fury instead. "His own family—there is no death cruel enough to punish such a crime."

Somehow, I understand that I am gazing upon the last living moments of King Arthur.

The man who was kneeling gently closes the king's eyes and begins to rise. I can no longer see the rise and fall of the king's breath. I hear the thundering of hooves, and a large knight rides up, flinging himself from his horse as he draws near.

"Percival," another greets him. There is no "well met" to accompany the greeting, and one glance at the king is all it takes for Percival to understand the gravity of the situation.

The large knight drops to his knees, reaching into a pouch at his side. He extracts an object wrapped in cloth, handling it tenderly. "I had a vision, telling me to divert my travels…telling me this would be needed…but I fear I am too late."

"What gift do you bear?"

"'Tis no gift, for I am but its courier. I carry the grail."

Silence ensues as the men's gazes all lock on the cloth-wrapped object. I wait for one of them to insist Percival unwrap it, but no one speaks.

A flutter of movement distracts me, and I see a woman in a flowing gown glide up to the gathering. I don't know who she is. Her hair is long and dark, unlike the golden Guinevere of the romances.

"My lady," the knights murmur, when she reaches them. "Pray, grant us your wisdom."

She, too, kneels at the king's side, beside Percival. She lays a hand on the king's forehead, letting it rest only briefly before she withdraws it. "A ruler brought down at the hand of a son...such evil cannot easily be undone. Arthur has left us for another realm."

"Dead?"

She tilts her head. "Death is difficult to define." She turns to Percival. "Good knight, though you bear the holiest of objects at your side, neither it, nor I, can accomplish what you wish. It cannot undo the course of events that led Mordred to inflict these wounds, nor can the wounds themselves be healed."

"Then we have failed." This is said by the same knight who shook with rage, moments ago.

The lady looks up. "Failure, too, is difficult to define. Arthur may yet have a role to play...I do not sense that his destiny has been fulfilled."

"My lady?"

She rises, and in my dream, the air around her shimmers. She tilts her head to the sky and her eyelids drift closed. "I believe King Arthur will rise again, to someday rule over a united Britain. It will be a time of greatest need, and also a time when the people are ready. That time is not yet come."

The men gathered around the king appear uncertain. "Maybe we should try the grail now," one suggests.

"Nay," Percival replies. "The purest of powers cannot be used to achieve something that was not meant to be. To try such a thing…it would sully the purity of the grail, and almost certainly mark the end of life for its bearer."

"You are afraid to die?"

"Not at all," Percival returns. "But I would die unsullied. The grail has been entrusted to me, that I might protect it. I would die in doing so."

Several of the men bristle, and I fear they will draw arms, but the mysterious lady intervenes. "Bury him with the grail, that he may call upon its powers when the time is right."

There is silence as the group considers.

"My lady…" Percival begins. His gaze drops to the bundle in his hands. "In my vision, I saw that the grail was needed. I thought the need immediate, but perhaps…" He reaches forward, placing the object on the king's breastbone, then folding his hands over it. No one moves to stop him.

Percival pauses, as though weighing the sudden emptiness in his hands and considering what he has just done. Finally he nods. "This is right. But we will have to do better than this to protect the grail, and with it our king's future. If anyone knew…"

They all scowl. "His would not be a restful grave," one says.

"You may think on it, Percival, as we bear him away," the lady says. "Good knights, you may entrust Arthur's final journey to myself, and your worthy knight, Percival."

Some of them frown, as though unwilling to let their leader go, but slowly they all take a step back, as though acknowledging their role is done.

"Come, Bors," Percival invites. "I would speak with thee."

The gruff knight looks surprised, but follows him. The two men walk a few paces, and because it is a dream, I can still hear them. "If I die without heir, I must know there is another who will protect the secret. You, above all others, I would trust. There will be rumors and misdirection, and men who continue to quest for the grail. If it becomes necessary to move it, we must be prepared for that as well. You remember the old code we used to use when we quested together?"

"Veritas, sanctitas."

"If you hear news of the grail, and it is not accompanied by that phrase, then do not trust in what you hear."

"You have my word."

They walk back to the group, where the remaining knights are assembling a rough litter under the watchful eye of the mysterious woman.

"How will we know when the time comes for him to rise again?" Bors asks.

She looks at him with sadness in her eyes. "You will not know, Bors."

His shoulders slump, but his expression is resigned, as though that was the answer he expected.

"His daughter will know. She alone will keep the watch." The lady lifts her head, and though I have been invisible this whole time, I am not invisible to her. Our eyes meet, and she holds my gaze long enough that I know it is no mistake. She tilts her head in the slightest of nods, and I wake up.

The dream leaves me unsettled. For every question it answered, it seemed to raise two more. Or perhaps there are no answers, and it was just a dream.

I feel foolish telling Tobias about it, but the images won't let me rest. To my great relief, he doesn't laugh. Nor is he angry with me for bringing Sam into our secret.

"Perhaps Our Heavenly Father sent you this dream, that you might better understand your own fate."

"Perhaps."

I must not sound convinced, for he asks, "What do *you* think it means?"

I have to admit I don't know. "Sir Percival never even unwrapped the grail," I complain. "I feel like I came *this* close to seeing it—even if it was a dream."

He smiles sympathetically. Tobias, more than anyone, would understand my frustration at my quest, even my dream quest, being thwarted. "But have you any lingering doubt as to your role? The Lady of the Lake all but named you Arthur's daughter."

"Lady of the Lake?"

"The one who made the prophesy? If the legends are true, who else would it be?"

My mind clears, as at least that part of the dream falls into place. Her gown was a pale blue, come to think of it. "Of course. I just hadn't realized." I finger the pendant about my neck. "I think I had already accepted my role, doubts or not."

"I suppose you have." He sounds proud of me. I like that.

I frown. "But there was no grail buried with King Arthur— was there?"

"Not that I've ever heard. You've seen nothing in the records?"

"No. In my dream, there was nothing of the cross. I thought…"

"What cross?"

Oh. I'd forgotten to tell Tobias about touching the lead cross, or why I thought the dream was somehow connected. Feeling once more like a fool, I say slowly, "I thought perhaps the cross was connected to the grail. I wondered why Abbot Whiting was so anxious to see it preserved, when we already know what it says. I went to look at it yesterday—*really* look. I didn't see anything new. But then I had that dream, and even though the cross wasn't in it, I feel like there's something I'm missing. If it were truly no more than a grave marker—albeit an important one—would it matter so much?"

"I think it would still matter," he answers, but I can tell by his measured pace that I've set him to thinking. "The grail couldn't be encased in the cross. It isn't thick enough, and if the chalice were of gold, forming the cross around it would have melted it."

"I don't know if it was gold. I don't even know if Percival and the lady carried out that plan…my dream ended too soon." I lean my head on his shoulder. "Thank you for not believing I've lost my wits."

"Who says I don't believe that?" he answers, drawing a giggle from me.

He sighs. "Unless you are in the habit of having such fantastical dreams, I would say this one came to you for a reason."

"Definitely not in the habit," I confirm.

"Can you remember anything else? Did Percival, say, happen to look like he might be my great-great-great-great uncle?"

I poke him in the side, and he responds by tickling me until we both are laughing so hard we have to stop to catch our breath.

Sam chooses this moment to come in from his chores, and he rolls his eyes. "Oh, excellent. Please, don't let me interrupt. There aren't chores to be done, or anything."

Tobias lurches up and tackles Sam, and the two are soon tussling and laughing. Usually people are too aware of Sam's limitations to engage him in rough play, and I can tell he loves that Tobias doesn't care.

"You two need to hurry up and get married," Sam says when he can breathe again.

"I'm working on it, little brother."

CHAPTER NINETEEN

The wedding day arrives at long last. It starts like any other day, except that when I awaken, my eyes pop open and I bound from the bed, rather than crawling reluctantly from the warmth of the covers.

"Excited, are we?" Sam mumbles.

"Yes." Yes, I am. The delay, and the weeks spent by Tobias's side at King Henry's court, have not only given me time to grow accustomed to the idea of marrying, but convinced me it is what I was meant to do. The days in which I thought I would never marry and become a nun seem like another lifetime ago. I have to admit, Sam and Abbot Whiting saw what I did not—that Tobias's ready-for-anything spirit is the right complement for my cautious nature. I am even fond of his family, even if his mother *does* think she knows what is best for everyone in her life. She knows nothing of our true purpose and has expectations for the two of us to rise high in the eyes of society. I cannot fault her for that. Most mothers are the same, when they have borne a son with prospects.

Still, my excitement is mixed with nervousness. Today I am to become a married woman. Wedded and bedded. It's the bedded part I worry about. Under Lady Seybourne's watchful eye, Tobias and I did little more than kiss, though quite a few of our kisses could have led to something more, had we not been careful. Given our near-escape in the garden at Richmond Palace, we even resorted to letting others think we were doing more intimate things than we really were. I enjoy kissing him, so that is a good sign.

I *do* want to do those things. Tonight I will. 'Tis only that I am all too aware that, unlike me, my husband-to-be is no virgin. Of course he's never told me this, but I know. If he's visited the whorehouses in recent weeks, he's been incredibly subtle about it. In truth, I don't think he has. But before we were betrothed? Such women would have been too enticing for a man like Tobias to pass up—unless his bevy of willing companions kept him entertained even without paid company.

I don't fault him for this. Truly, I don't. The reason it worries me is that I'm afraid I won't know how to please him—I don't know the things they did, or what he likes. I've come to the conclusion that, if I am to be married, I would prefer it be a true marriage. That means I have to make him *want* me, and continue wanting me. That is the unnerving part.

I am no fool—I understand the basics of the marriage bed. But my weeks at court have opened my eyes to the fact that there is much more to the games men and women play. Having spent the defining years of my maidenhood working in the shadow of monks, my education in this area was nonexistent—as it should have been. But now I find myself in need of that knowledge, and have no one to ask. Really, how does one even begin to ask for such advice?

Although Lady Seybourne loves to dispense advice on many topics she deems important for me to know, that is one topic I simply *cannot* ask her. An older sister would be incredibly useful. I've been paying closer attention to the conversations of girls my age, or slightly older, hoping to glean whatever knowledge I can. Lowdie is probably the closest thing I have to a sister, or a friend, since we worked in close proximity at the abbey. She's coming to help braid and coil my hair this morning, and I wonder if I can get up the nerve to ask her. She's not married either, but with so many siblings, she's bound to know more than me.

Except…I know the way his eyes went dark when we kissed, and the way his fingers lingered on my upper arms, as though he never wanted to release me. I was not the only one who felt something. So perhaps I am worrying for nothing.

When Lowdie arrives, we don't have much time because Lady Seybourne arrives too, with Binnie in tow. They all help me into the pale green silk, with the stomacher laced tighter than ever. Binnie and Lowdie arrange my hair in a crown of braids, which is covered by my veil, but Lowdie assures me they will still look lovely when I remove it later.

Finally, when Lady Seybourne leaves to go ahead to the chapel and see to whatever arrangements she has made, I am left with the two younger women.

"Lowdie," I whisper urgently. "How do I please him?"

"Hmm?" She frowns, but then her face clears. "Oh! You mean…*please* him."

I nod frantically.

Binnie's eyes dart between us, and I pray she has the good sense not to relay this conversation to her mistress.

Lowdie glances at her too. "Well, I've never…"

"Oh, come off it. You have sisters, and the married ones have given you probably half a dozen nieces and nephews already, so I know you must know *something*."

She licks her lips—whether nervously, or relishing what she's about to reveal, I can't tell. "My sister Ellie, then. She's always on about how she likes to lead her husband on a merry chase."

"What?"

"She teases him, see? Lets him get close, kiss her a bit, then sashays away. Or maybe she lets him catch her in a state of half-dress, so as to get him roused. Makes him work for it. She says they both have fun that way."

"Hmm. Like flirting."

"Like flirting, but more…touching, I guess. Like if he catches a glimpse of your bum, or your titties, when he's not expecting to have you, and he thinks maybe you actually *meant* for him to see…men like that." She flushes. "Or so Ellie says."

I picture myself sashaying around the bed while Tobias tries to chase me down. It sounds…complicated. But maybe if I just think of it as flirting, with less clothing, it will work out fine. "I can try that, but I'm supposed to eventually let him catch me, right? What do I do to please him when he takes me to bed?"

Lowdie hesitates, and Binnie nudges her aside. "Oh, heavens. If she won't tell you, I will. But this *never* gets back to Lady Seybourne, right?"

"Of course not." Lowdie and I are both wide-eyed.

"Right, then. I have a sister who…decided that being a lady's maid was not the method in which she wanted to support herself."

"You mean she—"

"Hush, Lowdie." I cut her off before she asks the obvious.

"Men like to feel desired just as much as women do—but pretty words don't mean much to them, see? Show him by touching him. Act like you can't think of anything you want more than to wrap your hands around his cock and stroke him." Binnie grabs my hairbrush and flips it upside down, using the handle to mimic a man's privates. She grasps the handle firmly, jerking upward.

My face must register my surprise at the violence of the movement. "Men like a little rough play—at least most of them do. If you've too soft a touch, he might grow soft, too, and then he can't…perform."

I nod slowly, and Binnie provides a few more tips on cupping his ballocks and using my hips to meet his thrusts. Finally, she drops her voice even further. "There's one other thing. My sister says the men all want it—so much they'll pay extra."

"What?" I can't help but ask.

"Take him in your mouth."

"What?!"

It's plain I heard her, so she doesn't bother repeating the words. "Like I showed you with my hand, but do the same with your lips around him. Drives them wild."

"Have you ever…" Lowdie blurts.

"This isn't about me. It's about Miss Thorndale, soon to be the young Lady Seybourne, wanting to please her husband, right?"

"Right." I shoot Lowdie a look, and she clamps her mouth shut. Of course we're both wildly curious as to whether Binnie has tried any of these tactics for herself, but I suppose she's right—that's her business. Regardless, I have new respect for Binnie—and what Lady Seybourne doesn't know won't hurt her.

❧

The wedding itself is a traditional ceremony. Abbot Whiting seems in better health, and the words of the ceremony flow over and through me as he speaks them. I'd like to remember every detail, but in truth, the whole thing passes in a blur, and then I am swept up in a throng of well-wishers who have come to help us celebrate.

There have to be at least twice as many people as Lady Seybourne told me she was inviting, but I find I don't mind that much after all. My uncles and a few cousins are there—likely because they never believed this would actually happen and have to see it for themselves. Even them I don't mind. Why should I? I have a handsome husband and land of my own. I can afford to be gracious.

The crowd slowly makes its way toward John's estate, and it is a good thing the weather has held, for most of the tables for the feast have been set outdoors. Tobias and I have the seats of honor at a table under a brightly striped awning, and I must say, Lady Seybourne does plan a good feast—peacock and all.

I don't know how the hours pass, but slowly, our guests trickle away, until only the servants and family are left. Lady Seybourne, happy but exhausted, gives Tobias one last pat on the shoulder before retreating to one of John's guest bedrooms.

John will keep Sam at his home tonight, so that Tobias and I will have some privacy. Sam can't help turning and giving me a smirk as they go inside—he knows exactly why he's not welcome tonight.

Tobias and I walk the lane to my old home alone. Old Meg has made sure the linens are fresh and clean rushes strewn.

When we reach the house, Tobias closes the door behind us and pulls me into his arms. "Finally, wife."

His lips meet mine, and I can taste the celebratory wine on him. I am half-drunk with it already—I am always eager for his kisses these days, and the wine makes me forget that I am nervous about what comes after the kisses. Binnie's advice flashes through my mind, but my thoughts are flying around so wildly—the day has overwhelmed me—that I cannot put them into action.

It doesn't matter. I feel him growing hard, nestled against my woman's place, and without thinking I press closer. He scoops me up and carries me to the bed, his fingers working to release the ties of my gown and then there are clothes everywhere and skin, and Tobias is touching me, and I stop thinking about anything else. No matter what dangerous secrets brought us together, the intimacy of our wedding night is everything I could have desired.

"What do you think?"

My breath catches. It's the day after our wedding, and as a surprise, Tobias has brought me to see our new land. It isn't what I'd imagined. It's better.

A small manor house, little more than a farmhouse, really, nestles up against a gently sloping hill. Green fields roll away, into the distance, dotted by clumps of trees. Inland, the trees turn to forest, while the land to the south and west gives way to marsh. The land seems to stretch on and on, unbroken but for rutted and overgrown paths out to the fields.

Tobias tips my chin up so that I am forced to look into his eyes. "Can you make your home here?"

I see concern, but also hope. He wants me to be happy. "If you are with me, I can make my home anywhere."

He pulls me in for a kiss. But too soon, he draws back. "I can't always be with you. I have duties—to my country and my king. Will this be too lonely?"

I look again at the swaying grass out by the marsh, and at the house by the hill. It *will* be lonely, but not in a bad way. Almost in the way I once imagined life in a convent to be. "No. I like it. Besides, I shall have Sam for company."

"True. There are neighbors nearby, and the town is not far, either, though you cannot see any of that from here."

"It's beautiful—and there is a house. I thought you said there was only a hunting box."

"A hunting box for a *king*," he points out. "Though I expect you'll still wish to make some refinements to the interior when you see it. The place was built to accommodate a large party, but it was not oft inhabited by women, and has too long sat empty."

"It's perfect."

He looks pleased. "Practical, too. The marsh may not be as ideal for farming as I suggested to John, but it will keep neighbors from encroaching, or desiring the land."

I nod, my respect for my husband growing as I gaze across the land. Tobias managed to talk King Henry into giving us all this?

He follows my gaze. "You don't have to stay here in hiding, though. In truth, you *should* get to know the people nearby."

The first part of his reasoning is obvious—our new neighbors will be less suspicious if we act like normal people would in a new place, getting to know those around them, settling in. But I sense more to my new husband's words. He's rubbing the seam of his chausses—the unconscious habit that means something is troubling him.

I catch his eye and give a little nod toward his thumb.

He whisks his hands behind his back. "I must stop that," he mutters.

I step closer to his side, understanding his concern. He wants me to know the neighbors in case anything should happen to him. He just doesn't want to say this aloud, and make me worry more than I already do.

"You will need a servant here, at least one at the house, and a farmer to work the fields. Not all of the land is marsh. The drier fields will have to be cleared for planting. I will be away, betimes for weeks, and it is too much for you and Sam alone. Especially if…" He glances at my belly.

Especially if he gets me with child. I press my hands to my suddenly hot cheeks. Silly. Every maid knows that marriage leads to babies. But our marriage is too new, our feelings too untested, for either of us to give voice to the possibility. There is so much we leave unsaid, in our daily conversations.

I admit, I welcome the possibility of having servants again. It brings back memories of my childhood, when my parents and my uncles and cousins were all on their way up in the world. Before all our bad luck. Of course, I know that some of my memories are colored by the fact that I was merely a child, and carefree. But even more recent are the memories of Sam and I trying to do everything on our own and struggling to keep up. An extra pair of hands is most welcome.

But I don't know how much we can afford. Tobias clearly has curried favor with the king, but how much of that was used to win us this land? The Seybourne family has money, but most of it belongs to John, as eldest. I don't know the extent of my husband's resources, and I am afraid to ask. I don't want him to think me so needy that he must stretch us thin.

"What?" he asks. "Something I said bothered you."

He is insightful—or my expression has given me away. I must be honest with him. I've already agreed to deceive the rest of the world. "Can we afford servants?"

He chuckles. "Dear Audrey. You needn't worry. We can afford to hire the help we need. Someday I hope to give you all sorts of luxuries. But for now, you may at least sleep soundly, assured that the wolves are not yet at our door."

He pauses. "There are some who work for the abbey that may not fare so well, when the time comes. Would you wish to offer any of them a position here?"

I think about it. Sam's fellow kitchen workers are the first to come to mind. Cook has released more of them since Sam. Jane and Mary, I dismiss quickly. They would think I was trying to lord it over them if I offered them work as my servant. I don't know the others very well. But…maybe Lowdie? I don't think she'd see things that way. She's the sort to take whatever work is available and be grateful for it. She's helped in nearly every part of the abbey at one time or another. "Maybe," I say slowly. "What do you think about Lowdie?"

It takes him a minute to recall her, but then he nods. "Aye. Nice enough girl, not too curious? Good worker, but not too aspiring?"

It's not exactly the most flattering picture, but it is accurate enough. "She's a friend, of sorts."

"Good. I should like to know you have a friend with you, when I am gone. I think you should ask her."

"I don't know about help in the fields. I don't know any farmers to ask." That's not entirely true…I know them by face and name, having seen many at mass over the years. I just wouldn't be comfortable asking any of them if they have labor to hire out. Aside from the abbot and Sam, and my father before his death, I hardly ever spoke to men.

"Not to worry. I'll get word out and hire someone appropriate. I want someone who can protect you, should the need arise. At the very least, I suspect there are locals who have poached freely from these lands for years, and may not be pleased to find them under new ownership."

I can feel my eyes widen. I hadn't even considered that.

"I've done it again, haven't I? Made you worry."

"I have a great talent for it," I admit, making him smile.

"Honestly, you'll be fine. This land may not have yielded the big game our king is so fond of, but the proximity to the marsh means plenty of waterfowl. Even if a neighbor occasionally makes off with an ill-gotten goose, we won't starve."

As if to prove the truth of his words, a great flock of geese startles up from the marsh, taking to a V formation overhead.

We spend the night in our new home, and while the lovemaking is wonderful, I am forced to admit Tobias is right—the interior of the house requires significant finishing and repair. I can hardly wait to begin.

When we return to Glastonbury, I get up the nerve to ask Lowdie if she'll come live in Bridgewater and work for us. "It's not so very far, really," I finish, rushing over the words. "You'll be able to visit your family often."

She pauses for a long minute, and my heart sinks. I've offended her, I'm sure of it. Trounced on our unspoken friendship by implying I think of her as a lower class. I've gone off and married a Seybourne, and now I think I'm better than her.

But she surprises me, lifting her chin and giving me a smile. "Aye. I think I'd like that."

Relief rushes through me.

"I'll have to ask Father, of course." She lowers her voice and leans in. "He's certain to agree, though. We all know the work at the abbey is coming to a swift end, any day now. I'd planned to start taking in laundry, but little Anne can do that as well as I."

Lowdie's father is a widower, left with a whole passel of children when his wife died in childbed. His work as a brewer is good work, but theirs is not a family that comes from money. Everyone must do their part. Little Anne is just ten years old, younger than Sam. Her hands will be ruined before she's twenty, taking in laundry. But perhaps she won't have to take in as much, if Lowdie has a secure position with Tobias and I.

Lowdie gives my hand a quick squeeze, and I realize it was still trembling. "I'm not too proud to serve in your house. You've been twitching about like you're about to leap from your skin."

I give a sheepish shrug.

"You're kind to think it, Lady Audrey, but I know a good offer when I hear one—and I'm not so mean as to begrudge you the good fortune you've come into. I've watched you work just as hard as anyone, and I know how things were for Sam and you when your parents died."

Her earnest sentiment makes a lump grow in my throat.

"Do you know, I've never been to Bridgewater?" she mused. "Never had a reason to go. And now I shall live there."

"It isn't far," I promise. "You'll be able to visit your family."

"Oh, I know," she assures me. A grin spreads across her face. "I was just thinking that, instead of piles of dirty laundry, I shall have a bit of an adventure!"

I smile back. If only she knew.

In spite of the condition of the hunting box-turned-manor house, I beg Tobias to let us move right away. We can't, though—not until the relics are ready to move. My desire to make a home of our new land renews my dedication to our original purpose as well. For once, there is more driving my actions than fear.

I start doing what I've always done best—making a list, planning meticulously. For safety, I keep the list inside my head, but it calms my mind to make it. First, the simple tasks. Moving the documents won't be difficult. People come and go from the abbey every day with papers. I already took some of my mother's records, but the abbot has indicated there are more, so we should do that soon.

Next is the cross. I know Tobias and Abbot Whiting are doing what they can to fix the problem of replicating it, so I have to trust it will be ready as quickly as they deem safe.

Then, there are the actual remains. Moving the whole tomb is too impractical—but we do need to protect its contents. That's when I realize we have another problem.

I wake Tobias well before dawn—I've been awake all night anyway. "We need to visit the abbot."

"Now?" He yawns and tries to pull me back down in the bed.

"Aye. Now. It's important."

"What's important?" His body becomes alert. "Did something happen?"

"No. At least, I hope not. Just trust me. I need to speak with you both."

To his credit, Tobias dresses quickly. He *does* trust me. We sneak past Sam, who, for once, is actually sleeping when we need him to be.

Bane—a new dog Tobias brought home the other day—lifts his head, but when he sees Sam is still asleep, he plops it back down. Traitor. He was supposed to be my dog, but as soon as he met Sam, his affinity became clear.

The only person we see on the way to the abbot's house is the lone monk standing the night watch near the abbey gates. He probably wonders at our arrival, but he lets us through.

Abbot Whiting is already awake when we reach his house. "I rarely sleep for long these days," he admits. "But you are too young to share that problem, so something else must have brought you here."

"Yes, Father Abbot," I say. We are alone, but I keep my voice low anyway. "The replica of the cross is important, but it isn't enough. We cannot just take Arthur's remains and leave behind an empty tomb."

The two men look at one another.

"The tomb itself is very fine, of course," Abbot Whiting says gently. "But it is not the true relic. It is only a work of stone, made to honor that which lies within."

"We could never transport it," Tobias agrees.

I shake my head. They think me featherbrained, if they think I want to try to hide that great marble tomb on the king's old hunting grounds. "That wasn't what I meant."

I take a deep breath, then forge on. "We're going to need bodies."

CHAPTER TWENTY

I clap my hand over my mouth, horrified at my own words. But now that they're out, I might as well finish the job. "Old ones. Skeletons. If the farce is to be believed, the replicas must be complete. The king's men will inspect everything, will they not? The tomb must contain bodies."

"With the tomb sitting in its usual place, they may not think to look inside. There's quite a lot of commotion at these…events," Abbot Whiting says.

"A lot of commotion means people will take unpredictable actions. The contents of Glastonbury have already been catalogued more than once, right? It's as if Lord Cromwell and his men already suspect you might try to hide things from them. If they suspect that, doesn't it stand to reason they will look *everywhere*?"

"And if they look in the tomb and find it empty, they'll know immediately something is up," Tobias finishes for me, then crosses himself. "She's right."

There's a soft tap at the door and we all freeze. Caught in the act.

The abbot is the first to relax. "That must be Robert. I was expecting him."

I'm eyeing the window. "Should we leave?"

"No. Robert is one of my remaining monks, and a trusted one. He's putting the finishing touches on our replica. He's quite good."

Abbot Whiting moves to let him in, and there is an awkward moment when he enters and finds the abbot is not alone.

Robert the Monk gathers himself. "Sir Seybourne, Lady Seybourne."

"Good morning to you," Tobias replies cheerfully, and I realize with a start that he's actually enjoying himself right now.

Abbot Whiting gives the monk a cursory explanation of the reason for our early morning visit.

The artisan monk glances between us warily, clearing his throat. "Do not look to me for this work. I can create a false cross. I cannot create a false human."

"No. I cannot think of anyone who could. Not a believable one," the abbot agrees.

"Then they'll have to be real." Tobias speaks the words we're all thinking—the same thoughts that kept me up at night.

No one replies.

"Well, look at it this way," Tobias suggests. "Compared to the crimes we could already be charged with, a mere incident or two of grave robbing is but a silly prank."

We tramp up a hill, the waxing moon our only light.

Never in my wildest dreams, had I imagined I would one day be robbing graves in the dead of night. Stranger still, that I would be doing so in the name of the Church. Or at least in the name of England. *God works in mysterious ways, indeed.*

But more than ever, I believe in our ultimate course of action. If I needs must disturb an ancient skeleton or two, well, then I pray their spirits will understand and forgive. I do actually mutter a few such prayers on my way up the hill, causing Tobias to shoot me a warning look. I settle for praying silently.

I only wish we could get this over with faster. But with Sam's limp, it's all he can do to keep up with our trudging pace. Uneven ground is harder for him than walking along a road. I wonder, not for the first time, if we should have left him home. Tobias carries the spades for the three of us, while I have a bundle of sacking to wrap...the replacements. That's what I've taken to calling them, in my head. It sounds less personal. I don't want to think about who they were...a mother, a son, a farmer, a cleric? I force my thoughts away from that tormented path, paying attention instead to how the damp grass is slowly soaking through my shoes, chilling my feet. It's uncomfortable, but I feel like I deserve that.

Tobias must sense my frustration with the pace. He puts one hand on my shoulder and I go still, giving Sam a chance to catch up.

"It's all right." He speaks into my ear, his voice the barest murmur. "There is no one about to see us, and it's quieter to move slowly, anyway. Ask any hunter."

I nod. His presence, more than his logic, calms me. I know that once we select a grave and begin to dig, the advantage of stealth will be lost. I just want to get there, get the job done, and get away. I realize I was the one who came up with this idea in the first place, but that doesn't mean I like it—or that I ever considered *I'd* be the one to execute the plan.

After our initial discussion, when we all agreed an empty tomb would give away our secret, Abbot Whiting sent Tobias out to scout for old, remote graveyards. Fortunately, he had several suggestions—having traveled the country and presided over any number of funerals in his years. Not any graveyard would do, of course. It needed to be old, for one thing. Preferably no longer in use. Even better if no one lived nearby.

Within days, Tobias found one that suited our purpose. It had once belonged to a small village, but the outbreak of the Black Death several generations ago had largely wiped it out. Over time, the remaining inhabitants had moved on. Only a few distant farmhouses remained, none directly in the line of sight from the old cemetery. Tobias, in his usual way, had befriended one of the farmers, chatting with him over mugs of ale, until the farmer parted with the information he needed— the old cemetery was not in use, and the nearest church only sent a grounds keeper once or twice a year to keep the worst of the debris away from the graves.

"Do you think it's safe to uncover these graves?" I'd asked. "What if we pick someone who died of the plague?"

"Plague victims are usually burned. Besides, we're looking for a grave older than the outbreak that killed the villagers."

I hope he's right. This is a dangerous game we play, in more ways than one.

We reach the top of the hill, and pause again while Sam catches his breath. Thick brush and trees have grown up around the old graves, which will help protect us from sight and muffle the sounds we make. The trees blocked much of the moonlight as well, and I'm barely two steps into the graveyard before I smack my shins on a headstone. *I can't believe we're doing this.*

"Which ones?" I whisper.

Tobias points. "The oldest part of the cemetery is back there."

He leads us deeper in. The headstones are lower here. I touch one, curious in spite of my trepidation. The edges of the stone are worn and crumbled with age, and moss has crept up over the bottom.

"Right, then," Sam says quietly. He sounds braver than I feel. "Shall we get on with it?"

"Indeed. I don't suppose it matters much, which particular ones we choose." Tobias uses the tip of his spade to indicate two markers. "How about these?"

Sam and I give a shrug of agreement. I say one last, brief prayer for the unfortunate souls whose long rest we are about to disturb. Probably they have long since gone on to their heavenly reward. There will be nothing but dirt and old bones here. Nothing to worry about.

With nothing left to say, we get to work. Tobias takes the lion's share, but I do my best. Sam drags over a round stone, using it to brace his weak foot. I notice that as long as he doesn't have to change position too often, he's strong enough to hold his own with a shovel. He's turning into a young man.

In spite of the cool night air, sweat soon trickles down my temples and pools in the hollow between my breasts. My arms and back begin to ache, but I can't stop. There was no way I was going to leave and come back to finish this job another night.

Finally, the deed is done. I am going to have nightmares, for certain, about lowering myself into dark holes.

I wrap the ill-gotten remains carefully, almost reverently. *Whoever you are, or were, you are now serving your country one last time.*

Tobias and Sam shovel the dirt back into the holes, and Tobias scatters grass, leaves, and pine needles over the bare dirt. With any luck, it will be months before the groundskeeper returns.

۞

Though our plans are escalating, we see less and less of Abbot Whiting after delivering the replacements. I suppose King Arthur is but one of his problems these days. I do see him often at prayer, though, and on the afternoon after we return from our midnight plunder, I find him on his knees before the high altar.

At the sound of my footsteps, he heaves a sigh and rises.

"Please, Father Abbot, continue. I did not mean to interrupt."

"No, it is well you did. You have been on my mind, and in my prayers as well."

I tilt my head, curious.

"When they come for me, Audrey—and we both know they will—it is possible they will want to question you as well."

"Me?"

"As my assistant, you will have been privy to my habits, and heard things I have said."

I scowl. "They'll want me to betray you."

He rolls his shoulders as though to ease an ache. "Whatever you do, my child, you must tell them the truth."

"What? But, Father—"

He lifts a hand, and I stop mid-sentence. "I only meant, if they ask questions about my loyalties, or my comings and goings, do not be afraid to implicate me. I did not mean to suggest you tell them *everything*."

My scowl eases, but only a little. I have no wish to implicate anyone. So I give him the only answer I can. "I will do my best, Father Abbot, whatever comes to pass."

"I know you will. I think it best we not delay any longer with the remainder of the plan. Your husband knows the details. If I seem to distance myself, my child, do not fear that I have abandoned this cause."

"No, Father Abbot."

"I do so to protect you—so that when they come to question me, no matter what methods they might use, I will not put you at risk."

I nod, blinking fast.

"Do not protect me the same way."

The time has come. The cross is the most critical, of course, for it sits in a glass case, on display for all to see. But when the replacement is made, even I cannot tell the difference. I think a raiding party, bent on destruction, will never even suspect. It is a shame, really. This replica cost a man his life, and yet the work for which he paid so dearly will likely not last the year…though whether the cross is lost to the king's collection, destroyed, or stolen for illegal trade remains to be seen.

The cross, despite being critical, is the easy part—aside from the documents, which are already tucked beneath the floorboards and under the mattress upstairs at home. More difficult are the actual remains. They have lain undisturbed in the marble tomb for centuries. And no wonder, because the tomb is not only heavy as sin, but its makers went so far as to seal the lit with mortar. Some tombs are simply build with a groove to fit the lid closely in place, but I suppose for Arthur's tomb, the prospect of curiosity-seekers warranted the additional caution.

For the second time, we will be robbing a grave in the dead of night. It's strange to think of becoming adept at such a thing. Glastonbury is even more dangerous than the site of our first robbery, of course. The last graveyard was in a remote corner of countryside, nearly abandoned. Glastonbury is the very opposite. For three days now, Tobias has been sneaking into the abbey in the dark of night, chipping away at the underside of the seal on King Arthur's tomb. He has to keep from damaging the marble, and he must take care to sweep up the dust as the seal crumbles.

"Tonight. I think I'll get the last of the seal tonight. Are you ready?" he'd asked.

I am. I wear my old mourning clothes and a heavy veil. When I arrive at the abbey grounds, I am able to slip past the night guard as he strolls the grounds. I have been practicing moving silently.

Tobias has already been here for some time. His plan is to open the tomb, make the switch, and give me the true relics. I will get out of there as fast as possible, while he stays behind to reseal the tomb, so that we leave no sign of our midnight venture.

The abbey is dark and the shadows darker. Only the glow from a single candle breaks the gloom. I approach, then suck in my breath and go still.

The man kneeling before the tomb, chisel in hand, wears the robes of a lay monk. He hasn't heard me yet. My heart beats faster. What happened to Tobias? Please, God, protect my husband.

I start to retreat, slow and stealthy, but then the monk reaches up and the candlelight catches a flash of gold. A ring. I frown, watching longer—and then I know. That *is* Tobias.

I sidle up, but this time he hears me. "Lovely robes. Very authentic. I nearly fainted, thinking it wasn't you."

He lifts the rough cloth, holding it away from his body. He rubs it between his finger and thumb, raising one eyebrow as he gives me a rueful look. "My apologies. This seemed like a wise decision, since I needs must linger in this place at such a strange hour. But in truth, I am not cut out to be a man of the cloth."

I laugh, careful not to make too much noise. "Nay, husband. You are not."

He drops the robes and they billow around him before falling into place.

This time, Sam has stayed home. His limp is too recognizable around here.

"Are you ready? We need to move the bodies."

"I'm working on it. Whoever put the seal in place knew what they were doing."

I have to bite down on my lip to keep the whimper of fear from escaping. What if he couldn't get the lid unsealed? "Do you need my help?"

"I don't want you in danger any more than necessary. If I'm discovered—alone—there's a chance I can talk my way out of it. But if you're here…"

"How much longer?"

He shakes his head. "Hard to judge."

"What if someone discovers the…replacements?" I still cannot think of a better word to describe the ill-gotten bundle of bones we'd borne home in the pre-dawn dark.

"They're well-hidden. It's killing me to work so slowly, but you know I daren't make too much noise."

"I know. I know." I can sense his frustration—and even by the light of a single candle, I can see the shadows beneath his eyes. The tomb of King Arthur, while not at all hidden, is nonetheless proving to be well-protected. Still, when the abbey falls, the very walls may well be torn down. We have to get in.

"Every little sound echoes in the cavern of the church. It's awful. And every time that one monk passes by, I have to stop what I'm doing and stay in the shadows."

Immediately, my guard goes back up. "What monk?"

"I don't know his name. One of the lay monks. Maybe he has trouble sleeping or something. He tends to wander the grounds at night. Never know when he's coming."

"Not the night watchman?"

"No. Somehow, the monk assigned the duty of night guard this week is poor of both hearing and vision."

We share an amused look, knowing the abbot had something to do with that assignment.

"The other one, though. You think he's a spy?"

Tobias shrugs. "Could be. The king has people in his pay just about everywhere…and he's not the only one. Or maybe he's just a monk who likes to walk in the quiet of night. Who knows. Either way, I don't fancy trying to explain what I am also doing up at that hour, on abbey grounds, tinkering with King Arthur's tomb."

"Hmm. Described like that, it does sound rather suspicious." I keep my tone light, though my heart is still racing.

His shoulders shake with silent laughter. "I am starting to like you, Mistress Thorndale."

I pout. "What? Just now? I thought you liked me all along."

He grins. "I did like you, in truth. But I admit, I did not know you as well as I thought. When Abbot Whiting first told me who he had in mind for this duty, I thought he'd gone cracked."

"I thought so, too," I admit.

"You didn't think me worthy?" He sounds surprised.

"I didn't think *me* worthy."

He shakes his head, reaching out to cup my face in his hand. Perhaps it is a trick of the candlelight, but I am struck by the tenderness and—dare I believe it?—admiration in his gaze. "What I was about to say, though, was that I was wrong. I think the abbot's judgment was better than I gave him credit for."

"Truly?" His approval warms me, through and through.

"Truly. You have a quality about you that…" he cocks his head, as if searching for the right way to put it. "I don't know. But somehow I think you were meant to do this."

"I hope so."

"I hope so too, because I've just about got the seal removed. One more night should do it."

"Another night?" I cannot hide my dismay. "But—"

Suddenly he flings out a hand, startling me into silence. He puts a finger over his lips, then indicates the far entrance of the nave.

I duck behind the other side of the tomb. Tobias does the same, pinching out his candle. Moonlight filters through the windows—just enough for me to see him mouth the words "Go, now." He tips his head toward the side exit.

If I move carefully, I can exit without exposing myself to the intruder. I assume it's the monk Tobias warned me about, though I didn't actually see him. I edge backwards, lifting each foot and carefully placing it back down. The side door is only a few more steps behind me on the right. The door presents another problem. Made of heavy wood and iron hinges, it is sure to squeak when I push it open.

I can see the night-wandering monk now, walking slowly behind the furthest row of pews, running his hand along the back edge. The moonlight isn't enough for me to identify his features. There is something sad about his movements, the way he lovingly touches the wood of the pews as though parting with a loved one. He hasn't glanced my direction, so I keep moving.

Tobias stays crouched in the shadow of the tomb. I can't see his expression at all.

My hand meets the wood of the door and I stop. I have to concentrate on slowing my breath—my heart thumps as though I've just run a great distance. In that moment of stillness, a new scent penetrates my mind. It takes my brain another moment to recognize it for what it is. Oil. Someone has recently oiled the door hinges.

Saying a silent prayer of thanks, I push, slow and steady, and the door swings open. I slip out the side and my instinct to run kicks in, but first I force myself to hold the door as it slowly swings shut. Then I run.

CHAPTER TWENTY-ONE

I am not sad to leave our old home behind. It was home once, but for too many months it has been a burden, a place full of memories and laden with responsibility. When the abbey falls, John Seybourne will annex our land to his, paying Tobias and I a small fee for use of the fields, just as the abbey has done. I don't know what will happen to the house. I suppose that could be rented out as well. Maybe another family will fare better there.

We've spent the past few days preparing the house to be vacant. Tobias has taken one load of furniture to the new home, leaving the house feeling almost as though we have already left. We've put covers on the items that will stay here for now. Only our personal belongings are left to pack. Since the seal on the tomb has taken so long, we are nearly finished—we can be up and gone to our new land as soon as our mission at the abbey is complete.

Being married is a funny thing. I've begun looking forward to Tobias's return each evening. Nights when he is away seem empty. My days have been filled with more physical labor than I have ever done, and I fall into bed each night with barely enough stamina to engage in marital acts—but I do, and willingly. I've calmed down enough to remember some of Binnie's advice and, well, I suppose I shall have to thank her when I see her again. Tobias claims he is a very happy man.

Sam seems almost happy at the prospect of moving—I suspect he likes the idea of a fresh start, where although he'll still have a limp to deal with, he will not have the weight of the rumors to bear on top of it.

We are clearing the overgrown tangle from the hedge surrounding the house one morning, and I hear him humming. He has the sort of face that *should* look happy—happy and often mischievous—but too often his features are furrowed or pinched. Today, his features have lost their pinched look. What's more, when he straightens from tugging up a tough root, I realize we are standing eye to eye.

"When did you get so tall?"

He grins. "It snuck up on me. You as well, apparently. Did you notice my new crutch? I had to make it while you were away. The old one wasn't tall enough."

"No, I didn't. I should've, though. That's fine workmanship." It's true…Sam is really developing a knack for shaping wood, and the new crutch is smooth and well-formed. "No wonder I've had to get more and more at market each week."

"Especially now that I'm not working in a kitchen, with meals provided and easy access to food."

"You miss it?" I ask in surprise.

He gives me an impish look. "Only the food."

"Huh. You're still scrawny, though."

He screws up his face at me. "Not much scrawnier than you."

I make a face back, and for a moment it's like we're both children again. "You're happier now, aren't you?"

"Aye." The impish look returns. "Plus, you need me."

I play along. "I do?"

"Certainly. For protection."

I surprise a giggle. "Protection? Isn't that Bane's job?"

"That great brute of a dog your husband left with us?" he scoffs, trying to keep a straight face. "Another mouth to feed. Like as not, he wouldn't harm a fly."

We both break down at the same time, grinning at one another in our shared moment of mirth. I'm pretty sure Bane would like nothing better than to rip an intruder to shreds and feast on the carcass—especially if Sam gave the word. His loyalty to and fondness for Sam defies explanation.

When Tobias comes home, we are still feeling spirited. This will be the last evening we spend here—though instead of leaving at first light, as our neighbors understand our plan, we will leave in the wee dark hours, stopping by the abbey for our final actions.

As the hour draws near, some of my mirth fades as I think of the task ahead. It's not the actual theft of the relics that I fear so much anymore…it's being entrusted with their care for—very likely—the remainder of my life. The dream I had, the one where I observed King Arthur's death, keeps resurfacing. I keep hoping that one night, the dream will pick up where it left off, but so far, that has not happened.

I find myself gazing out the window as the light fades, as though I could see across the years and back to that ill-fated moment.

"Sad to leave?" Tobias asks, coming to stand by me.

"No."

"It's understandable if you are. It's the only home you've known."

I turn back to him. "No, really. I'm not sad to leave. I only worry for the future. I know what our task is tonight, but what comes after? How will I be worthy of that with which I've been entrusted? What if the time for Arthur's return comes and I do not realize it?"

"His son brought him low…when the time is right for his return, only his daughters will know." Tobias paraphrases the lines from the folk song that changed my life.

"But how? How am I to know?" I am aware my voice is petulant, but I cannot help it. "I want to do my best, Tobias—truly, I do—but I hardly know what to do at all."

"Well," he says reasonably, "I suppose you start with the simple part—the abbot has entrusted us to tend Arthur's grave, as it were. Once the relics are safely moved and hidden, that part is easy enough."

"If you say so."

"As for the rest, you could start where your mother, and hers before her, did—by passing down the song."

I frown. My mother and grandmother may have sung the song enough for it to work its way into my memory, but they weren't exactly diligent about explaining its meaning—or the duties that came with knowing that song.

I guess he can see my skepticism, for he shrugs and replies, "Aye, well. Perhaps you'll want to do a bit better job of it."

I know how Sam feels when faced with questions and problems too big to surmount—it is easier to retreat, at least for now. I want Tobias to distract me. "I suppose, before I can pass on the song, I shall need a daughter to receive it. Perhaps I should start there."

Tobias's eyes twinkle. "Or a son. You could pass it to a son, as Abbot Whiting's mother did."

"I could," I say lightly. "And I suppose, if I aim to do better than those before me, I should aim for both a son and daughter—or perhaps even several of each."

"You should." He maintains a straight face, but barely.

My own lips quirk. "I will need some assistance in getting started."

"I aim to serve."

❧ ❧

Thanks to Tobias, we leave on a lighthearted note, full of plans for expanding our young family. The warmth of those plans lingers with me as our cart reaches the back entrance to the abbey's grounds, and Tobias and Sam clamber down.

We've worked out a plan. Tobias and Abbot Whiting will take care of the heavy lifting—literally lifting the marble lid of the tomb and replacing the real remains with the fake ones. Sam will stand guard in the shadows. I am to wait outside the gates with the cart and two horses. Sam and Tobias have spent hours ensuring the axles of the cart are well-greased, and the horses' harness and every bit of metal and leather is in good working order. Good preparation for any journey, but especially a journey that depends on leaving in the dark hours of night, and keeping as quiet as possible.

Our new home—and the new home of the relics—is near Bridgewater, a good fifteen miles from Glastonbury. An easy half-day's ride for a horseback rider, but considerably slower with a horse-drawn cart.

I perch at the front of the cart, waiting for Tobias and Sam. As the time passes, the warmth of our earlier conversation ebbs away once more. I can't stop tapping my foot, or wondering what is happening. Have they lifted the lid? What if they encounter a problem? Are they almost done? I've pulled the hood of my cloak low over my face so no one will recognize me, but that small measure of safety has done naught to calm my rising fears.

England is not a safe place. King Henry has put men and women to death for lesser offenses than the one I commit now.

Finally, I see two dark-cloaked figures, one with an unmistakably uneven gait, making their way toward me. Tobias settles Sam and the cargo in the back, then nimbly hops up to the front. I give the reins a slap before he can even sit. The horses start forward and he lands with an *oomph*. I look at him and widen my eyes in apology. I can't even manage a whisper.

He just gives me the barest shake of his head. *Apology granted.* Funny how I can read him so well after such a short time.

I try to concentrate on the way forward, knowing Tobias will be straining his eyes in the dark, keeping a lookout for any signs of danger. Sam, too.

The horses, though, are the first to know. We've passed the abbey grounds and the close cluster of town dwellings has given way to farms and woodland when the ears of the horse in front of me perk up—just as the other horse tosses his head and takes a skittish, sideways step. They keep moving, though, and for a minute I think we will be all right. Perhaps an animal in the woods startled them—but then I hear it, too. The soft *clop* of hoofs striking dirt. Hoofs that don't belong to our own horses.

"They've seen us."

"Who?"

Tobias just shakes his head. "I don't know. Pollard, if I had to guess. Highwaymen, if we're lucky."

"This close to town?"

"Probably not," Tobias admits.

Sam utters a word I would have sworn he didn't know.

Look after Sam. I cringe. I'm trying, truly—but right now, I'm not doing very well at fulfilling my mother's wish.

"Come on. We've got to hurry," Tobias nudges my hands, and I realize I am gripping the reins so tightly my knuckles ache.

"The faster we go, the more noise we'll make," I warn.

"That doesn't matter now. Just go," he urges.

I give the reins a slap. The horses pick up the pace, but there is no way we will outrun men on horseback.

"We just need to make it further into the woods," Tobias tells me. "We'll hide if need be."

The horses are moving at a good clip. They're making an awful racket, and everything in the cart seems to rattle and creak. My throat tightens with fear. I try to focus on Tobias instead. "I didn't know Pollard was in town."

"He wasn't—until today."

"What? But how could he know?"

"I don't know what he knows, or suspects. His arrival may be a coincidence."

"Then maybe it's not us they're after," Sam says, ever hopeful.

Hoofbeats in the distance betray his hope.

"It's definitely us," Tobias mutters grimly. "If it wasn't before, it is now."

The cart bounces along, jarring my jaw, my bottom, and every place in between.

One wheel hits a rock, and the cart gives a great lurch. I fly up from the bench, but Tobias grabs my arm firmly, pulling me down. We bounce, and then the cart rights itself. For a moment, I feel relief. We may still be all right...but with the next turn of the wheel comes a *crack* that sounds like gunpowder in the night.

The cart veers and tilts. The horses whinny in fright, pulling at the harness, but the wheel has broken from the axle.

We're stuck.

This is it. This is how I am going to die.

CHAPTER TWENTY-TWO

Tobias mutters an oath that makes Sam's earlier expletive sound like a child's prayer. "Everyone out. There's no fixing this now."

"What are we going to do?"

"Walk."

"They'll catch up with us."

"Not if I can help it."

I never knew a whisper could sound grim, but I know now.

"They'll find the cart." I hate the fear in my voice, but I can't help it.

"Aye. They will." He hefts the bundle containing the carefully wrapped relics and fixes me with a look. "But they won't find these."

Sam slides down the side of the cart, crutch at the ready. If Sam can do this, so can I. I gather my wits as Tobias grinds our torch into the dirt, plunging us into darkness. It takes a moment for my eyes to adjust, and then I see him beckoning ahead of me.

I follow him down a path, away from the main road, moving as quickly as we dare. The path narrows quickly, until it is little more than a game trail. The canopy of trees overhead blocks the light of the moon, and we are traveling blind.

I hear Sam behind me, his breath harsh as he tries to keep pace with us. His crutch scrapes against the brush and bramble that creeps across our path.

We keep moving, and it is all I can do to find the way before me. I wonder if Tobias knows this path, perhaps from some past adventure—or if we are wandering blindly in more ways than one.

I'm listening for hoofbeats. The men who hunt us will have to dismount to follow this trail, but I'll hear them first. I hope. If I can even hear anything over the pounding of my heart. It batters against the walls of my chest, its beat so loud I know it will give our position away.

So loud that I don't notice, at first, that Sam's labored breath and uneven footfalls are no longer right behind me.

It's when I pause and look back, expecting to see—or at least sense—him there, only he's not, that I begin to panic. I strain my eyes, trying to see through the dark. When did he fall behind?

Away from the town, the darkness is nearly complete—only a sliver of moon, barely enough to make out the branches directly in my path, lights the landscape around me. Our enemy, perhaps sensing his quarry was about to escape, has extinguished his torch.

I hear hoofbeats—the sound I'd been straining for moments ago—and my fear magnifies the sound until they seem to be coming from all around me.

Take care of Sam.

Sam. Sam, Sam. It's like a chant running through my head, though I daren't speak——let alone call out——his name.

I hear the mutter of men's voices and the clink of something metal. A harness, maybe. They must have found the cart. They'll search it first. That should buy us a few precious moments. But I can't find Sam in the blackness that surrounds me. I can barely make out the ground at my feet. Unconsciously, my feet turn back, moving slowly in the direction of the road.

My breath comes more slowly, now. Or perhaps fear has stopped it all together. At least I can hear.

Away in the distance, the flare of a torch suddenly pierces the dark. My heart drops to my feet. Standing in the middle of the road, silhouetted by the flame, is a slight, crooked figure I know only too well.

I start to cry out, but a hand claps over my mouth before the sound can carry. *Tobias.* He's stopped, too, realizing something is wrong.

How did Sam make it all the way back to the road? Hadn't he been following?

"What's he doing?" Tobias mutters in my ear.

We both watch as Sam takes a step toward a shadowy figure on horseback. His arms, even his right arm holding the crutch, are spread wide. A gesture of innocence.

And then I know. Beyond a shadow of a doubt, *I know.* My brother's twisted body is no match for his noble heart. "He's giving himself up."

"*What?*"

This time it is I who turn to clasp a hand over my husband's mouth. "He'll never make it. He knows this. He's giving us a chance."

One of the shadowy figures has dismounted. He gives Sam a shove that sends him stumbling. I can't tell if it's Pollard or not. In the night, everything looks and sounds different.

"No." I take an involuntary step forward. I know he means well. But I can't let Sam do this.

My body stops moving forward, though I will it otherwise. It's as though an invisible wall has sprung up between my brother and I, and I can do nothing but look on in horror as the shadowy play of silhouettes unfolds before me. Oh, dear God. Oh, dear God. I fall to my knees as one of the men grabs Sam roughly and slams him up against the cart.

No. I can't let him do this.

I push myself up, stumbling forward, not caring that I must be making enough noise to wake the whole forest.

Sam's captors don't even notice. They have their prey. One of them holds Sam by the throat while the other searches the cart. As I get closer, I can hear them.

"Where is it?"

Sam makes a strangled sound, and the man holding him loosens his grip.

"Where is what, sir?"

"Whatever you're stealing."

"I—I haven't got anything stolen."

The man hits him—a vicious backhand that knocks Sam off balance. His bad leg can't handle the change of weight, and he lands on his bottom in the dirt.

"I was running away," he mutters. I have to slow down, straining my ears to hear his words.

"Then you're a fool as well as a cripple. Aren't you the Thorndale boy? The one with the sister what just married a Seybourne. You think you're going to find a better life somewhere else?"

"Yeah, that's me. Exactly. You think my sister wants me around, getting in the way? She's newly married, and I'm nothing but a burden to her. Couldn't even hold a job helping in the abbey kitchens." He sounds for all the world like a sulky boy.

I bite my lip against the pain of his words. They could so easily be true, but they aren't. Not really. Sam knows that. He *knows*. Doesn't he?

The man rummaging through the cart pokes his head up. "There's nothing in here but broken chairs, and a bag of carrots and bread."

Broken chairs? I'm confused. I thought Tobias and Sam had loaded up goods for our new household. Why would he bring broken furniture? There's more going on here than I knew. I stop trying to reach Sam. I feel Tobias come up behind me, his hands on my arms to steady me. Was he a part of this plan?

"Are you sure? Check again." The man sounds irritable now. He gives Sam, who has just grabbed his crutch and is using it to lever himself up, a kick that sends him tumbling again. "We saw you leaving the abbey, boy."

"Well, yeah…I m-mean, yes, sir."

"Of all the treasures of Glastonbury, you stole broken chairs?"

Sam straightens. His movements are slow, painful. "I—I wasn't stealing. They were broke anyway, an' I asked for them. Thought I could fix some of 'em and sell them. Prob'ly sell the rest for kindling. Give me something to start from, until I get settled."

"Then why take them in the middle of the night."

"On account of the running away. Audrey would never 'ave let me go if I'd of told her. Cook and Father Tom were doing me one last kindness, see, since they had no job for me anymore."

"You really are an idiot. What about the horses? That's thievery for certain."

"Nay. I never meant to keep 'em. I'd 'ave sent 'em home soon as I could."

The man checking the cart straightens. "Nothing here, boss."

The man growls in frustration. "Let's get out of here, then. We're wasting time. The movement was supposed to happen tonight."

Sam's ruse appears to have worked. My brother is no idiot— he may have just saved us all. But what did that last comment mean? The movement—as in us moving these relics? Or something else…like the grail.

The second man mounts up. The first whistles to his horse, which has meandered past the edge of the light cast by the torch. The animal approaches, but before the man mounts, he growls again and lands a vicious kick to Sam's side. "Devil's spawn," he spits. "You have no idea what you might've cost me tonight."

He grinds the torch into the dirt, and a moment later I hear the thundering of hooves as the men ride off.

I wait, straining my ears, until they are gone. What I do *not* hear is Sam getting up.

CHAPTER TWENTY-THREE

I push forward, trying to get to Sam, but Tobias holds me back. I struggle, desperate in my need to reach my brother.

Tobias's arms come around me, pulling me in close, my back to his chest, and I feel his breath warm on my neck.

"Trap," he whispers.

I go still. Somehow, a shaft of reason pierces the haze of my desperation. It's a trap? I will myself to think. Did the sound of the hoofbeats fade away just a little too quickly? Maybe. I was focused on Sam, not on the men who kicked him. Did they suspect him of falsity, even as they rode away? Did they kick him, knowing it would draw us out?

I press forward again, and once more, Tobias stills me. "A few more minutes," he whispers, low in my ear. "It won't make a difference to Sam. But it might keep us all from getting killed."

I know he's right, but my whole body trembles with the need to deny it. Even if I run to Sam, I have no way to transport him—not without damaging him further. Tobias is strong, but to carry him all that way?

We wait, and it's the hardest thing I've ever had to do. My arms and neck feel like ants are crawling all over them, but I know it's just the cool night air drying the nervous perspiration on my skin. Tears stream freely down my face. How could I have let this happen?

"Audrey." Tobias's whisper brings me back to the present moment. He indicates the road. "I think it's safe. Let me go first."

I watch Tobias approach Sam. No one comes thundering after him, so I assume we are safe and follow quickly. I drop to my knees at Sam's side. He's conscious, but pale. Maybe it's the moonlight. "It worked," he says to Tobias. His eyes shine with something more than pain. *Pride.*

"Wait." I look between the two of them, then at my husband. "You were in on this? You knew he was going to…to…" Fury chokes off my words.

"I didn't know what would happen. This was one option of many. Even now, Abbot Whiting should be approaching our Bridgewater home, carrying with him the lead cross and the documents."

"He…what?" I glance back at the woods.

Tobias follows my gaze. "We were carrying the human artifacts. Everything else left the abbey hours earlier."

"You could have told me! We were…what, a decoy?"

"You never would have agreed," Sam says.

"Of course I wouldn't. I—" I clamp my mouth shut. What he says is true. Tears of frustration spring to the corners of my eyes. How am I supposed to protect him?

"Audrey," Tobias says quietly. "Your brother has done a great service this night. I need you to honor that. Our best hope at this point is to stick with Sam's story. We're too close to the abbey still to try for Bridgewater tonight. I need you to ride back to your old home, and then at first light, you must go about town, asking if anyone has seen Sam. Say that we had intended to leave this very morn, but he slipped off in the night, and you are frantic with worry."

"That is no lie," I whisper back.

"Comb your hair, too—you can't give the appearance of having spent the night crawling through the underbrush."

I make a face at him in the dark, but he's right.

"I'll care for Sam, and see what I can do to mend the wheel. I'll bring him home."

"Can you carry him if the wheel can't be fixed?"

"Maybe, though I'd have to leave the relics behind. It looked like he got kicked in the ribs. If they're broken, it would be better to lay him flat in the cart until we can transport him that way."

"Pretty sure they're broken," Sam mutters. His paleness has taken on a waxy sheen. His initial euphoria at the success of his plan has faded, leaving only pain.

I chew on my lip in worry. There are still a lot of unknowns to this plan. Will people believe my story? Will the relics be safe? And most importantly, will Sam be all right? I don't like the idea of stashing the remains somewhere in the woods. But King Arthur is already dead, and my brother—God willing—is not.

"Audrey? Go."

I go. My eyes have adjusted to the night, now, and I quickly free one of the horses and mount up. By the time I approach town, the damp weight of my skirts and the sleepless night are taking their toll, but I press on. As the sky turns from black to pre-dawn gray, we slip through the fields, approaching home from the back. The baker and other merchants will be up and starting the day's work, and I daren't be seen.

At home, I peel off my sweaty garments and sluice water from the wash pitcher over myself, scrubbing dry with a thick fold of linen. I run a comb through my hair and dress as quickly as I can in a fresh chemise and a faded black dress. It seems an ill portent to wear mourning clothes with my brother lying injured in the woods, but they are the only garments left here—I'd planned to come back for a few things at some point, though not so soon. Briefly, I wonder what *has* happened to the things I'd packed, since they aren't here and they obviously weren't in the cart that the men searched…but I have bigger worries at the moment.

Following Tobias's plan, I run about town, asking frantically after my brother. Of course, no one has seen him, but they express their concern. I do this for what feels like hours before finally trudging home. I want to run back out to Sam and Tobias, but I follow instructions. Tobias said he would get Sam home. I trust he will do so—even if he couldn't trust me with last night's plan. I hate that they did that. They tell me this is *my* destiny, but then they insist on keeping me in the dark. I know why, but I still don't like it.

I circle the house multiple times, uncertain whether they will approach from the front or the rear. Finally, a horse with two riders appears at the edge of the back meadows. As they draw closer, I see Sam's figure is slumped in Tobias's arms.

"Couldn't get the wheel straightened," Tobias explains when they get close enough. "Got it just enough to pull the cart off the road, but we'll need a new wheel before it goes anywhere else." I can see the strain in his arms and on his face. Sam is no small child anymore, and to hold him steady while riding a cart horse bareback…I don't think I could have done it.

I help ease Sam from his arms, and together we get him inside to the bed. The movement rouses him to consciousness, and the agonized wail that emanates from his throat sends shudders down my spine. He quiets quickly, seeing myself and Tobias at his side.

I crouch next to Sam and pull up his shirt, ignoring his grimace. The right side of his torso is already bruised and swollen. He cranes his neck to get a glimpse, then lets his head fall back at the sight. "No hurry on that cart, now," he whispers. "I've had enough for a while, thank you."

Incredibly, Sam's story of attempting to run away works, and although his character is much maligned amongst the townsfolk, no one seems to suspect that more nefarious events actually took place that night. We explain away Sam's injuries by saying he fell from the horse. With his weak leg, no one questions that, either. The only others who know the truth— the men who accosted him—have not returned.

Matrons pat me on the shoulder sympathetically. "You've been through so much," they say—meaning they remember it is my parents' deaths that left me with the burden of caring for a boy who might never be independent. "Thank goodness you've married a Seybourne now."

There is something in the way they say it that makes me uncomfortable, but they have a point.

While I sit at Sam's side, Tobias is busy. Riding solo with a spare mount, he retrieves the relics and delivers them to their intended destination. He is gone at dusk and back the next morning. Next he Tobias takes care of replacing the broken wheel, and in a few days' time, we attempt the journey to our new home once more. This time, we bring Lowdie with us, since she is to come work in our house—and since this time, we are traveling in open daylight and without any questionable goods.

Sam's side is still a horrible purple color. Tobias gives him whisky before the journey, but he still moans whenever we hit a large bump. Lowdie chatters to him, telling him little stories of her siblings and their misadventures. It seems to distract him.

We make it, though it takes all day, and as our little manor comes into sight, I feel—for the first time in days—hope. I'm tired of the intrigues of court, I'm tired of the constant fear of living at Glastonbury, and I just want a place we can *live*. I think that place is here.

Sam doesn't get better, though. His ribs should be mending, the bruises fading to green and yellow, before finally fading altogether. Instead, his whole right side remains dark purple and swollen. It is painful just to look at. I can't imagine how it feels.

Lowdie does the work of two men—or at least her own share and Sam's, besides. She throws herself into cleaning up the old hunting box as though it's her own home, and she oversees the various laborers and deliveries that Tobias arranges. I try to stay at Sam's side as much as possible, but whenever I am not there, Lowdie happily takes my place, telling Sam all about his new home and the things we are doing to improve it. Bane, too, spends most of his hours at Sam's feet. I have to force him to run outside every so often—Tobias says he needs to get the feel of the land, so he can protect us when he's gone, but Bane seems mostly interested in protecting the foot of Sam's bed.

Tobias, meanwhile, has secured the relics and procured the rest of our belongings from wherever he'd spirited them off to the night Sam was injured. Everything is coming together—except Sam.

When a full sennight has passed since the attack, I can no longer push my worry aside. I send Lowdie to summon the physician, giving him the same story we told in Glastonbury—that Sam fell from the horse.

The physician is named Dr. Goode. He is slight and meek in appearance.

"That must have been a nasty fall." He probes the darkened flesh lightly. "I believe at least two of the ribs are broken. Sometimes such damage takes a long time to heal."

"But he will heal?"

He casts another glance at Sam. I can read the doubt in his eyes. "Lady Seybourne…"

"What else can we do?" I am not ready to give up.

"I could call the barber to bleed him," Dr. Goode says. "It might reduce the swelling. Give him some comfort. Also I can give him a tincture for pain. That's all we can do…help him rest easier, and pray. The rest is in God's hands."

I swallow. "Give me a moment to think this over, please."

"Of course, my lady."

I am unused to being called "my lady," but I hardly notice it now. I just want the doctor to go away. But of course that's not practical. It's just that his very presence sets me on edge and reminds me of my failures. I lead him to the front room, where Lowdie has thoughtfully left a tray with ale and bread. I leave him there, escaping gratefully into the yard.

I lean back against the door and breathe deeply as a wave of dizziness washes over me. I hate having to make this decision—having my brother's fate in my hands.

Tobias has ridden to Glastonbury today. He is still looking for a couple of trustworthy laborers and, like I picked Lowdie, he hopes to find them amongst those who will be affected by the abbey's pending doom. I suspect he is also still collaborating with Abbot Whiting, garnering any last information he can. If Pollard's prediction was correct, our time is nearly up.

For the moment, though, my biggest fear is whether Sam's time is up. I don't know whether to trust this doctor's recommendation. Tobias has already admitted he doesn't know what to do aside from make him as comfortable as possible and hope for the best, so I know that waiting for his return will bring no fresh ideas.

I consult with Lowdie, who, though technically my servant now, is sensible enough.

She shrugs. "Bleed him? Maybe. I know remedies for the earache, and the headache, but I don't know anything that would help Sam." She sniffs, and I notice that her eyes look watery. "My uncle got bled once. Hard to say if it helped or not."

"Did he live?"

"For a few weeks more. But who's to say whether he'd have lived longer, or died sooner, if they hadn't bled him?"

I sigh. Lowdie is no help at all.

Finally, after churning the matter like butter in my mind, I go inside and reluctantly give the order. "Go ahead. Call the barber."

CHAPTER TWENTY-FOUR

The bloodletting does ease some of Sam's swelling, but it also weakens him. We try broth and tinctures, but before two days pass, his side is swelling up again, and I know that Sam is going to die.

The realization shakes me so badly, I can hardly hold the spoon up to his lips the next time I try to give him broth. My hand trembles so violently, the drops spatter on his cheek.

Sam reaches out and grasps my wrist. Surprised at his unexpected movement, I drop the spoon. The rest of the broth dribbles onto the blanket.

For a second I feel a flare of hope at his sudden strength.

"Audrey. D-did you know? When I dream now, I see Mother."

"That's…" I don't know what that is. Not good, at least in terms of an indication of his own fragile mortality. "How…does she seem all right?"

"She does. She seems peaceful. She doesn't say anything, though. Just sort of smiles, and just now, before I woke up, I dreamt she reached a hand out to me."

"It sounds like a nice dream." I wish, for a moment, I could share it. I've begun to forget little things. I wish I could touch her hand, smell the scent that was uniquely her. I can't quite recall it to memory, but I know if I were to smell it again, I would recognize it in a heartbeat. But there is a reason Sam is being granted these dreams and I am not.

"Audrey. I'm dying, aren't I." It isn't a question. My brief flare of hope dissolves as quickly as it appeared. I don't trust myself to speak, but I manage a nod. Sam's face blurs in front of me as my eyes well up.

"Audrey." He keeps using my name, like he wants to hear it, to stay focused in this very moment. "This was my choice."

"To die, Sam?"

His eyes hold mine, and he gives me a small smile. We both know that's not what he means.

"I'm supposed to take care of you, Sam. It's the only thing Mother asked of me." My voice breaks. "I don't want to fail her, or you."

He squeezes my wrist, though without the strength he once had. "You've done what Mother asked, and more. You've always looked out for me. I knew what I was doing when I walked back to the cart. This time, I was looking out for you."

I shake my head. That's not how it's supposed to be.

"Listen, Audrey."

The intensity in his voice makes me focus. His eyes are bright, but not with the feverish light I've come to fear. They hold the spark of passion, of boyishness that is so…Sam.

"I knew, when I walked back to the road that night, that it might be the last thing I did. But Audrey, I knew why I was doing it. I knew what I was protecting—and it was something worth dying for."

My eyes well up again, but he gives my wrist a little shake. "Boys like me, we don't join the lists, we don't fight in wars. We don't often get to choose a hero's death. But I did, Audrey. I got that chance, and I took it. I walked back to that road to save the lives of a knight and his lady, and to protect the legend of King Arthur. How many people in all of history can say that?"

Tears stream freely down my face now. When did my little brother grow up? How did I never see that beneath the freckles and impish turn of his nose, there lived such a fiercely honorable spirit?

"You are a hero, Sam. The best of heroes. I love you, my brother."

❧ ❧

Lowdie, without being asked, summons a priest to give Sam his last rites. She and Tobias stand with the priest as he performs this duty. I can't watch. I try, but I can't.

After that, Sam slips away quickly. By morning he is gone, and I fall apart. I can't even lift my feet to drag myself from his side.

Tobias comes upstairs. When I see him, I just stare. He takes one glance at the bed, and he knows. My pain is echoed on his face.

The next week passes in a stupor. Lowdie is the only reason I get through it. That sounds terrible, because Tobias is there, trying to provide comfort, but I cannot forget his part in this. He knew what Sam was doing—they *planned* it together. I know he feels horrible about this, but he knew, and he let it happen. We are so awkward in our grief that neither of us knows what to do or say. Tobias rides out to notify our family members, and I am selfishly glad when he is away, because it relieves me of the awful burden of trying to form words when there are none.

Lowdie is grieving, too, more than I would've guessed, but she keeps moving, keeps tackling the mountain of tasks that come with our new home, which to me suddenly seem too enormous to overcome. She even holds herself together enough to make the arrangements for Sam's burial.

"Have ye selected a place to lay him to rest?" she asks.

I just stare at her numbly. I think I manage to shake my head "no," but I am not certain I even do that. I am brought back to the death of my parents, not even two years' past, when I had to do this for them—or let my interfering uncles take over, the threat of which was all that kept me functioning back then.

"Right, then." Sympathy fills her gaze. "I think I know a place he would choose, if he could. Peaceful, like. There's also the question of the funeral…do ye wish we should summon one of the priests from back home?"

I am so relieved to have Lowdie here now.

"I don't suppose Sam would have a preference."

"Right, then," she repeats. "I'll just take care of it, then."

"Thank you," I manage to tell her. My voice is hoarse, and I realize I haven't spoken in the better part of two days. Sam should have a hero's funeral, but no one besides Tobias and myself can ever know that.

"I liked Sam," she says then. "He could be funny, sometimes. An' I never minded his leg. I'd even wondered, once or twice, when he got a little older…"

I come out of my stupor enough to realize she had feelings for Sam. I never realized. Lowdie might not be the best catch either, but she has a good heart. It makes me feel worse for Sam, because now he'll never grow up and have that chance.

He only got twelve years of life, and most of them difficult. God has called him home, and he is in a better place now.

I tell myself that, and townspeople who I've barely gotten to know say it when they offer their condolences, but the words are hollow. Sam is gone, and I have failed utterly. *Take care of Sam.* It was the only thing she asked of me, and I failed. I know he made his choices, and I believe with all my heart that he died a hero, just as I told him—but it should have been me. I should have been the bigger hero, more clever and more protective, so that he never would have had such a choice to make.

With Sam gone, I throw myself into what I know he would have wanted me to do—finding out as much as I can about my own history and that of King Arthur. Sometimes, my grief is still too fresh, and I find myself staring blankly at words, or watching them blur as tears fill my eyes. But other times, I am able to focus. I start to think there is only so much pain the mind can handle before it seeks escape. For me, the stacks of old documents, while frustrating, provide that escape.

I learn some interesting facts. Apparently, when the original excavation took place—the one during which King Arthur's grave was unearthed—the monks shrouded the site in white sheets. The ancient accounting is unclear as to why. Secrecy? Protection from the elements? It makes me wonder. It also reminds me of my dream. More and more, I believe that what the dream was trying to tell me is that there was, or is, a link between the death of Arthur and the holy grail. I suspect he was buried with it. But there is no mention of that in the monks' records of the excavation. Then again, there wouldn't be, would there? Just as Arthur's daughters were given the charge to look after his legacy, I *know* that the knights who found the grail would have set in place similar safeguards—much more reliable ones, even. So maybe their descendants were the ones to initiate the excavation in the first place…or, when they learned of it, found a way to whisk away the grail before it was discovered.

Of course, I could be completely wrong. I am turning suspicious, anticipating a plot behind every person, every move made. And on what basis? A dream? The insinuations of the scholar-spy Hutton, who didn't even live long enough for me to learn *why* he thought the grail might be attainable? What else? A stack of documents that, even if I translate them correctly, may not be reliable? Can I trust those who wrote them? Can I trust my own translations? Most of the time, I feel like I am missing something important…as though what is *not* plainly written is as important as the words committed to ink.

I am worse than my grandmother was purported to be. Soon I too, will lose the ability to distinguish between fiction and reality. In fact, I wish I could have spent some time with my mother's mother. My own tenuous grasp on the truth makes me wonder if that lady did not know more than she was given credit for.

It is about two weeks after the funeral that I notice Tobias seems restless. We have been moving wordlessly around one another each day, going through the motions of the day, but not knowing how to do anything more. My anger has begun to fade—I know Sam understood the choice he made, even if I would have chosen for him differently—but my grief is still overwhelming.

At dinner, there are several times where I think Tobias is about to say something, but then he changes his mind and goes back to eating. I know what is on his mind—with the first hint of crisp air in the mornings, autumn is near. The king will return to London before long, and he will expect his loyal courtiers to do the same. *It's too soon*, my heart protests. But the life of a courtier is not a life of freedom.

I wait until the meal is over, and Tobias is standing pensively in front of the fireplace. When he still doesn't say anything, I tell him, "You should go to the king. There's nothing you can do."

He crosses the distance between us and I brace myself, but he gathers me in as delicately as if I were a freshly picked flower. "That's not true. I can be here for you, now."

My eyes well up. "That's not true. We both know you can't."

"Then come with me."

The last thing I want is to return to court. "King Henry is fond of you because you cheer him. I would be but a dour presence in my mourning clothes."

"Certes, everyone would understand. There's nary a soul at court what hasn't worn mourning black at some time or another. Even King Henry himself."

"Maybe. But I cannot leave the relics. Sam *died* to protect them, Tobias. I can't let him have done so in vain."

He pulls me close, tucking my head under his chin. "I know. Truly, I do. I feel the same way. I propose a deal, then…I shall stay long enough to dig out the cellar. We'll store the relics, then brick up that portion of the cellar and cover the wall with dirt. The hiding place will be secure, and invisible to anyone who should come looking. Then you can rest easier about coming with me."

I weigh the idea, testing its merits and flaws. I realize my initial reaction was not entirely true—returning to court is not the *last* thing I want. It may be unpleasant, but staying here alone with the fresh grave of my little brother would be sheer torment.

"Will the king be angry at your delay?"

He shrugs. "I need an heir—a sentiment with which the king, of course, is only too familiar. I cannot help but linger in the clean country air, where our chances of conceiving a healthy baby seem best."

I have to give him credit…the king may not *like* it, but Tobias's stated sentiments match his own exactly, so he can hardly blame Tobias without sounding like a hypocrite. Then again, he is the king, and hypocrisy is only hypocrisy when someone else is being accused of it. Nonetheless, I know Tobias will charm him into understanding.

He touches my cheek tenderly. "Audrey, I need more than an heir. I need *you*."

My eyes well with tears. I haven't been there for him of late. "I know," I whisper. "I need you, too."

His hand slips down my neck, curving around my shoulder as he draws me toward him, toward the bed we now share. I go to him willingly, almost eager for his touch.

Afterward, I lay awake, feeling both guilty and relieve that I feel *alive* again. I still have a husband and a mission worth living for, no matter how big a hole has been left in my heart. How strange to find such comfort at the side of this husband of mine, this husband I never wanted. Now, I not only want him, I fear for him. I do not like it when he goes away, though I know he must. I am no more alone, in numbers, than I was this time last year. But everything has changed, including me. I am the wife and mistress of the household—I am *supposed* to feel an emptiness when the master of the house is away, and I do. As much as I detest the court, I'll be going back with him.

CHAPTER TWENTY-FIVE

September 1539

Tobias wastes no time in bricking up a small enclave within the cellar. I send Lowdie on several shopping trips into town, purportedly to purchase supplies for our trip to London. Rarely has she had a coin to spare, so she goes happily enough, giving Tobias and I time to finish the work underground. We smooth dirt and clay over the brick wall, and when it is dry, it is indistinguishable from the rest of the cellar. The relics are as safe as can be, for now.

Lowdie's excitement at shopping for London is soon eclipsed by excitement at the prospect of actually traveling with us.

"Truly, my lady? You want me to come with?" Her eyes lit up like a child with an unopened present. "I'm no lady's maid, though. You should have a proper maid."

"You'll do your best, though, won't you?"

She nodded eagerly.

"Then you'll come. I'd rather travel with a loyal companion than someone I barely know, just because she might know how to knot a ribbon into a rosette." And that was that.

As we pack, I notice her pack a stack of clean rags—the sort used during a woman's monthly courses, and I realize I should have needed those last week. The realization stops me. It is too soon to tell, but I may be with child. It is a thought both frightening and exhilarating. My life is full of secrets, but this one I gather in and hold close, for it has the promise of hope. I will keep it my own until I know for certain.

Our first stop is in Glastonbury, of course, to let our family members know our plans. The morning is cool, and the ride goes quickly. Lowdie goes straight to her family, but Tobias and I cannot help but make a stop at the abbey.

It turns out we are a day too late.

The guards, who have surely seen us dozens of times, acknowledge us with suspicion. "State your business."

"We are travelers, stopping to pray for safe journey," Tobias answers.

The guard drops his voice. "You can go in, but don't stay long. Everything's run amuck since the inspectors arrived."

A buzzing sound fills my ears. My whole body vibrates with it. We'd known this was coming.

"What inspectors?"

"The royal commissioners. Pollard, Layton, and Moyle."

"Is everyone safe?"

The guard looks troubled. "For now."

"Explain yourself."

He grimaces. "We have not surrendered. But they've taken the abbot."

My heart feels heavier than the lead cross which is so entwined with my fate. "Taken him where?"

"To the Tower."

Tobias glances at me, assessing. "We won't stay long," he assures the guard, who lets us pass.

When we are a safe distance past the guard, Tobias mutters, "We need to find out what happened."

"We shouldn't be here," I protest. "What if they know? It's too risky."

The grounds are more sparsely populated than normal, and everyone we pass has a worried look on their face.

"If they suspected our involvement, they would have come for us."

We approach the chapel and enter, just as we had told the guard. My eyes go straight toward the black marble tomb, but there is nothing abnormal about it—nothing that can be seen, anyway.

Tobias's gaze follows mine, but he puts out a hand to gently stop me from moving toward it. For a moment we just stand there, gazing at what only we know is our handiwork. The lead cross has been replaced, and the bodies inside the tomb are those we unearthed from the country cemetery. My eyes drift to the other parts of the great abbey…the soaring ceilings, held up by strong pillars, the stained glass, the high altar. I think of the generations of men who toiled to build it, a monument to glorify God, and I wonder what they would think if they could see it fall.

Tobias is still looking at the tomb. "The deception is complete."

I cast a quick glance around, but there is no one to hear us.

"Do you regret it?" I ask him. I cannot name the expression on his face, but it concerns me. "I do not look at you and see a deceitful man."

He gives a low laugh. "You once called me 'the veriest of courtiers.' If that were true, then you would never look at me and *see* deceit, though I were rotten to the core with it. You would see only that which I wanted you to see."

I wait. I know him better than this.

He sighs. "Nay. I do not regret it." He turns to me, puts a finger beneath my chin, just enough to draw my gaze up to his. "And whoever I may be called upon to deceive, know that I will not deceive you, Audrey."

I swallow and nod.

"Stay here and pray."

"Where are you going?"

"To find out what happened."

Tobias is not gone long. Still, the moment I see him, I shoot to my feet, grasping his wrists, looking for reassurance.

"We're safe," he says. Gently, he detaches my hands from his wrists. "They went through the abbot's papers."

"We kept nothing there," I protest. "They wouldn't have found—"

"No. They were not looking for…that. Not at all. They were looking for an excuse to hang Abbot Whiting."

My heart falls like an anvil. "Hang him?" I echo weakly.

"Any excuse will do. They dredged up some letters—years ago, Abbot Whiting once supported Katherine of Aragon in her unwillingness to accept an annulment. That alone is probably enough. We should leave now."

"So many others did the same," I whisper.

He puts a gentle hand at my back, turning me toward the exit. "And how many of them are still alive?"

I shiver. Not many.

"He was also accused of hiding a gold chalice from the men who cataloged the abbey's treasures."

That makes little sense. "What would he want with such a thing?"

"I am nearly certain he did it on purpose."

Oh. "That will seal his fate, then."

"And if we are lucky, throw them off the course."

"You don't think it will make them search harder for other things which he might have hidden?"

"No. I think they are so full of glee at finally having something to stick against one of their most powerful holdouts, they will rush to the conclusion for which they have so long waited."

"Perhaps God will have mercy on him and let him meet a natural end, first." It sounds cruel, wishing death upon him, but I do not mean it that way. Abbot Whiting is old and ever more sickly. The angst of these last years has weakened him. He is certain to die soon—I only wish for him to suffer as little as possible.

"Perhaps," he agrees, though from his noncommittal tone I can tell he knows the same thing I know—Cromwell's men will find a way to make his suffering public.

"He'll get a trial, at least, will he not?" I'm grasping at straw, now, looking for any ray of hope and I know it. Such trials—when they happen at all—are a farce. The outcome is already decided.

Tobias knows this, too. I hear it in his troubled sigh. "As a member of the House of Lords, he is entitled. Only an Act of Parliament can condemn him. But…he chose this, Audrey," he reminds me. "He knew what he was doing. Trust in that decision, my sweet."

I'm trembling. How many of the men I know and trust must make such a choice? First Sam, and now the abbot. Tobias would do it, too. I pray to God that will not be asked of him.

Tobias

The remainder of our journey is uneventful. We arrive in London before King Henry and his entourage, though from the high level of servants' activity, it is clear they expect him soon.

Audrey has not said anything, but I suspect she is with child. Her courses have not come in well over a month now, and her breasts are swollen and tender to the touch. I do not dare voice this hope by asking her, though I take care not to discomfort her when we are intimate. Too many pregnancies end early and in disappointment. I don't think I can bear to see Audrey saddened by any more loss. I do not pretend my grief is as keen as hers. How could it be, when I have only just come to know and care for Sam, and she was everything to him, and he to her, when they were on their own. But I feel the same guilt she feels—only worse. It was *my* job to protect them both. That is why Abbot Whiting selected me—to use my wits, intellect, and strength to supplement Audrey's quiet determination. Sam…Sam should have never been at risk. I should have stopped those men, no matter what he wanted— no matter what choices he made.

I was afraid Audrey would hate me. I think she wanted to, at first. She, too, knows how I have failed, and will never look at me the same way again. Maybe it would be easier if she was still angry. The quiet aura of sadness that blankets her is almost worse. I would do anything to see her happy again.

If I am right about her condition, it will be months yet before the child will quicken, but I pray every night that it will happen. A child would be more than just an heir—it would be the first truly good thing to happen in a long time. It might make her happy.

In the meantime, Lowdie is doing her best. She insists upon dragging Audrey out to the markets and merchant shops, the confectioners and purveyors of exotic goods. It is presumptuous of a servant, insisting her mistress take action, but it gets Audrey out of her gloom, so I say nothing. Sometimes I even go along, when I am not pasting a smile to my face and bantering with the king and his men. Lowdie is built from the salt of the earth. Her own life has never been easy, but she keeps going and forces us to do the same. I admire my wife for having the good sense to choose such a servant, when other women would pick someone more comely and accustomed to a lady's needs. Lowdie's gifts are less obvious, but no less valuable.

So it is that I hardly notice when, one sunny afternoon, they leave the house with baskets tucked in the crook of their elbows. It never occurs to me they would be foolish enough to visit the Tower.

Audrey

We listen for any word of Abbot Whiting, but there is none. His fate may as well be decided.

The trouble is, I still need answers. Answers about my own relatives, I hope to find in Kent, just as soon as we can manage to travel there. But answers about the relics themselves…I know only one man who might have them. Even if he does, I am not at all certain he'll be willing to share.

There's no rule against visiting those being held in the Tower—only the uneasy awareness that your presence will be noted, and subject to speculation. There's also no rule that says the Yeomen Warders have to let me in.

I've thought about it every day since we arrived. Two days ago, we got close enough to observe the steady stream of people coming and going from London's most infamous prison. There were more than I expected—enough to ease my fears. Of course, many were probably on official business. The Tower houses military stockpiles, the Privy Wardrobe, and more official administrative offices than I can keep track of. Yeomen of the Guard patrol the whole enclosure, while the warders are charged with securing the prisoners. Since the Tower was not originally built as a prison, the prisoners are housed wherever room can be made, and according to their station in life. Common criminals, of course, are relegated to the horrors of Fleet Prison. The Tower is reserved for prisoners of state. Some, I have heard, even have servants to attend them. Others, they say, are dragged to subterranean chambers and subjected to the rack.

I have to try. A year ago, I would never have dared.

The Tower is a busy place today. People move with purpose, seemingly unbothered by the the many ghosts that must haunt these grounds. The walls have housed too many of the condemned for there not to be some residual spirits, some lingering despair.

We try the White Tower, the largest of them all. Our arrival is noted on a register, but we are not stopped. Indeed, when I see the long list of visitors on the registry, I breathe a little easier. I feel safer as one among many.

We have guessed correctly, and are shown to a chamber with a heavy door. The warden knocks loudly and unbars it, indicating we may proceed. I push, and the door slowly swings inward. Abbot Whiting rises, equally slowly, from a tufted stool near the hearth. He appears unharmed, and the room is sparse but clean—no servants here, but far better than I'd imagined. Still, the skin sags beneath his eyes and the hollows of his cheeks. He has lived a thousand lifetimes in the past few years. A rush of relief—*I am not too late*—and sadness washes over me. I keep a hand on the door to steady myself.

"Lady Seybourne, and Miss Brewer." His eyes light when he sees Lowdie behind me, and I am glad to have brought her, if only to brighten his day.

We exchange pleasantries, but he knows I have come for more. He raises an expectant eyebrow. I turn apologetically to Lowdie, who makes herself scarce.

I waste no time—though I keep my voice to a whisper. "When King Arthur died, the grail was buried with him. That's where the prophecy came from, that he would someday return?"

In spite of his haggard appearance, his eyes begin to twinkle. "I am old, but not old enough to have been present at that death," he whispers back.

I bite back a smile. "But you have records of the excavation upon Glastonbury's grounds, Father Abbot."

"So I do. There is no record of the grail being retrieved from Arthur's grave."

"Not everything makes it into the official record, though."

His eyes twinkle more. "No, not everything does."

"That night—the night Sam was…was…" My throat closes and I have to stop and take a few breaths before I try again. "Was that the night it was moved?"

He considers me for a moment. "Many events occurred that night. Does it matter?"

"If I am correct, and the grail is tied to Arthur's return, then yes, it does matter. You have entrusted me with protecting his remains, and I would do so for honor alone, but if the greater cause is lost…"

"It is not lost."

"So it is safe?"

"For now. That is the best any of us can do, for the future is ever uncertain." He touches my shoulder. "Audrey. The grail may bring about the return of the king, but it has value beyond that. Beyond measure. It is all that is faithful and pure. It is…hope. And hope must always be protected."

I swallow, nodding. "But…must they be together, in one place, do you think, for the prophecy to come true?"

"Now that is an interesting question. What do you think?"

"I think maybe…I don't know."

"In truth, neither do I. Lady Seybourne, remember what I told you."

I frown. "That I need not know everything?"

"That…and also what you must do if questioned. You have taken a risk today. I doubt it will go unnoticed."

"I could never…"

"But you must." He sighs and reaches into his robes, glancing first at the door. It is open part way, but the guard is not in sight from where we stand. He lowers his voice further. "In spite of the risk, I am glad you came today. I want to give you this." He holds out his gold pendant—the one that matches mine.

"They didn't take it from you?" I'm surprised his captors would leave him with anything of value.

"It was well-hidden—sewn into a seam in my heavy robe. They would have found it eventually. I should have given it to you months ago."

My throat is tight as I accept the pendant and quickly tuck it into my stomacher.

"I hope God will bless you with many daughters. If he does not, find someone worthy."

"I will," I whisper.

"I grow weary, my child. May I say goodbye to your companion?"

I slip out and find Lowdie, who is chatting about root vegetables with the guard. Abbot Whiting bids us both farewell, and when we would linger, he gently gestures to the door. "Go now."

I nod. "God be with ye, Father Abbott."

"And with you."

I can't stifle the tears running down my cheeks. Lowdie doesn't even try. She bawls freely, messily, more at home with expressing such emotion than I will ever be. I wonder if all her tears are for the abbot, or if her grief is just as much for the passing of the life we both once knew.

Our visit over, I am anxious to leave the Tower, where the very walls echo with the lament of lives cut short, and our muffled footsteps thunder over silenced voices.

A guard approaches me as we turn to depart. "Miss Thorndale?"

"Lady Seybourne," I correct him.

"Right. You need to come with me, now."

A hollow dread fills my body. Abbot Whiting's warning was too prescient. I look to Lowdie. Even her lazy eye is alert. I mouth one word. "Tobias."

She nods.

"Where are we going?" I ask.

"One o' the offices. Sir Moyle has some questions for you." He leads us down the hall, around a corner, and up a set of stairs. He stops in front of an open doorway, giving me a nudge forward. From the corner of my eye, I see Lowdie get a good look at our surroundings, then speed off in the direction of the exit. No one stops her—she is not the one they want.

With trepidation, I enter the room. *I've done nothing wrong.* I remind myself of this with each step. It may not be entirely true, but if I don't believe it, they won't either. A small fire burns in a grate, making this room marginally more pleasant than the chill pervading the prisoners' area.

Both Moyle and Pollard are in the room, though Pollard is absorbed in some other task, pouring through some kind of ledger. Only Moyle is looking at me. I remember him from the day he came to summon Tobias to court. Nothing has been simple since.

"Lady Seybourne, is it? Formerly Miss Audrey Thorndale?"

I incline my head, acknowledging him. "What do you want?"

"I want to know what you know."

I'm trying to stay calm, but I'm so scared I'm afraid I'll faint, and then they can kill me or abduct me and I won't even be able to fight back. "I don't understand."

"Don't play me for a fool, girl. You were the abbot's assistant." His tone is impatient, but he makes no physical threat. I recall what I have learned—thankful, finally, for the lessons from Tobias's mother. Sir Thomas Moyle is a loyal servant of the king, or at least as loyal as any amongst the court. His true zeal, though, seems to be in expanding his own wealth. He started by marrying an heiress, and has added to his estates by assisting in the dissolution of monasteries, then accepting grants of the former monastic land. Unsavory, but not a man known for direct violence. The recollection helps me gain the composure to answer.

"I—I was, yes. My family was very fortunate to have the work."

"Being around him so much, you will have learned things. Or perhaps you knew them all along…after all, there is that pendant you wear."

Oh, no. Please, I pray silently, *let him only be guessing. Please tell me he doesn't really know.* The pendant was supposed to attract fellow protectors—not their enemies.

"This?" I finger the pendant, since there's no use in hiding it now. "It's just something passed down from my mother. Sentimental of me, I suppose, but I have little left of her but memories."

A flicker of some emotion I can't name passes across his face, but is gone just as quickly. "It's more than that. I think you know it, too."

I'm thinking as fast as I can. I know what the abbot would do. Tobias, too. They would go to their grave with their secrets. There is a part of me that would accept that fate—a part of me that thinks death is what I deserve, after all, for failing Sam so terribly.

But these men wouldn't kill me quickly. They would find another to do the dirty deed—but only after they try to make me give up my secrets.

I don't know if I am that brave. If I die, and the abbot too—for he is not long for this earth, one way or another—what then? There would be no protectors left. I can't let that happen.

"I don't understand. What is it you want?"

"Tell me why, if that necklace is just a family trinket, Abbot Whiting owns an identical one."

Damn. I am not given to cursing, but it is the first word that comes to mind. How does Moyle know? Maybe he doesn't. The hard lump of the abbot's pendant presses into my rib. Tucked as it is beneath the curve of my breast and behind the stiff fabric of my stomacher, there is no way it shows. No one saw it change hands. I force a smile. "That was a matter of great curiosity to us, as well. My mother was assistant before me, and before her death, she was tracing our family history. She thought perhaps we had an ancestor in common with Abbot Whiting—an artisan who made both pendants."

All this time, Pollard hasn't looked up. I wonder if he has already written me off—as good as dead.

Sir Moyle looks skeptical, as if my story makes sense, but is not what he wanted to hear.

"May I leave, now? My husband is expecting me."

He glances back toward Pollard, who finally speaks. "There is one other who wishes to speak with her. He may have more success in gaining the information we seek."

"Right. Wait here. Don't even think about going anywhere."

Both men rise and leave.

Alone, I am left to wonder if I will ever leave this place. My stomach grumbles, and I am bewildered that I can even feel hungry at such a time. I stand and pace. Perhaps I *should* just leave. I poke my head out the door, but a guard stands at the end of the hall. He gives me a warning shake of his head, and I duck back inside. More time passes. I am hungry and thirsty. I see a pitcher on a stand. The mug next to it appears clean enough, so I help myself to some water. It helps, but only a little.

The pacing isn't helping. Finally, I do what I know best. I drop to my knees and pray.

After what seems like an eternity, the door opens, but it is only another guard. "There has been a delay. I am to show you to a room where you may wait."

I frown. Isn't that what I had been doing? Why must I do it somewhere else? "The hour grows late, and my husband, Sir Seybourne, is surely expecting me."

Is there a flicker of sympathy in his eyes, or am I only imagining it?

"I only follow orders, Lady Seybourne."

I follow him to a chamber disconcertingly similar to the one where we left Abbot Whiting. "'Tis only while ye wait," the guard promises—but there is no mistaking the dull thud of the bar falling into place when he leaves.

I won't be going home tonight.

CHAPTER TWENTY-SIX

The walls close in, and my breath starts to come in shallow gasps. I *must* keep my wits about me...but I feel as though I've left them scattered in bits and pieces all along the road from Glastonbury to London. I must have done so, or I would never have been so foolish as to come here in the first place.

Surely, Lowdie has reached Tobias by now. He'll come for me.

The chamber has no windows, making it impossible to measure the passing of time. He should be here any moment. What if they will not allow him to see me? Or, God help me, what if they hold him, too?

All these thoughts run through my head in the first moments after the door closes behind me...and repeat themselves a thousand times or more over the next days.

The guards bring food and weak ale, but I have no appetite. It is hard to say if my constant queasiness is born of fear, or of the tiny life I am now almost certain is forming in my womb. I beg the guards for information instead, but they have little to share. I have not been charged with a crime. I am only being held for questioning—though by whom, they cannot say.

Cannot, or will not. I suppose it makes no difference. At least they do not subject me to the horrible forms of torture I have heard whispered about by those who have never been inside these walls.

On the fifth day, I am allowed a visitor. I leap to my feet at the sharp rap on the door, not knowing what to expect. I crane my head to see around the guard, praying for the sight of Tobias, but when the guard steps aside, only Lowdie stands behind him.

Lowdie. Not the looming threat of the unknown interrogator, but not who I'd hoped for, either. Still, I am glad to see her.

Her one good eye darts this way and that, while the lazy one had rolled off to her right. "Are they treating you well?"

She asks the question just as I ask one of my own. "Tobias?"

She gives a slight shake of her head. The guard actually moves off to give us some privacy, and I wonder if she's bribed him. For someone I once deemed slightly dim, Lowdie is surprisingly well-equipped to get about in the city. I've come to respect her. There are freedoms granted to those dismissed by the upper echelons, and Lowdie knows how to use them.

"Your husband is doing what he can, my lady."

"Which isn't much," I guess.

She winces. "Not without endangering himself as well. He says the king is busy with other matters and is unaware you are being held…and that this is better, in truth, than calling his attention to it."

My mouth falls open, unable to believe Tobias would betray me so. "Better?"

"The king is quick to believe in conspiracies, especially those directed against him." She speaks the lines as though she has rehearsed them, which she probably has. "If no one *else* has told King Henry of your imprisonment, it means they have no real evidence against you. They may hold you for a while, but eventually, they will lose interest."

"So I just wait? How long until they lose interest?" I don't like this plan at all.

She makes a sympathetic grimace. "Who can say?"

My heart sinks. "What about Tobias? If he cannot free me, he might at least visit?"

Lowdie drops her gaze. "To be honest, my lady, he is right angry with ye for coming here in the first place."

Some of my anger deflates. "I suspected that," I admit. "Will you tell him I am sorry, and that I have recognized the error of my ways?"

She nods, and I realize I owe her an apology, too. "I am sorry to put you in the middle of this, Lowdie. That was never my intention."

She gives me a wry smile. "When I think, I could have stayed home and taken in laundry, and missed out on all this adventure?"

The twinkle in her good eye tells me she means what she says. She hands me a bundle with a fresh shift and stockings, and a much of dried figs. "'Tis little enough, but they inspect everything, you know?"

No doubt.

"Don't lose heart, Audrey Seybourne. You'll be going home soon."

I don't know how she can be so confident, but I straighten my shoulders and lift my chin. I can be strong. I must be strong.

When Lowdie signals the guard she's ready to leave, I don't miss the way she sidles past, brushing against him, or the little glance they exchange. I may have underestimated her, but I am ever so glad to have Lowdie on my side.

The bar falls back in place, and in the sudden silence, I can only reflect that I wish my husband were equally on my side.

I am held captive for twenty-one days in the Tower. In that time, Lowdie visits every third or fourth day. She bears food, and fresh clothing, and occasionally a note from Tobias—who never comes in person. His notes are bland, saying things like "stay strong," "know that I am thinking of you," and, once, "I am certain this misunderstanding will soon be rectified."

I know the notes are being intercepted and read before Lowdie delivers them, but they still feel cold and uncaring. If he truly thinks this is just a misunderstanding, then why not show everyone by not being afraid to visit me?

Someone before me—whether prisoner, guest, or resident, I do not know—has left a slim volume of poetry behind, which serves as my only entertainment for days. I spend hours in prayer, more than ever before, and try to shove aside my doubts that God is even watching over England anymore.

On Lowdie's second visit, I beg her to bring needle and thread, which she does, giving me one more way to pass the time. I wonder how many prisoners have gone mad within these walls.

I am not too far down the path of madness—I hope—when the yeomen warden finally comes and lead me back to the office where Moyle and Pollard confronted me three weeks ago. My escort lets me precede him, and I sink into a chair to hide how badly my knees are trembling. Just as the warden is about to leave me alone once again, I see the black robes of a priest swoosh in. The door slams shut behind him.

"Rise, my child."

I look up to his face and suck in a breath. *I know that face.*

Quickly, he claps a hand over my mouth. He reaches into his billowy robes and extracts a quill. He gestures to me, indicating I should remain quiet. I nod, too frightened to do anything else.

Satisfied I will comply, he releases me, grabbing a thick sheet of paper from the desk where Pollard sat the first time I was here. He dips his quill in an inkpot. I watch as he quickly scratches the words:

You recognize me. That is good. Do not say anything. No doubt they are listening.

Friend or foe? Friend or foe? My mind is awhirl. The man is a prior. I last saw him three years ago, nearly four now, in Abbot Whiting's study. I want to believe him an ally, but his presence in this place could mean he works both sides.

"Lady Seybourne," he says, in a voice I know is intended to carry through the walls. "You are a loyal servant of this realm, are you not?"

"Yes, sir."

"Then you understand the importance of the king's undertaking…the religious reform spreading through the land. The king must have an accurate accounting for the possessions of the Church, so that he has all the tools of power and may best bring his people unto glory." He is gazing directly at me while he speaks, but I have the sense this speech is prepared for the benefit of others. "You come from Glastonbury, which has long been associated with the stories of King Arthur and the Holy Grail…yet I do not see the grail listed amongst the abbey's possessions."

"No one has seen the grail in centuries, sir."

"I want you to think about that for a moment…measure the truth of your words. Perhaps you can recollect something that would suggest it *has* been seen, and hidden."

I frown, but as I consider his words, he dips his quill again and scratches out another message.

Answer only what anyone would already know.

Friend, I think…though one who apparently has gained the trust of my foes. "We…we have the tomb of King Arthur, Father Prior."

"Indeed. The Arthurian relics are priceless. Why do you think kings still fight under the banner of the red dragon, and spend inordinate sums to prove their lineage traces back to King Arthur?"

He isn't expecting an answer, which is good, because I have none to give. I know just how important those relics are, whether they are linked to the grail or not. I lost my brother for them.

"Men would kill to possess such a treasure."

Yes, I know. They already have.

"You cannot protect the relics, girl. Nor can Abbot Whiting. But you can protect the good reputation of your new husband." He raises his voice, and the hint of threat grows stronger.

I refuse to rise to his bait, remaining stubbornly silent.

"You would do well to listen, Lady Seybourne. I am not the enemy you seem to think I am." He clasps his hands together, and zeal lights his eyes. "Indeed, I would see no harm come to our great ancestor, either. I want to know his remains, his memory, will be kept safe. That is why I ask—tell me the plan. What will happen when Glastonbury falls?"

I lower my gaze. "There is no plan."

"You know I don't believe that."

"When Glastonbury falls," I say, slowly and deliberately, "all contents of the abbey's treasury will go to King Henry. Glastonbury's possessions are well-catalogued. How do you think we could do anything *but* turn them over?"

He narrows his gaze, assessing whether or not I speak the truth. "I could protect them."

"How?" I shouldn't encourage him, but the word slips out before I can stop it. For all I know, he would sell the relics to the highest bidder without a second thought.

"They are not safe in England."

"No one is safe in England."

A bark of wry laughter escapes him at that. "I see why the abbot is fond of you. No, you are right. No one is safe in England, least of all King Arthur."

"Then how…"

He points at the door and cups a hand to his ear. *They are listening.* "He could be safe in France. The French have long revered your king of old, and I have many connections there who would consider it an honor to play even one small part in his story."

He is play-acting for the benefit of those listening outside the door…I think. But if he's working with the king's minions, why would he voice such a disloyal offer? Maybe he is testing me. I am a fish, and he is holding out bait. I don't know. My few weeks at court were insufficient training to play at games such as this.

I am a protector, too.

"I know," I whisper in response to the freshly scripted phrase. But the French? I pause, as though I am thinking about his offer. He starts writing again, but a flick of his wrist is my cue. I must answer, play my part in this farce.

"I—I understand and cannot fault your French allies for such a sentiment. But Father Prior, I cannot help you, or them. The disposition of the relics is not my decision to make."

The safety of my charge is linked to the safety of yours.

He knows.

He knows, and he's studying me with a curious look. "You would really let them go to the king's men? Wait. No. Don't say anything. You have someone in the king's employ, is that it? You'll let the relics go to him because you know they'll be safely delivered into the hands of another?"

Now, that does sound like an intelligent plan. I actually wish it were true. For now, it is enough if he thinks it is true, so I keep my mouth shut and look away, trying to give the impression that he's guessed correctly—but I don't want to admit it.

Aloud, I let my voice break and whimper, "I don't know, I swear to you. I just want to go home."

Slowly, he nods. "One moment, and then you may leave."

I will tell them I have tested you, and you know nothing.

My heart leaps. I don't understand what just took place, but somehow, I've passed the test.

You need to get far away from here, and do not return.

I completely agree.

The prior dips the pen into the ink one more time, and puts it to the paper. Two words.

Veritas, Sanctitas.

He meets my eye, then takes his paper, folds it once, and drops it into the small fire. We both watch the flames lick the edges, then catch hold. The paper blackens and crumbles to ash. The prior nods to the door.

CHAPTER TWENTY-SEVEN

I'm shaking by the time I get home. I don't have any money, so I have to walk—normally something I would enjoy, but three weeks with little exercise and little appetite have left me weak. Then there's the overwhelming relief of being free. It's dizzying. So is my anger and disappointment at my husband. My emotions are flying wildly about, soaring, then swooping and diving like birds at the dock.

I almost hope Tobias won't be home, so I can settle myself, but he is. At the sound of my entry, he comes and wraps me in his arms. Lowdie, displaying uncommonly good sense, makes herself scarce.

I'm trembling in his arms. His chin rests atop my head, and in spite of his steady breathing, the accelerated pace of his heartbeat gives away his tension. At least that signal won't be obvious to his enemies, the way his unconscious habit of rubbing the seam of his chausses was. It's a strange thought for the moment, but after all the swooping and diving of my emotions, my thoughts have also decided to act like a flock of birds—or rather, what happens when the flock is startled and flies off every which way.

The silence grows and it's not a comfortable one. I need to say something.

"You didn't come for me." Probably not what I should have started with. But also the truest combination of my thoughts and emotions.

He steps back, dropping his hands from my shoulders, and I feel the physical loss of him keenly.

"I couldn't. It was too big a risk."

"I'm your wife. Am I not worth the risk?" I hear the plaintive tone in my voice and I don't like it, but I can't seem to help it.

"That's not it, Audrey. You know that." His mouth settles into a grim line, as if he's expected this argument. "As you have often pointed out, I am a courtier. That means everything I do is seen by others. And while that gives me some leverage to provide for and protect you, it also goes against the very nature of *your* duties."

"You really think they would condemn a husband for visiting his wife?"

"I don't profess to know *what* the king or his top advisors would do. That's exactly the problem." He drops his voice. "Think about it, Audrey. The abbot is done for. I know you don't want to hear it, but deep down, you know it's true. That leaves you and I. If there are any other Daughters of Arthur out there, we haven't found them yet—and they could be just like you, not even aware of their legacy, or their duty to protect it."

I feel deflated. Maybe I should focus on finding the others, if they exist, instead of clinging to a life already lost. "I understand. I just…I felt so abandoned, and I thought you would find a way. What good is it to charm everyone if they still don't trust you?"

"No one who has been in that court more than a day trusts anyone. Not if they have any sense of self-preservation. I know what you think of me—that I go tripping merrily through life, and good things simply come my way." He lets his head fall back and expels a breath. "It doesn't work that way. It never has. I've worked for years to get to where I am now, always balancing on the fine tip of a sword. Somehow, I've managed to stay upright, and I'll be damned if I'm going to fall now because my *wife* has more loyalty than sense!"

I cringe at the snarl in his tone, but I have few words with which to defend myself. Even though I am no happier with him than he is with me, he is right about my recklessness. I always thought that, of the two of us, I was the careful one, and he was the reckless one. Now I can see that his recklessness is just a charming facade, while mine—in spite of being driven by loyalty, a virtue—is far more dangerous.

"I am sorry. I know I was wrong. I was just so worried for Abbot Whiting, I did not think of the consequences of my actions."

His expression softens—barely. "Audrey. I know you care for him like a father. He protected you when your parents died. I know that. But, don't you see? That's *my* job now—the abbot himself intended it that way. But I can't do my job if you sneak behind my back and place yourself in danger."

"I didn't mean to—"

"You knew the risk. Otherwise you and Lowdie would have told me where you were going, that day. You didn't want me to spoil your plans."

Shame floods my body and my eyes sting with tears. I hate that he's right. "I won't do it again."

He stares at me for a long time. "I don't believe you would mean to," he says finally, "but to be certain, I'm taking you back to Bridgewater."

Tobias goes early the next day to seek permission for an absence from the court. He says he'll hire an escort for me if necessary, perhaps one or two of his cousins, but he would prefer to take me himself. I wonder if the king will grant the request. If he does, I sincerely hope he will not insist on us returning any time soon. I am growing ever so tired of this back-and-forth, back-and-forth travel between the court and home. I don't see the allure of the lifestyle my husband lives.

Though Tobias and I have not exactly reconciled, I'm not opposed to returning home, if I can stay. I get the sense he does not wish to argue with me any more than I wish to argue with him—though he did insist I not leave the house today. Not that I wanted to, anyway. We did not make love last night, but he did pull me to him when he came to bed last night, and I awoke this morning with his arm still thrown over me and my head nestled in the crook of his neck. He still cares for me. We just don't always know what to say, or what to do.

"Permission granted," Tobias announces as he strides through the door shortly after noon.

"Truly?" A smile steals across my face for the first time in days. I'm free from the Tower, and free to go home.

Tobias moves closer, his expression sheepish and hopeful. "I might have indicated that you were with child, and I felt it best to get you settled in the wholesome country air before travel became uncomfortable. It's true, isn't it?"

My jaw drops. "How did you know?" I'd been meaning to tell him, and then with everything that happened…

"I suspected when we first came to London. But I know sometimes the early signs don't work out, and I didn't want to pressure you or make you feel bad if anything happened. Especially after..." he pauses and clears his throat. "After losing Sam. But it's been longer now, and I held you last night. Your body is changing."

He puts his arms around me. "Don't stay angry with me, love. We'll get you back safe where you belong, and put all this behind us."

I turn into him, and my lips find his. I want nothing more.

Lowdie has us packed immediately. She's had her fill of the city, as well. We stop in Glastonbury to see Tobias's mother and brother, while Lowdie spends time with her own relatives. Tobias tries to tease John about the maid he's begun courting, but the mood stays somber.

Two days later, we make the final leg of our journey, and I am relieved to be home. The laborers have made good progress clearing a patch of land. It will be ready for planting in the spring. They've kept Sam's grave well-tended, too, which both warms my heart and hurts it.

We settle in, and our days fall into a comfortable pattern. My appetite has returned, and with it, some of the weight I lost in the early weeks of this pregnancy. I am hoping for a daughter, of course. I have begun to believe that I am, indeed, descended from Arthur's daughters. This calling, this duty to protect, beckons to my very blood. This quest was meant to pass from mother to daughter, safeguarded by those who nurture and protect. Tobias says he will be happy no matter what—after all, both Sam and Abbot Whiting proved that the legacy of Arthur's daughters can be upheld quite well by a son. That is true, of course. If it is God's will that I have only sons, then I shall raise them to be good and worthy men like my husband and my brother. I will be content with that, should it come to pass. But in the meantime, I hope for a daughter.

Tobias has another hope, as well, that he only dared whisper in the dark of night.

"Surely, Britain's need has never been greater. What if the return of the king is nigh? What if…what if…it is time for him to be reborn?"

"Reborn?"

"I don't know, but I was thinking…Christ was only dead a short time before the Holy Father raised him, right? So his body was still…him. But King Arthur? It's been hundreds of years. You don't think his bones will suddenly rise up and take on flesh again, do you?"

I cringe, trying not to recall that those very bones are walled up in our cellar. "Please don't say things like that."

"My apologies. I cannot imagine that is how the prophecy will play out. I imagine Arthur's spirit will be born into a new body, a child destined to play the role that was cut short when the king was murdered by Mordred so long ago."

The idea makes sense—except for where he's going next. "You think…*my* baby?"

"*Our* baby," he corrects me. "Audrey, I honestly don't know. But Abbot Whiting as good as confirmed that Arthur's grave and the holy grail are connected, and he went to an awful lot of trouble to see that both would be protected after his death, and I just think…I think it's possible."

I'm quiet as I roll that around in my mind. I've never been with child before, obviously, but I don't feel like my situation is any different from my peers. Would I even know if the life growing inside me was destined for greatness?

Finally, I give him the only response I can think of. "I like that you believe in miracles. Abbot Whiting always said he did, too."

❧☙

In spite of our comfortable routine, I have the uneasy sense of being caught in a moment, waiting for something to happen, something beyond my control—and it has nothing to do with my unborn child. I almost wish that whatever it is, even though my intuition says it is unlikely to be good, it would just happen already—that would be better than waiting, not knowing. We've had no news about the abbot since my ill-fated visit to the Tower.

So when Tobias comes through the door and announces without preamble, "They will bear him home tomorrow," I know immediately to whom he refers.

"Bear him?" I echo. My voice cracks. Emotions wash over me. Relief, that the waiting is over. Grief, at the loss of a trusted mentor. Uncertainty, for what this will mean. "He is dead already?"

"Nay." He closes his eyes briefly, and I know his is trying to find a gentle way to tell me whatever it is he has to say.

"Tell me. I am strong enough to hear this."

"His arrival in Glastonbury will coincide with his execution. This is a triumph for Cromwell. They will make a spectacle of it."

My heart plummets and I am silent for a moment. My next words…I can hardly believe they come from me. I am not the woman I was a year ago—even six months ago. "We must attend."

Tobias gapes at me. Lowdie, who has sidled up to the edge of the conversation, does too.

"Absolutely not," my husband says.

I don't want to argue with him, but I am passionate about this—I feel the conviction down to my toes. "It is the right thing to do."

"Are we going in support of Abbot Whiting, or in support of the men who will hang him?" Lowdie asks warily.

"It matters not. The public attends executions. The Seybournes are no different. We do not have to declare support for anyone. But we do have to attend. To do otherwise might be viewed as a vote of disapproval, an indication we do not fully support the king's orders…or even an indication of fear—that we have something to hide."

Tobias nods slowly. "I can go and represent our family."

Lowdie moistens her lips and ducks her head. "If I might have leave to attend…"

My husband looks between us. I don't dare say anything, but I know he can tell from my expression that this is important to me, too. "All right," he grumbles. "There are certain to be crowds. We stay within them, and do nothing to stand out."

We both nod dutifully, and say nothing when he mutters something about "willful women."

Tobias and I pass the hours of the night with very little sleep. He tries to lay still, but I can tell from his breathing that he isn't sleeping any more than I am. When daylight comes, he takes my face between his hands. "You look pale."

"I'm only tired."

"Stay here today, Audrey. Please?"

"No. I need to do this."

He leans over, whispering his argument in my ear. "But the baby," he says. "I don't like to think of you becoming overwrought."

Since he got me with child, he's become ever more protective. It is rather sweet. But I feel fine—or as fine as one can feel, knowing that a great and good man is about to go to his death.

"I am in good health. This is important. Abbott Whiting…" I choke up, then clear my throat. "He did this for us. For all of us. I need to be there."

I do not expect the king to grant mercy, and my expectations are not wrong. King Henry has shown time and again that he will not tolerate those he deems to be standing in his way. Even if the doomed party was once a trusted adviser, a friend—or his own wife. The only thing that surprises me is that Abbot Whiting is not alone. Two others, both monks, have been summarily tried and found guilty, as well. Roger James and John Thorne, according to the man who calls out their list of offenses. Familiar faces, but neither are men I have spoken with. Other than the abbot, I was always too shy to speak to those in positions of power.

The two monks do not look afraid—if anything, the men who will die beside Abbot Whiting look proud to do so. They stand taller than the abbot, who is feeble now and broken in body—though his face is resolute.

What happens next, though, does surprise me, if only because I prayed for a quick and merciful end. That prayer will go unanswered.

A cloaked man leading a horse comes into the courtyard. Over his shoulder are slung three wooden hurdles. Another man leading two horses follows.

I watch in horror as Abbot Whiting and the two monks are roughly grabbed and trussed up upon the hurdles, which are attached by lead lines to the horses. Pollard gives a nod, and the second man cracks a whip.

The horses take off, following a rider—unseen until now—to the top of Glastonbury Tor. The abbot and his men are bumped and dragged brutally, but if they make a sound, I cannot hear it over the screams, moans, and exclamations of the crowd.

We follow along behind the horses, moving as though in a trance. There is nothing merciful about this. Cromwell will make an example of him. But why? There are hardly any abbeys left—hardly any men to follow the abbot's path by defying the crown.

Someone has erected a gallows atop the Tor.

Abbot Whiting is a good man. I know this in my gut. I know, if there is anything he regrets, it is that these two men will die with him. For him. Cromwell's thirst for blood cannot be satisfied by the abbot alone.

I want to look away when the platform drops, but I force myself to watch. I will bear witness to this tragedy.

The abbot's body swings free, and my own body echoes with a sudden, hollow feeling. He was not my father, but I feel his loss like the loss of a father, just the same.

I bend my head in prayer.

They put his head on a spike. Dear God in heaven, they put his head on a spike. It is fastened over the west gate of the abbey in a grotesque warning to those who would resist the will of the crown.

I think I'm going to be sick. The ground sways beneath my feet and I sink to my knees, folding over as I wait for the waves of nausea to pass me by. Tobias hovers anxiously beside me, murmuring small words of comfort as his glance flicks nervously around. He is anxious to be rid of this place, and I am too.

The warning serves no purpose. The abbey itself is already deserted. It is a mark of cruelty, of the desire of the King of England to inspire terror in his subjects. Even if the Catholic church was corrupt, so is this. Reformation is a far bitterer brew than any of us could have known, when the first whispers began.

Shakily, I stand, and we leave before the looting begins. Lowdie rejoins us—I had lost her in the crowd earlier—and we move in silence toward our mounts. I needed to be there for Abbot Whiting, to stand witness to the events of his death. But his spirit has passed on, now. I do not need to see them cart off everything of value, until they tear the very stones from the walls, then light fire to all that will burn. No doubt I will see it in my dreams anyway.

On the way home, I feel oddly light. Then I feel guilty for the lightness, but it is there just the same. On top of the profound sadness, there is a certain relief in knowing it is over. Glastonbury is no more.

Strangely, I feel safer. I am a nobody, and will remain a nobody. There is a hidden power in this.

No one will come looking for me. No one will think that I, meek and mild Audrey Thorndale, now Audrey Seybourne, could be involved—let alone integral—to such subversion. The relics are safe.

EPILOGUE

The tomb is gone. What remains of Glastonbury Abbey is but a shell, stripped of any material that might prove useful elsewhere. The shrine of King Arthur was deliberately despoiled and his grave in the monastic church was soon lost among the rubble. I cannot say on what day this happened—indeed, it was done with very little fanfare. King Henry put forth no edict to protect the tomb. For him, it had already served its purpose.

A few of the former abbey's outlying properties have been granted to one John Thynne, much in the same way my own home and land was granted to my husband. I have not met Thynne. Wisely, he does not frequent Glastonbury, where some wounds still fester.

The main grounds of the abbey lie abandoned, which is just as well. Too much has happened here for the people to forget so soon. Someday, I am certain, the crown will release the land,

and it will find new use as the memories of those who live nearby begin to fade.

I would like to say the turmoil has died down, but in truth it has only shifted focus. King Henry has married and disposed of two more wives—another annulment and another beheading. Lord Cromwell, too, has been tried and executed for treason, though his legacy lives on. Religious and political uncertainty are a way of life, now.

Someday, our king will come to his senses. He will remember that not all value lies in gold and silver. That some things, things great and good, are not meant to be forgotten. In truth, it may not be this particular king who remembers that.

I may not live to see it. I probably will not. But I like knowing I played a part in ensuring England's destiny lives on. My search for my grandmother's sisters, and possible descendants, continues. Tracing a family's maternal line has never been easy, considering the change in surnames each time a woman marries, but now it is doubly hard, because so many church records have been lost or destroyed.

Despite Tobias's secret hopes, our young son shows no signs of royal aspirations as he plays with his baby sister. I do not let that worry me.

Someday, Britain's one true king will rise again.

Until then, I keep the watch.

Thank you for reading *Entrusted*. **I hope you enjoyed it. If you did…**

1. Help other people find this book by leaving a review at your preferred retailer.

2. Sign up for my new releases e-mail, so you can find out about the next book as soon as it's available.

3. Join me on Facebook at: Allegra Gray's Facebook

Thank you for supporting my books. I truly appreciate it!

Other Ways to Connect with Allegra:

Visit Allegra's website at:
www.AllegraGray.com

Amazon author page:
Allegra's Author Page on Amazon

Goodreads author profile:
Allegra on Goodreads

Also by Allegra Gray:
Nothing But Scandal
Nothing But Deception
Nothing But Trouble
The Devil's Bargain

Page forward for a sneak preview of *Beguiled*, Book 2 in the Relic Guardians series, coming in January 2016!

Beguiled - Book 2 of the Relic Guardians

James

London, 1810

"That cross hasn't been seen in centuries. It was lost, with Arthur's tomb, when the monasteries were dissolved."

"Not lost, exactly. More like…hidden," my brother replies, holding the lead cross before the wide-eyed antiquities dealer. "My family has preserved it as part of our private collection for nearly three hundred years."

I hate that he is doing this. Selling off the trinkets, the paintings, even the furniture? I have no problem with that. They are only objects collecting dust in the cavernous rooms of a rambling old mansion. The cross that marked King Arthur's grave is different. To part with it, after protecting it for so long, feels like betrayal.

Charles scoffs at my youthful fancy. After all, he is the one who will someday inherit a barony gone to ruin—a fate brought on by generations of ancestors educated in spending money, but not earning it. As the second son, I will have to make my own way in the world—which means I will *not* have to deal with the creditors and debt collectors salivating at the doorstep of the Madrigal estate. Charles will. So, whether I like it or not, I choose to hold my peace.

Mr. Somerset, the dealer, reaches for his magnifying glass. "May I?" His hands tremble with eagerness.

"Of course." Charles hands the object over.

Somerset examines it closely, while his daughter Kate—my sole reason for attending this shameful transaction, makes eyes at me from her perch behind the counter. She has the pieces of an intricate clock disassembled and spread before her. She deftly handles them, using tools to reshape warped metal, her young eyes performing the work her father can no longer manage. Kate does not care about my family's circumstances—as long as there are funds to finish my education before we can be together. Until then, she delights in tormenting me…and Kate is a woman with a shape designed to bring a man to his knees.

Her father sets down the magnifying glass. "It looks old enough to be authentic," he pronounces. "I'll have to do some research, compare it with the drawings from the last known chroniclers…and I should very much like to consult with a colleague of mine—one who specializes in ancient relics."

"I understand."

"Do you have any other documentation to assist in verifying it?"

"An accounting." Charles hands him an old ledger book. "My ancestor who brought the item into the family kept track of all his…acquisitions from that time."

What he means is that our ancestor kept a log of each abbey and monastery he looted as they fell, during the Dissolution of the Monasteries during the reign of King Henry VIII, and the haul from each. Then again, he was one of the few in the family line to actually add to the Madrigal family coffers, so perhaps I should not judge. Such enterprising spirit has been lacking in our family ever since.

"Excellent, Mr. Madrigal. If this cross can be authenticated, I can no doubt find a buyer willing to pay a hefty sum. Indeed, I shouldn't be surprised if it sparked a bidding war." His eyes light with glee at the prospect. My brother's do, too.

My gaze drops to where Kate's shapely bosom strains against the neckline of her gown. She notices, and her eyes sparkle as well, a knowing smile playing at the corner of her lips.

Charles may be selling the family legacy, but I suppose it cannot be helped. On the bright side, everyone in this room is going to get what they most want.

That afternoon happened six years ago. I had no idea, at the time, how badly I'd been duped.

Look for *Beguiled* in January 2016!

About the Author

Allegra Gray grew up with her nose in a book and her head in the clouds—that is, when she wasn't focused on more practical things like, say, learning calculus. Perhaps all those stories inspired a spirit of adventure, because at the age of seventeen she embarked on a career journey that has (so far) included serving as an officer in the U.S. Air Force, grad school at Virginia Tech, teaching English, and managing defense contracts in the Middle East. The best thing about this breadth of experience? When she tried her hand at writing novels like the ones she'd always loved, she recognized at once that she'd found a *true* passion. Her newest series, *The Relic Guardians*, is genre-bending mainstream/historical suspense, inspired by her long-held desire to unveil things obscured by the mists of time. Allegra is also the author of four historical romances, including the "Daring Damsels" trilogy of *Nothing But Scandal, Nothing But Deception, and Nothing But Trouble.*

This book is a work of fiction. Names, characters, places, organizations, events and incidents either are products of the author's imagination or are used fictitiously.

ISBN-13:
978-0692486146 (Silverthorne Entertainment)

ISBN-10:
0692486143

Published by Silverthorne Entertainment

Proof

Made in the USA
Charleston, SC
08 July 2015